LOVE BEYOND TIME

BOOK 1 OF MORNA'S LEGACY SERIES

BETHANY CLAIRE

Editor: Jonathan Baker
Cover Designed by Damonza

Available in eBook, Paperback, Hardback & Audiobook

eBook ISBN: 978-0-9899502-0-6
Paperback ISBN: 978-0-9899502-4-4
Hardback ISBN: 978-1-947731-39-4

http://www.bethanyclaire.com

PRAISE FOR LOVE BEYOND TIME

"Be swept away by Bethany Claire's miraculous
love story that transcends time and space.
Sexy, Scottish, time-travel.
It doesn't get much better than this."

DeWanna Pace
NY Times & USA Today Bestselling Author

DEDICATION

For Mims

CHAPTER 1

austin, TX - Present Day

Sun beamed against the windows as I walked down the line of tiny faces peering up at me. I knelt before each one, holding up a number between one and ten on my fingers, looking over each little body to ensure that laces were tied, backpacks on, and lunchboxes were in hand as I waited for their answer. As each called out the right number with a prideful smile, I gave them their daily sticker and moved on to the next student.

I could see Anthony three students down, pestering the unfortunate Harrison, who was standing in front of him and blowing in his ears every time he turned around to face the front of the line. As Grace called out number seven and asked for help with her laces, I threw my most stern *cut it out* look in Anthony's direction. The ornery-but-exceedingly-bright child caught my meaning and returned the look with a sheepish grin as he stepped away from Harrison and stood still as a statue.

Two students later, I stood in front of Anthony. He rattled off the number nine that I was holding up in front of him before I even had a chance to look him over. Both laces were undone, and he had split his zipper so that only the middle of his jacket was actually closed.

"Good job, Anthony! Here's your sticker. Still haven't mastered the old shoelaces yet, I see?"

"No, Ms. Mothgomfrey. I been working and working at it, but I just can't seem to get that rabbit to go around the hole."

I repressed an eye roll as I bent to tie his shoes. Anthony's speech was better than all of the other kindergarteners in his class, and I knew he could say my name, Ms. Montgomery, without problem, but he just lived for the giggles of all the other students every time he said my name that way.

"Well, those rabbits can be tricky that way, but you just keep working at it. You'll get it soon."

"I sure will! I promise! I sure am tired of watching you tie my shoes every day. Ya know, I'm five years old, it's humilly-aten."

"Well, Anthony. That's sure a big word. Where'd you hear that?"

"That's what my Mama said to Daddy the other day. She said it was humilly-aten to be married to a man that thought it was okay to watch television all day long on Sundays while she cleaned and cooked and did laundry and that he needed to get his fat, lazy a . . ."

The bell rang, interrupting his speech and saving the day as far as I was concerned. I should've seen that coming. I knew better than to ask Anthony an open-ended question.

I quickly checked the last few in line and went to the front of the classroom, motioning for the day's leader, Izzy, to hold open the door while everyone walked outside. Once everyone was out of the classroom and Izzy had returned to her place in the front of the line, I led them down the hallway, smiling at the sound of their tiny, squeaky shoes as they pitter-pattered single-file behind me.

*T*wenty minutes later, when the last child had been picked up, I shut the door to my classroom and plopped ungracefully down at my desk. I gently pressed my fingertips against my eyelids in an effort to push away the day's stress. It seemed to help a little, so I stood up, stretching mildly before I tucked my long, dark hair, which was now frizzing after being out in the wind, behind my ears.

I pushed my chair in and circled the room for a quick sweep before I headed home. I bent over every few feet to pick up the various crayons, chunks of Play-Doh, and construction paper scattered across the carpet. I knew the custodian would come along behind me shortly, but I just couldn't bear for her to see the classroom in this state of dishevelment. As I looked over the mess that scattered from one work center to another, I thought to myself, not for the first time today, how glad I was that I had decided against adding finger-painting to the day's lesson plans.

With my arms filled to capacity with various craft litter, I deposited the load into the trash can next to my desk. With a glance around the room, I decided I was satisfied enough to call it a day.

I stacked the handwriting exercises for the letter "G" on top of my desk to grade first thing Monday morning, and I was buttoning my jacket when my classroom aide Mitsy opened the door and stepped inside.

"Are you ready for your big date tonight? I talked to Brian and he said Daniel is super-excited!"

I spun quickly to face her, panic settling in my gut. "What? Oh, Mitsy, I totally forgot! Look. Maybe you could just call him and see if we could do it next Friday? You know, I'm really swamped right now. We'd both have more fun if we did it when I wasn't so distracted."

Mitsy placed her hands on both hips and narrowed her eyes as she spoke to me again, "I will do no such thing! And if you think you are going to get out of yet one more date, well, let me tell you, Miss I-have-no-problem-dying-alone, I am not going to let you weasel out of this one! He's a great guy, Bri. I haven't actually met him, but Brian's known him all of his life. His wife died two years ago, and he needs to get out of the house just about as badly as you need to. Just look at it as something that will benefit you both."

I turned away from her as I closed the coat closet and walked

3

back over to my desk to grab my purse. "I'm not trying to weasel out of it. I just really need to work on lesson plans for next week, and I think I'm catching a cold."

Mitsy blocked the door to the classroom and grabbed my wrist as she dragged me back over to the filing cabinet beside my desk. I knew what she was about to grab before she opened the cabinet.

"You are not catching a cold, and don't you dare try to tell me that you have lesson plans to work on." I watched as she paused briefly to yank open the first drawer. "Let's see. What do we have here? All of Monday's lesson plans in this folder? Check. Tuesday? Check. Wednesday? Check. Do I really need to go on, Bri? You should just make it easier on yourself and tell me you're going, because you are either way. All there's left for you to decide is how soon you want me to get out of your hair." She smiled sweetly and placed my folders back into the cabinet, slamming the drawer shut with immense satisfaction.

Reluctantly I grinned and held my hands up in surrender. "Fine. Fine. I'll go. But you're going to let me pick out my own bridesmaid's dress for you and Brian's wedding, right?

Mitsy thrust her hand in my direction, "Deal."

I'd just zipped up the back of my dress when the doorbell rang at 7:30. *At least he's punctual,* I thought as I tried to put an earring on with one hand while attempting to slip myself into my heels with the other.

Taking a quick glance in the mirror, I slathered on some lip gloss, held my hand in front of my face to check my breath, and headed to answer the front door.

Daniel held a bouquet of flowers so that they covered his face, and as he slowly lowered them I had to swallow the audible gasp that crept up my throat. I was able to manage a polite, "Hello. Please come in," as my eyes combed over the thick, gray hair that covered his head.

As he made his way through the doorway I spotted a few thick, wiry hairs sticking out from the opening in his ear, and the abnormally large nose that some men get when they age was evident from his profile.

He was handsome . . . for a man in his sixties. As I shut the front door, I found myself wishing I'd had that glass of wine I'd thought about when I got home from work.

Steeling myself, I turned to face him. "It's nice to meet you. The flowers are lovely. Thank you. Why don't I go put them in some water, and then we can leave?"

He extended them to me and as he grinned slightly, I could see that his eyes looked exceedingly kind. "I can tell I wasn't exactly what you were expecting. I guess Brian and Mitsy didn't tell you much."

I walked quickly into the kitchen, keeping my back to him so that he couldn't see my face as I spoke. "No, not too much. I know that you're a dentist and are related to Brian. I assumed you were a cousin."

The old man chuckled slightly, and his cheeks reddened as I walked back toward him. "My sons are his cousins. I'm his uncle."

"Oh." I stared down at my purse awkwardly, wishing I actually had something to look for inside it.

"Look. I don't want to make you uncomfortable, but we've both gotten all dressed up. Why don't we go ahead and go out to eat and visit with each other a little bit, then I'll bring you back here and we'll forget this whole thing ever happened. No harm, no foul. What do you say?"

He extended a hand in my direction, and sympathy washed through me as I reached to take it. He obviously had no more idea of what he was getting himself into than I did. "Good food, nice company. What could it hurt? Let's get out of here."

As he held the front door open, I walked straight into the person walking rather purposefully toward my front door.

"Mom?" I said.

I repeated myself for good measure as the uncomfortable feeling of shock ran down my spine for the second time. "Mom? What are you doing here? You're supposed to be in D.C., aren't you?"

She stepped back so that we could look at each other from a more appropriate distance, "Well, I'm happy to see you too, Bri. I'm glad I caught you before you left. I don't have a key to your new place. We need to talk right away. I have some very exciting news!"

I watched as she bounced up and down, the same thirteen-year-old trapped in a fifty-year-old's body that she'd always been. I knew the exact instant she spotted Daniel, still holding the door wide open, watching the spectacle.

As her eyes widened, she stopped bouncing, and immediately went into flirt mode; another one of my mother's classic qualities. "Well, hello sir. And who might you be?" She slowly stretched a hand in his direction.

"Name's Daniel. I was just leaving." He paused to pat me on the back and then walked through the door. "It was nice to meet you, Bri. I'll see you at the wedding."

I waved politely in his direction and ushered my mother inside, shutting the door behind me. She spun on me just as I'd latched the door.

"Who was that? Very handsome, but a little old for you, don't you think, dear?"

I leaned against the back of the door and exhaled loudly. "Very long story, Mom. But remind me that I need to have a conversation with Mitsy about what exactly it is that she thinks my standards are."

She laughed, obviously understanding the situation. "Well, seems like she understands my standards just fine. Do you have his phone number?"

I rolled my eyes and made my way into the living room. "No, Mom, I don't, but I'm sure Mitsy will give it to you if you want. Now, what's going on? Is everything okay?"

We sat down on the couch facing each other, and Mom excitedly reached for my hand as she told me her news.

"I got the grant!"

I couldn't help but smile at the excited expression on her face, "The grant to resume your work on Conall Castle? That's great, Mom!"

She squealed as she continued, "Yes, Bri, that grant. It's been nearly twenty years, but I'm finally going to get to go back and figure out what really happened."

My mother, Adelle Montgomery as most people knew her, was a world-renowned archaeologist. Her big break had come while working on an excavating project near the remains of Conall Castle in Scotland.

The tragedy of Conall Castle was one of the most well-known legends in Scottish history, and the mystery behind the destruction of the Conall clan had remained unsolvable for over four hundred years.

Within weeks of beginning her first lead dig at the ruins, Mom had discovered an underground library that, due to the strong stone base of the castle, had survived the infamous fire. It took weeks for Mom and her team to dig their way into the library, but once inside, they found countless archaeological treasures that had brought Adelle into the forefront of archaeology. Dozens of journals, hundreds of letters, and countless documents detailing family lineage with birth, death, and marriage certificates were all found within the library.

The find had propelled her career into overdrive. While the documents found in the basement shed a great light on the mysterious clan, none of the documents had solved the mystery of who had murdered the Conalls, afterwards burning the ancient castle to the ground.

After years of unsuccessfully solving the mystery, she moved on from her work on the Conall dig to other projects that sent her all over the world during the past twenty years; all the while she had been hoping for a reason to resume her work on Conall Castle.

"And I haven't told you the best part!" She squeezed my hand and bounced up and down like my kindergarteners before recess.

I sat quietly, waiting for her to tell me, knowing it would drive her crazy.

She stopped bouncing. "Aren't you going to say, 'what'?"

I laughed and indulged her. "What's the best part?"

"You're going to Scotland with me! I've already registered you as my assistant on the dig."

I jerked up off the couch, hitting the coffee table and sloshing water out of the cup that sat in front of me. "What? You know I can't. I have school. I teach kindergarteners. That's like asking a substitute to walk straight through the gates of Hell!"

"Oh, hush! You exaggerate. You haven't taken a personal day since you started teaching six years ago. I know you have a ton of days built up. Besides, we'll only be gone a couple of weeks. And you have Mitsy. Your students will be fine. You know you've always wanted to go to Scotland."

I reached up and squeezed the bridge of my nose with my fingers. Last minute travel plans did not appeal to me at all, but she was right about one thing. "I have always wanted to go to Scotland."

"Great! I'm going to go book our flights now. We leave Sunday."

Before I could put up a fight, she was on her way back to her car to grab her computer. Recognizing I'd been beaten, I walked back into the entryway and sank down beside the front door next to my school bag. Reaching inside, I grabbed my planner and tried to figure out what I was going to tell my principal.

CHAPTER 2

*S*cotland—*1645*

*T*he eldest Conall brother paced back and forth outside his father's chambers, reluctant to leave his father's side but understanding the laird's desire to speak to his youngest son alone. After what seemed like hours Eoin heard the door begin to creak, and Arran Conall emerged from their father's room.

Standing at over six foot four, Arran was still at least two inches shorter than Eoin. With blond hair that fell to his shoulders and vibrant blue eyes, Arran was very popular with the lasses of Conall Keep.

Although Eoin knew his own good looks were a fair rival to his brother's, he was careful not to earn such a reputation for frivolous lovemaking. His younger brother, however, embraced his reputation; it was a rare night that his bed was empty, and even rarer that the same woman was found there twice.

Arran's carefree nature and love of life were contagious, and there were few times when Eoin had seen his brother without a smile. But this time, when he exited their father's room, Arran's smile was gone. The red tip of his nose and the strain in his eyes revealed that Arran was too proud to let the flood of tears flow.

Knowing any attempt to comfort would only embarrass him further, Eoin looked at the ground as he entered their father's chamber. Eoin had been only five when his mother passed away while giving birth to Arran, and all Eoin remembered about her was spending afternoons in her beloved garden, watching her tend the plants with exquisite care.

His father, on the other hand, had been his constant companion. Eoin was the spitting image of his father: same long, dark hair and ebony eyes; same quiet-yet-confident demeanor, so different from his brother's loud and boisterous way of life. As children, Eoin and Arran depended on their father for everything, and although his father had spent the past thirty years preparing him, Eoin had never expected to be laird of Conall Castle so soon.

He would have done anything to prevent his father's fate, but as his gaze fell upon the laird, Eoin knew there was nothing to be done. While he had been thrown from horses many times in his life, the fall his father had taken that morning tossed his aging body onto a rocky hillside. The damage inflicted was too much for his body to heal. His father was dying, and all Eoin could do now was sit at his bedside and comfort him during his last minutes.

---

*A*lasdair prepared to impart his final wish upon his eldest son as he watched him enter the room. He tried to sit up as Eoin approached his bedside. The thought of his heir seeing him in such a weakened state pained him almost as much as the crushed ribs and deflated lung that forced his breath to come in short rasps. He was a warrior, built strong like both his sons. He found it difficult to believe that it would be a creature as gentle as a horse that would send him to his deathbed, but he supposed that was just another sign that while the body and mind age, the soul often remains oblivious to fragile bones, creaking joints, and moments of forgetfulness.

Despite grayed hair and failing body, Alasdair knew in his heart he was still the youthful, handsome lad who wanted nothing more than to steal another kiss from his beloved wife. It had been twenty-five years since Elspeth passed away, and he still couldn't think of her without tears springing up in his dark eyes.

He pushed thoughts of her away, for he knew he would see his beloved soon enough. As his son sat down beside him, Alasdair allowed his thoughts to drift to the burden he knew he must place upon Eoin's shoulders.

Alasdair would not tell his son the true reason for his insistence upon a marriage between Eoin and Blaire MacChristy. For while he knew the true nature of Morna's predictions, Eoin had never known the witch. Alasdair knew if his dying wish for his son was based on some crazed long-dead aunt's predictions, it would only make Eoin even more resistant to the marriage.

It had long been believed that his son's betrothal to Blaire was to ensure the protection of the MacChristy territory. Donal MacChristy was laird over the smallest castle and territory in Scotland. With poor people and few provisions for safety, the MacChristy clan was ever in need of help from neighboring allies. It had been great fortune that Alasdair had always been good friends with Donal as it had made arranging the betrothal that much easier and more believable.

Alasdair knew that if Morna's predictions and spell came true, Blaire MacChristy would soon be replaced with a lass from the twenty-first century, and he was certain Eoin would not remain oblivious to the strange happenings. To help ease his son's shock, Alasdair had ensured that all of Morna's journals detailing her prediction, spell, and wish could be found in the witch's beloved secret room in the castle's basement, along with the spelled plaque showing Blaire's picture. He had also told the prediction and story to his beloved housemaid, Mary, but he wasn't sure if she'd believed his outrageous tale.

After Morna's death, Alasdair had discovered her journals detailing the enchanted plaque and how she planned for the swap to take place. The identity spell had already been set before Morna passed. Regardless of what happened, there would be a girl born many years from now, identical in appearance to Blaire MacChristy. The exchange of the two girls hinged upon the plaque Morna placed in the center of her sanctuary. If both Blaire and the identical girl were to see and read the words on the plaque out loud during some point in their lives, their paths would combine, and they would switch places in time. This part of Morna's plan was entirely dependent upon fate, and Alasdair strongly doubted if any such fantastic occurrence would ever take place. Regardless of his misgivings, he refused to betray his sister's memory.

"Son," Alasdair's chest began to weigh down on itself, begging him not to say anymore, but he refused to let his body fail before he said his peace, "I doona want ye and Arran to mourn me for long. I have had a full life. Everything I ever wanted, I have possessed."

"I don't want to hear ye say another word about that, Father. Just get some rest, and ye will feel much better come morning."

"Ye can hold your lies, son. My body may be weak, but my mind is sharp. Ye know as well as I do that I am dying. I need ye to make peace with that as well. For I expect ye to continue with the wedding plans as if nothing has happened. Ye will be laird of Conall Castle within the hour. It falls to ye to watch over not only our territory but the MacChristy's as well, by marrying Blaire."

*D*read crept up Eoin's spine at the thought of going through with his marriage to Blaire, but he refused to dwell on such things right now. He had never argued or denied his father anything, and he certainly wasn't going to start tonight.

"I want ye to send word to Laird MacChristy come sun up. Suggest that Blaire come to reside here at once, so that ye can make yer preparations together. I believe the wedding should be set for three weeks' time. I know she tries yer patience, but I expect ye to treat and cherish her as I did yer mother."

Eoin didn't believe himself capable of showing anyone the kind of adoration that his father had shown his mother. He didn't really think anyone other than his father was capable of loving that deeply, especially not himself. Despite having had significantly fewer partners than Arran, he was no less talented at lovemaking. But he had never met a lass who made him, even for a moment, dread spending the rest of his life without her.

He would not tell his father that, so instead, just as Alasdair Conall took his last breath and left this world to meet his beloved Elspeth once more, Eoin vowed, "I promise Father. I promise to marry her, and I promise to try."

CHAPTER 3

 *ver the Atlantic Ocean—Present Day*

"*B*ri, they're about to serve breakfast. Why don't you wake up and we'll talk about our plans for after we land?"

I started at the sound of my mother's voice beside me. I was in a deep sleep, and—as I tended to do when I slept sitting up—I snorted slightly as I came awake and threw my arms up to stretch, smacking the man sitting beside me as I did so. Only semi-conscious, I didn't take notice of my mistake until I caught the man's glare out of the corner of my eye.

"I'm so sorry." By reflex, I reached over and touched the man's arm as if he were one of my students who had fallen down on the playground. "Are you okay? I was still half . . ." I trailed off when I saw the man's glare transform into a lingering smile, urging me to snatch my hand away with a little more force than was probably necessary.

"That's alright, sweetheart." The man's eyes roamed over me as his grin spread.

I quickly faced my mother and scooted away from the man as much as was possible in the few inches that lay on either side of me.

"I was having the most horrible dream. I dreamed that Anthony, my ornery one, led a class revolt against the substitute. They had her tied to a chair and there was finger paint everywhere." I cringed at the images of sticky wet fingers smearing themselves across the classroom rug and bookshelves.

Mom laughed as she took a cup of coffee for each of us from the flight attendant. "Honey, they're five years old. They can't even tie their own shoes. They won't be taking the substitute hostage."

"I know, but the finger paint is certainly a possibility. I really should've locked that up in the cabinet. I'm just exhausted. I was up at the school until one this morning planning lessons and getting materials organized and making sure Mitsy had a handle on all of the plans."

"It's all going to be fine, Bri. What did your principal say when you asked for time off?"

"He wasn't thrilled, but I think more than anything he was shocked. The only personal days I've taken since I started were when I came down with pneumonia last winter, and then it was only because I truly thought I was going to die. He knew it must be important. He just asked that I try to be back by the Monday after Thanksgiving and to make sure that the substitute had adequate plans."

"Well, that's great. See? You have nothing to worry about. Just try and put all that out of your mind, dear. I really do need your help. I can't let this grant money go to waste."

"You're right. I won't mention it again. I'm here to help in any way I can." I smiled when I saw my mother's eyes lock on the food cart that was headed our way, and I knew our conversation was over. Mom was one of those few blessed people who could eat all she wanted and never gain a pound.

I watched as she inhaled the powdered eggs and cold croissant that sat untouched on my own tray and tried to focus my mind on something other than the pity I felt for the courageous substitute that was filling my shoes.

As I tried to rack my brain for something to ponder, I realized the sad truth: I had little in my life that was out of the norm to focus on. My drastic social decline since moving to Austin had me well on my way to becoming the Miss Havisham of the Lone Star State. I spent every spare second either working on my home or working on my classroom. While I loved the kiddos in my class, I was ashamed that I'd let my life get so unexciting.

I was at a point where many of the goals I'd set for myself had been met. I'd worked my way through college. I was happy with my job, happy with myself, and I owned my own home. But I was ready for my life to encompass more than just myself.

I wanted a friend, a husband, a lover. I wanted children in my life who'd call me "mom" rather than "teacher" or "Ms. Mothgomfrey." But with my social circle filled with PTA moms rather than eligible bachelors, my chances of finding anyone were pretty dismal.

Maybe a handsome Scot will sweep me off my feet? Because that happens to teachers from Austin every day, and there's sure to be a lot of eligible bachelors at the castle ruins . . . where no one has lived in four hundred years.

I shook my head, embarrassed at my little daydream, and tried to pull myself back to reality. "Okay, Mom. What's the plan?"

"Well . . ." I watched as she spoke in between mouthfuls of food, "When we land in Edinburgh, we'll pick up our rental car and drive to the National Museum of Scotland. They've been keeping all of the documents we found at the site. I already have clearance, so I should be able to take a lot of things with us. We'll start there by combing through the documents we already have and see if that brings to light anything we might have missed during the first dig."

"Ok, sounds good to me. Did you make any hotel reservations when you booked our flight?"

"No. I don't want to stay in Edinburgh, I think we should go ahead and try to get into the Highlands, closer to the ruins. I remember a little bed and breakfast we used to pass that was on the side of the road leading to the site. It was so charming on the outside. I always wanted to stay there, but never got the chance. We always just camped out on the grounds. I have no idea whether it's still there or not, but I'd like to take a chance and see."

"Alright. Anything else I need to know?" My blood pressure rose slightly when I learned that our night's accommodations were anything but certain, but I swallowed my panic and set my mind to go with the flow.

"Yes . . . you're going to need to drive. The rental's a standard." The corner of Mom's mouth pulled upward as she suppressed a grin.

"Okay, no problem." I chuckled slightly. Mom was an infamously bad driver even with an automatic transmission. I had never intended to let her drive us in the first place.

A chime overhead warned us we were beginning our descent into Edinburgh, and the captain came over the speaker system to ask everyone to return to their seats.

"Are you ready for this, sweetheart? I've always wanted to take you to Scotland, but you were always either in school or teaching school when I was here. I just know you are going to love it." She stood and motioned for me to switch her seats. "Here. I want you to look out the window. It's beautiful."

I obediently scooted over by the window and raised the plastic shade to look outside. I stared out over the lush landscape and immediately understood Mom's love for this country. It was where she belonged. I knew if I didn't live in the United States, she would have moved here permanently after her divorce.

I watched as the ground slowly came closer, and as the wheels touched down on the runway I felt a small tug deep inside. Maybe this was where I belonged as well. Excitement built as we taxied to the gate.

Scotland was going to be good to us. I could tell.

CHAPTER 4

*S*cotland–1645

*E*oin heard his brother's footsteps before he saw Arran plop down next to him and swing his feet over the side of the stone wall that surrounded the castle's exterior. The rocky coast that encircled their home calmed him, and Eoin often escaped here when something troubled him.

"Cheer up, brother. We haven't seen Blaire in over ten years. Just because the two of ye were determined to make each other miserable back then, doesn't mean ye will now. After all, ye certainly aren't the foolish lad ye were a decade ago."

Eoin turned to look at his brother. "Perhaps, but I canna stop thinking about the young lass who shot me in the arse with an arrow because I refused to let her have my horse. I still bear the scar! I canna imagine that she could have changed enough for me to feel anything for her."

Placing his arm around his brother's shoulder, Arran smiled as he spoke. "Who said ye have to feel anything for her? All ye have to do is marry the lass and take her to yer bed. Blaire was quite the beauty and, from what I've heard, she has only gotten prettier since we last

19

saw her. I feel sure a number o' lads would gladly take yer place. Consider yerself lucky, brother. Ye could be betrothed to Laird Kinnaird's eldest daughter. Ye would be, if the old toad had anything to say about it. If I remember correctly, she was just as disagreeable as Blaire but not nearly as comely."

"You're right, o' course," Eoin admitted. "It's not as if I expect love, but I'd rather not attach myself to someone I barely know. And as for taking her to my bed, if she is even remotely as difficult as she was as a young lass, I doona think her beauty will be enough to entice me."

As Eoin listened to Arran's laughter at his own disdain for his fiancée, the sound of footsteps made both men turn their heads to the trail leading to the castle.

"Here she comes. Let us go find out if the betrothed is apt to be as difficult to live with as ye seem to think she will be. I, for one, look forward to having a lass about." Arran stood and waited for Eoin to lead the way.

"As if there's been any lack of lasses about the castle with the way you parade them in and out every night." Eoin placed his hand on Arran's shoulder. "But let me make one thing clear to ye, brother. Regardless of how I may feel for her, she will be my wife. Ye are not to touch her, understood?"

"I would never! I may love the company of women, but I am quite looking forward to ye having a lass of yer own. Come. Ye best get that look off of yer face before we get down to greet her, or I predict that ye will start things off with yer bride on a bad foot, no? I doona think most lasses enjoy being greeted with a look o' pure dread and disdain."

"Right." Eoin plastered the largest grin he could manage as he stepped back through the side window from which he had climbed out onto the wall and made his way to the castle's entrance. He had just stepped into the hallway in front of the grand staircase, when he heard Blaire's voice echoing through the hallways.

"There is no use in standing here staring at me all day. Unless ye expect me to carry all my things to my room myself, and surely the laird has more manners than that. But then again, I'm having a hard time remembering very many good qualities about him. He couldn't even be bothered to greet me upon my arrival. I doona know what he has instructed ye, but I demand to be placed in whatever room is farthest from the laird's. We are not married yet. I will only share a room after the wedding, and even then, only if I'm forced."

Eoin stepped onto the staircase where Blaire could see him and interrupted her before she could berate the old stable master further. "Hello, Blaire. Welcome to Conall Castle. I apologize for not being here when ye arrived. I was sitting out on the wall when I saw ye headed this way." Reaching the bottom of the staircase, Eoin stood before Blaire and placed her hand in his. Flashing a smile that would make the most beautiful of women melt, he gently kissed the top of her hand, his dark black eyes piercing her own.

"I'm not interested in yer charms, Laird Conall." Jerking her hand away, Blaire bent and began piling her belongings into the stable master's arms. "Believe me, this will be a marriage in contract and nothing more. Any man who would agree to such an arrangement is obviously deranged. If it were up to me, I would be laird of the MacChristy keep after my father's passing. I would do a fine job, most likely better than him, but everyone seems to think women are only capable of breeding and pleasing a man, so I'm being married off. Do ye not think ye and my father could have made an alliance of safety without me being part o' the bargain?"

Eoin watched as Blaire stopped fooling with her things, only just noticing that the old man was already holding more than he could carry. He didn't move as she walked right up to him and jabbed two of her fingers right into the center of his chest, her eyes flaring with anger.

"But no. The great Eoin is too small a man to find a woman of his own. He is happy to wed someone who does not love him, care for him, or like him."

Eoin's temper rose as Blaire's fingers continued to jab into his ribs. Seething, he grabbed both of her wrists. "Ye can set the lass's belongings down, Kip. Go see that her horse is tied safely in the stables, and show her escorts to the dining hall so that they can have a good meal after their journey."

"Right away, sir." The old man struggled to set the large pile down neatly, then took off as quickly as he could out the grand doors.

"As for ye," still holding her wrists, Eoin backed Blaire into a column that lined the entranceway. With their bodies touching and his face close enough to feel the heat off her breath, Eoin continued, "Has it ever occurred to ye that I may be as reluctant toward this marriage as yerself?"

"Not possible," Blaire muttered under her breath.

"Aye, tis very possible. This betrothal was arranged between my father and yers. I was informed of it as a young lad and was as helpless in the matter as ye. As for yer other demands . . ." he tightened his grip and leaned in even closer, his lips brushing her ear as he whispered huskily, "yer belongings are to be brought to the room directly across from mine, and upon our wedding night, ye *will* move into my chambers immediately, that I can assure ye, Lady Blaire. This will be a real marriage in every sense o' the word. Ye will bear my children, and ye will quickly see just how capable I am of wooing any lass of my choosing."

"Ahem . . ." Arran cleared his throat as he walked into the room. "Well hello, Blaire. Had I known the two of ye were going to get along so quickly, I would have given ye some privacy and welcomed ye in the morning. I apologize for the intrusion."

"Do not make the mistake of assuming this is how it appears, brother." Eoin released Blaire's wrists and faced his brother. "Please help me take Lady MacChristy's belongings to the Lavender Room."

"But I have not yet had the chance to properly greet yer fiancée." Arran stepped to take Blaire's hand, but she quickly jerked it away.

"Doona bother. I'm sure beneath yer welcoming façade ye are equally as lacking in manners as yer brute of a brother." She snarled her upper lip. "I have often heard it said that ye were the fairer of the two Conall brothers, but I would have to disagree." She quickly whirled to face Eoin once again, "Now. I have had enough of both of the legendary Conall brothers for one evening. If ye can simply point me in the direction of food, I can assure ye that I can find the way myself."

Beyond stunned, both brothers pointed to the double doors to her right, staring wide-eyed as she stormed out of the entranceway and through the doors to which they'd pointed. Arran was the first to speak. "By all the saints, brother! I do believe ye were right about the lass. She is quite the beauty, but I'd be wary of taking her to my bed as well."

"Aye. I told ye so." Bending, Eoin began lifting Blaire's belongings, leaving half for his brother, and nudged his head to the staircase so that Arran would follow.

"I know just what ye need, brother. Let us ride out in the morning and spend the fortnight before yer wedding enjoying yer last few days of freedom! It would do ye good to get drunk and tup a lass or two before ye're strapped down with the wench now sleeping across the hall from ye. Mary would be more than happy to help with the wedding preparations, and if what I have seen of yer future bride tonight is any indication, she willna be wanting yer help even if ye are here."

"Nothing sounds better, but I doubt that would do anything to improve the lass' mood." Before he could get another word out, the doors out of which Blaire had gone burst open once more as Blaire stepped back into the grand entranceway.

"If ye call that slop that was waiting in the dining hall 'food,' I shall starve to death during my imprisonment here! I refuse to eat one bite of it. I expect much better out of the morning's meal. Now if ye don't mind, I will follow the two of ye to my chambers, where I will spend the rest of my night."

As they trudged up the staircase, balancing the loads of her belongings, Eoin leaned over to catch his brother's ear. "Ye're right. It's just what I need. We will ride out at first light."

*M*iles away Ramsay Kinnaird stood before his large stone fireplace, downing yet another goblet of whisky, when his personal messenger entered the room.

"I'm afraid tis true, sir. Blaire MacChristy moved into Conall Castle this very evening, and they are to be married within a fortnight. It was arranged between the laird's father and Donal MacChristy himself. From what I hear, neither Eoin nor Blaire are looking forward to the marriage."

"I doona give a damn about their feelings toward their marriage!" roared Ramsay, slurring his words as he continued. "How dare Alasdair make such an arrangement? Donal MacChristy is laird over the smallest keep in all of Scotland, while my territory is by far the largest. With both Donal and myself having daughters of the same age, it is an insult of the deepest accord that Alasdair would pass over arranging a marriage with my daughter for Blaire MacChristy."

"I . . . I believe, sir, that the arrangement was made so that Alasdair could ensure protection for his good friend. As ye know, the MacChristys have been facing difficult times for years. Their land is too scarce and their people too poor to provide adequate protection should their territory be in danger. I do not believe Alasdair meant any disrespect to ye, sir."

"I know perfectly well what Alasdair's intentions were when he made the arrangement, you damn fool!" He threw the metal goblet into the flames, sloshing the contents of his cup, forcing the flames to heighten and roar at the alcohol's touch.

"I . . . my apologies, sir." The man backed up a few steps, fearing that the laird's temper was about to grow completely out of control. Far too many servants had disappeared simply because they had been in the wrong place at the wrong time when the laird flew into one of his violent rages.

"This will not stand, I can promise ye that. This marriage will provide no protection for the MacChristy clan, for I will wipe out all of the Conalls. Afterward, it will only be a matter of time before the MacChristys wither and die of their own accord. Once his precious

Blaire is murdered before she is comfortably settled in her new home, the old laird will be so heartbroken, he will care for his territory even less than he does now." Storming from the room, Ramsay paused briefly, grabbing his messenger by the throat. "If ye so much as breathe a word of my intentions to anyone, I will wipe ye and yer entire family from the face of this earth."

Shoving the servant to the ground, Ramsay Kinnaird flew out of the room, his murderous plan taking shape as he went.

CHAPTER 5

*S*cotland – *Present Day*

*A*s usual, everything took twice as long as planned. Despite the fact that our plane had landed early that morning, it was close to six PM. Dusk was beginning to set in as we loaded the documents from the museum into the small compact rental and headed out of the city.

Several hours later, hungry and exhausted, we finally spotted the small inn that Mom had remembered. I parked in front of the charming two-story home and flipped on the interior lights of the cramped car as I pulled out a map.

"What do you think? Are we close enough to the ruins to stop for the night?"

Yawning, Mom stretched and nodded.

"Yes. We're only about thirty minutes away, and I've always wanted to try this place out. It looks great, doesn't it?"

"Yes it does. Let's go. I'm totally exhausted."

We unloaded our suitcases and made our way to the inn's entrance. Stepping inside the old wooden door, I smiled as the warmth of the fireplace to the left washed over me, melting away the icy feeling in my fingers and face.

I was loosening my scarf and unbuttoning my jacket when I heard a voice coming from the top of the stairs.

"Jerry! I think there's someone here. Go see if they will be wanting a room and, for God's sake, ask them if they want something to eat."

My stomach growled immediately at the mention of food. I hadn't eaten anything since the plane, and the one bite I'd had of the soggy powdered eggs hadn't held me for long. I reached down to pat my stomach, hoping it would stop growling at my request, just as the most miserable-looking man I'd ever seen walked our way from what appeared to be the kitchen.

Hunkered over, with a head covered in gray hair, he was far too skinny. He had the most severe-looking face, with a long, pointed nose and a chin that jutted far outward. I couldn't help but think that he more than slightly resembled Ebenezer Scrooge.

"Well, hello lassies," the man said with a large smile. "The two of ye look like ye're about to freeze to death, shivering in the doorway. Please, come in and I'll get ye something warm to eat, as I assume ye'll be staying the night." He quickly patted me on the shoulder and then walked back toward the kitchen, waving his hand so that we would follow.

I was certain my jaw visibly dropped, and it took me a few good seconds before I could follow. I glanced at my mother, who was staring back at me with a look of pure satisfaction.

"Never judge a book by its cover, Bri." She smiled and finally followed me.

Once inside the room, we were quickly whisked to a small table in the corner. Two steaming bowls of soup were placed in front of us, then the man's questions began.

"We're so glad to see the both of ye. First guests we've had here in a long while. Out o' the way as I'm sure ye know. Where are ye from? And what brings ye to this part o' the world?"

Mom spoke up first. "We're from the States—I live all over. Bri's my daughter, and she's a teacher from Austin, Texas. I'm here to do some archaeological work on the ruins of Conall Castle. I convinced Bri to come along and help."

"Ahh . . . Texas ye say?" The man turned and looked in my direction. "I know the whereabouts. My wife Gwendolyn grew up in San Antonio. She came here to visit her uncle as a young lass, about eighteen I think she was. I worked for the old man; from the second I saw her running through the field, trying to catch one of his sheep . . ."

He started laughing a deep, belly laugh that shook his whole body. I couldn't help but smile as well, the man's love for his wife evident with each heave of his shoulders.

"Well . . . I fell in love with her right then, and I knew that she wasn't going back to the United States."

"What's that, Jerry? What lies are you telling these poor women?" A petite woman, with striking green eyes entered the kitchen, and after planting a kiss on her husband's cheek, came in our direction, to greet us.

"I hope he's not boring you two to death with his tall tales. Let me guess, he was telling you about how he swept me off my feet; rendered me so senseless that I never went home. Well, he knows good and well it was this scenery I fell in love with, not this blithering old fool."

She winked over her shoulder at him, and I could tell by the twinkle in his eye he didn't believe a word of her teasing.

The rest of the evening flew by in a blur for the both of us. The old couple talked for hours, and I found myself captivated by the stories of their years spent together.

Finally, at half past eleven, we carried the last load of documents to a small room at the top of the stairs. Gwendolyn had attempted to give us each our own room, but Mom asked that we share, insisting that it would be easier to do research if we were in the same room.

As I listened to Mom mess up the covers while she tossed and turned in the antique bed, I washed my face, brushed my teeth, and pulled on my favorite flannel pajamas. Exhausted, I crawled into the bed and stuck my icy cold feet up against the warmth of my mother's sock-warmed toes.

I sighed and rolled over in an effort to claim back some of the covers that were disproportionally on the other side of bed.

"I know what you're thinking, darling. You'll get it someday."

"What's that?" I rolled over once more to face her.

"You want a relationship like Jerry and Gwendolyn. I could see it in the way you looked at them the whole evening. You'll get it someday. Not every relationship is like mine was with your father."

"I know. You're right. I just worry sometimes that it isn't ever going to happen for me."

"It will. But, sweetheart, you might want to ditch the retainer and buy some sexier PJs first."

***

*T*hree days later, and I sat surrounded by piles of yellowing parchment and dust.

I blew a rogue strand of hair out of my face that had slipped free from its binding with my lower lip. So far, we'd spent our days in Scotland poring over the boxes of documents without luck.

I glanced over at my mother, who with each passing day grew more restless. "I think we should take a break. Let's drive to the ruins and poke around there. Just start digging. Perhaps, we'll have more luck that way."

I was certain she hadn't heard a word. Her brow was creased in concentration, and her mind was clearly elsewhere as her eyes frantically searched the document in front of her. "Mom. Are you . . . ?"

"Oh my God! Sweet Mary, Moses, and Joseph! I cannot believe it!" She jumped up, screaming and dancing awkwardly around the room.

"What?" I stared at her, startled and slightly worried by her strange outburst.

"Bri! Come and look at this. I'm so tired, I wouldn't put it past myself to be imagining it. Quick. Come and see!"

"Everything all right in there?" Gwendolyn's voice called to us from the other side of the doorway, concern clear in her voice.

Mom ran to the door and swinging it open, threw her arms around the innkeeper. "Oh, yes. Everything is fantastic!"

"Okay, then. Good. Umm . . . there's some lunch for you both on the stove. But, please, take your time. It will be there when you're ready." Gwendolyn slowly backed out of the room, shutting the door behind her, obviously confused.

"Mom. What's the matter with you? You scared her to death!" I chuckled as I reached for the thick, yellowed piece of parchment she was extending in my direction.

"I don't know how I never noticed it before. It must've fallen out of one of Alasdair's journals. I'm certain it's in his hand."

I scanned the crumbling paper, struggling to make out some of the faded lettering. "Do you think it's true? Could there really be another room, a secret room in the basement that was never found in a previous dig? I thought you all had cleaned everything out of that basement."

"I don't know. I would be surprised, simply because we spent so much time excavating the basement, but it's the most promising thing we've found so far. We have to go and check it out."

"Absolutely, we do. Let's get cleaned up, go eat lunch, and hit the road."

"Yes. Let's! You take the shower. I'll take one when we get back here tonight. I'm just going to splash some water on my face."

I turned on the shower and stepped away to grab a towel and a change of clothes while I allowed the water to heat up. As I turned from the tub, I caught a glimpse of Mom's smiling reflection in the mirror and thought for a moment it was myself. All my life, people had told me how much we resembled one another, but I'd never been able to see it until that very moment.

Her eyes were glowing with excitement and, with her grinning broadly, I could see the young woman my mother once was, and the resemblance between us was undeniable.

I hurried in the shower, knowing my mother was anxious to get to the site, but I still felt warm and refreshed when I turned off the steamy spray. I reached around the curtain to grab a towel and saw my mother sitting on the edge of the bed twiddling her thumbs and tapping her feet.

She's always been good at subtlety, I thought to myself as I rushed to get ready as quickly as possible. Her jittering reminded me of my kindergarteners when they've waited too long to go to the restroom.

I pulled out my favorite pair of jeans and a v-cut blue t-shirt that matched the color of my eyes, donning them as I went back into the bathroom to throw on some makeup.

Quickly glancing at myself in the mirror, I pulled the hair away from my eyes with a clip, and walked back to the suitcase to retrieve my tennis shoes. I hadn't even bothered to pack any other pair. I knew that for the work we'd be doing, practicality was key.

I motioned in Mom's direction, waving her to the door so she would know I was ready. Together we made our way down the stairs. As we entered the kitchen, I saw my mother's eyes widen as she noticed the steaming pan of lasagna on the stove and Jerry and Gwendolyn sitting at the table.

"I decided to pull out one of my mother's recipes from the States for our American guests. Hope you enjoy. Come and sit down with us." Gwendolyn scooted over next to her husband and motioned to the two seats on the other side of the table. "I also packed you both a bag of sandwiches. From the commotion earlier, I figured you ladies might be out the rest of the day."

"Thank you." I filled my own plate and sat down across from Jerry. "You really don't have to cook for us every meal."

"Oh, doona worry, lass. We're charging ye for every bit of it." Jerry chuckled as Gwendolyn smacked his arm.

"Oh, you hush. It's really no problem. You wouldn't be able to find any other food anyhow. We're pretty much in the middle of nowhere."

"Well, thank you. This lasagna is delicious." I shoveled the steamy goodness into my mouth, grateful it hadn't been haggis awaiting us.

"Well, good. I'm glad you like it. I haven't made it in a very long time. Not Jerry's favorite, but it sure brings back a lot of memories of my mother's home cooking."

"Bri doesn't have very many memories of that, I'm afraid. Not much of a cook myself. Bri's very good though. Guess she learned to fend for herself once she got tired of boxed macaroni and cheese every night." Mom laughed as she got up to get her second serving of lasagna.

"It wasn't all that bad, Mom. You were a whiz at navigating take-out menus."

Gwendolyn laughed and got up to clear her and Jerry's plates. "Well, you ladies have a good rest of the day. Jerry and I are off to town to pick up a few groceries. We'll see you two in the morning. I'll leave the key by the front door if you don't mind locking it and placing it under the mat on your way out."

"Sure thing. Thanks again!" Mom shouted as we watched the couple leave. "Okay, sweetheart. You ready? I want us to have plenty of time to search around before nightfall."

I watched as mom pulled my plate away from me and placed it in the sink, not waiting for my reply. Obviously, I was through whether I wanted to be or not. "Sure, Mom. Let's get out of here."

I could feel the excitement emanating from my mother as I locked the front door to the inn and climbed into the rental. Together, we mapped out the route to the castle and set off toward the ruins.

CHAPTER 6

*S*cotland—*1645*

*B*laire yawned and stretched generously over the luscious feather bed that was covered in a color of lavender that matched almost everything else in the room. She had never seen a room more delicately decorated for a woman's tastes, and she suspected that it had once been Elspeth Conall's place of refuge. It certainly had been hers since she'd arrived at the castle. Upon learning of the brothers' quick departure after her arrival, she'd been so furious Blaire had decided not to leave the room until they were back at the castle.

This morning, they'd arrived.

And the end of her life, otherwise known as her wedding day, was set for three days' time.

Eoin was certainly handsome enough, but even as he had her pinned up against that column in the entranceway, with his breath coming in bursts against her ear and the side of her neck, not even a hint of a tingle had rushed down her spine.

Different from most women she'd grown up with, Blaire's life did not revolve around men, and her biggest worry was not finding a suitable husband. Blaire MacChristy dreamed of independence, of living on her own, of making her own way in life. As a result, Blaire had been endlessly chided anytime she voiced her desires, and her father made it very clear from an early age that her wishes mattered not anyway. Blaire didn't want to get married, and she had decided the first time she'd heard a crying child that she would always prefer a good lap dog to a suckling babe at her breast.

She never particularly like Eoin, but the moment she found out she was going to be married to him, she decided to put all of her effort into resenting his very being.

Arran, on the other hand, she wanted to make amends with. She needed a friend in the castle and one with enough power to sway things in her favor if she was going to reside here for the rest of her miserable life.

With Arran set as her number one task for the day, she quickly got dressed and pinned up her hair so that loose curls fell around her face. Wearing a light blue gown that beautifully framed her full breasts and trim waistline, she glanced in the mirror and decided that she was satisfied enough to exit her chambers.

As she wandered the many halls and corridors that wound through the castle, she couldn't help but be struck by the castle's great beauty. It had obviously been built by someone with great attention to detail and lived in by people who held great pride for their property and land.

Rounding a corner while absentmindedly looking around, she ran into a friendly-faced, plump, elderly woman carrying fresh lavender linens, obviously on her way to freshen up her bed. She hit the woman with such impact that the servant dropped the pile she was carrying and immediately flew into a string of apologies.

"Beggin' yer pardon, miss. The bedding was blocking my view, or I would have seen ye coming around the corner. I should not have been so careless. Are ye alright, miss?"

Struck by the woman's apology, Blaire immediately bent and began to help her gather the load. "Doona apologize. I was the one who was too busy looking up. I should have been paying closer attention. What is yer name?"

"My name is Mary, miss. I am pleased to make yer acquaintance. In person, that is. I've been talkin' to ye through the door for a number o' days now."

"Oh! Thank ye for bringing all of my meals. I wasn't quite feeling myself. Do ye know where Arran is? I was hoping to apologize for the way I treated him, the night I arrived. Also, I believe there is a stable master that I should apologize to as well. I doona believe I made the best impression."

"Oh . . . the stable master is my husband, and his name is Kip. But doona worry about him, miss. He needs someone to give him a hard time every now and then. Lord knows he does the same to all of us most of the time."

The woman's belly jiggled as she chuckled, and as the corners of her eyes crinkled with her smile, Blaire could see the woman's kindness seep from her eyes.

"As for Arran, I expect ye'll find him in his chambers, miss. I saw him leaving the stables a few moments ago. Just so ye know miss, I told them it wasn't a good idea for them to be running off like they did, but they never seem to listen to anyone but themselves. Stubborn, thick-skulled boys, the both o' them. But don't ye worry, miss. Mary's given them a lecture, like they've likely never had in their lives before. They're awfully sorry for the way they've treated ye, and they willna be doin it again, I can promise ye that."

"Well, thank ye Mary, but I suppose I'm to blame as well. Now, which room is Arran's?"

"Just on the opposite wall, one door down from yer own, miss. Right next to the laird's."

*B*laire paced back and forth in front of the door waiting for Arran to answer. When she received no answer, she knocked more loudly, and resumed her pacing once more.

Knocking a third time, she decided to try the bolt. It was unlocked, and she slipped inside the door, slamming it loudly behind her in an effort to draw attention to herself. Before she could even look around the room, her back was slammed into the door behind her, and she screamed as the knob jammed into her lower back.

Immediately, the hand gripping her arms relaxed as she slumped to the floor, landing on her bottom. She peered up at Arran, watching as recognition flittered across his face.

"Ach, lass! I'm verra sorry. I thought ye were Eoin, coming to give me a hard time for sleeping in the middle of the day. But I expect he's having as hard a time staying on his feet as I am." He swayed slightly and, hovering over her, propped both hands against the doorframe. "But why the hell would ye walk into my bedchamber?"

"I . . . I'm sorry," she managed. Her back throbbed from the impact of the knob on her spine and the pain had her on the verge of tears. But she never cried in front of others, and she certainly was not going to start now. "I was just coming to apologize to ye."

Arran chuckled slightly. "Why would ye be doing a thing like that? I was quite certain ye'd be ready to tan both of us when ye saw us next."

"It's not ye that I'm upset with. I'm sure ye felt obligated to accompany Eoin when he decided to philander around the countryside. But as to my behavior the night I arrived here, I had no reason to speak to ye so. I hope ye can forgive me."

"Lass . . ." he reached down to grab her shoulders and helped her to her feet. Once she was standing, he resumed his position against the doorway, leaving her trapped between his arms. "Ye shouldn't be so hard on Eoin. It was my idea for us to leave. I talked him into it."

She interrupted him, shocking herself at the pitch of her voice. "Ye what? I just arrived! I didn't even know my way around here when ye two left! Not that yer confession in any way excuses Eoin, but I canna believe both of ye could be so thoughtless."

*A*rran stared down at her as she continued screaming. She was even more beautiful when she was angry, with her face flushing pink and her eyes a vibrant blue. No wonder his brother had pushed himself against her when she'd screamed at him. He couldn't think of doing anything else, and with his head pounding and his thoughts still mushy, he couldn't resist the temptation to silence her by crushing his mouth to hers.

---

*S*he knew she was making a fool of herself, she didn't even know what she was screaming anymore. It wasn't until Arran's lips moved against hers that she was shocked into silence.

Her body reacted to his kiss in ways she didn't even know were possible. All of her anger melted away, along with every other sensible thought in her head. She knew she should stop him, but when his hands dropped from the door to cup either side of her face, she found herself leaning into him, desperate to get closer.

When he pushed her into the door with his body, she realized that despite the urgency of his kiss, he was taking special care not to hurt her back again. As his tongue slid deeper into her mouth, the feeling of his velvety lips undid her completely. Surrendering, she wove her fingers into his hair, clinging to his body and gently scratching his scalp. He groaned into her mouth as she tugged at his hair, grinding his hips toward her.

It wasn't until his hand dropped to cover her breast that Blaire returned to her senses. *Oh God. This must stop.* Doing the only thing she could think of to break his kiss, she raised her knee, throwing it into his groin. The second he dropped to his knees, she ran out of the door and back to her bedchamber without stopping to look back.

Slamming the door to her own bedchamber, Blaire sank onto the edge of the bed and stared blankly at the wall until her breathing returned to normal. Reaching up to brush her fingers over her lips, the rush of emotions she'd felt only seconds ago came back to her.

Blaire had always prided herself on not being driven by the mindless need for men like most women seemed to be, but perhaps she'd just been kissing the wrong men.

Before Blaire's engagement to Eoin had been announced, Blaire had her fair share of suitors at her father's home. Many of them even kissed her, but she had always found the kisses to be only tolerable, if not mildly pleasant. Arran's kiss was far more than tolerable, and it ignited the first glimmer of hope she'd had since arriving at the castle.

*rran couldn't begin to imagine how he could have been so daft. She was engaged to his brother. She was the one person forbidden to him, and he had pinned her against the wall and kissed her with such passion he still couldn't catch his breath.

If it hadn't been for her kneeing him in the groin, he knew he would have taken her to his bed. He couldn't remember the last time he'd wanted a woman so much. He could blame it on the ale, but he knew that was not what had made him kiss her.

He had been captivated the moment he saw her in the entranceway with his brother and had suggested they leave town as much for his own benefit as for Eoin's.

The heat between them had been indisputable. The moment their lips touched, she melted into him. He briefly allowed himself to imagine where that kiss was leading before shaking himself out of it. She was Eoin's. He would never tell his brother what had occurred between them, and he would make damned sure Blaire wouldn't either.

He couldn't bear the thought of hurting his brother, and although he found it hard to believe he would be able to resist her, he swore to himself he would do his utmost to avoid Blaire MacChristy altogether.

CHAPTER 7

$\mathcal{J}$ust one more drink and he'd be brave enough to have the conversation he'd been putting off for three days. He couldn't figure out what it was about this lass, but his whiskey consumption was leaning on the side of excess ever since her reentry into his life. Arran's plans to avoid Blaire had gone about as well as his plan to take Eoin away until the wedding.

It didn't matter how many excuses he made to avoid the main building, he ended up with Blaire wrapped up in his arms. Whether he was working with Kip in the stables, shooting arrows in the field, or even helping Mary in the kitchen, they seemed to run into each other. And without fail, moments later he'd have her up against a wall or in a closet, trying to show her with his kiss just how much his body wanted her in his bed.

And each time, she returned his passion with full force, begging him to marry her instead of Eoin. He couldn't believe how much he wished he could do just that. Marry her and have children with her, and wake with her beside him every day. He loved her fiery spirit, the way she said what she thought without hesitation; he'd never met a lass who was so forceful with her words.

Her beauty was another matter entirely. She made his heart race so fast that he could hardly breathe, but it was her wild spirit that he knew could tame his own wandering ways. She fit perfectly in his arms, in his heart. And the knowledge that he had to deny her for the sake of his brother caused him to reach for yet another glass, downing it quickly and standing to make his way to Blaire's room, just down the hall.

*H*e was surprised at how quickly she answered the door, or perhaps it just seemed as such with the way his head was swimming. His lips were warmed by the touch of Blaire's lips. As she pressed herself up against him, he had to force himself to push her away, holding her arms tightly so that she couldn't come closer to him. Cruelty was the only way she would accept his rejection and willingly marry his brother.

"Blaire, ye know we canna do this, lass. Ye're marrying Eoin tonight. I canna be the one to marry ye. The contract was drawn between my father and yer own. It isn't for us to be changing it, lass, as much as ye'd like me to." He released his grip on her arms as she ceased trying to move closer. He stepped away as he watched her slowly turn her face so that it showed no emotion. He'd expected no less from the fiery, wild lass. He knew she'd rather die than show him a weakness.

"But ye canna tell me ye wouldna like to. Perhaps, the knowledge of that will be enough to keep me content in between our days together."

"Lass, I can tell ye I wouldna want to marry ye. That's what I've come to say. Ye are beautiful, Blaire, and I've enjoyed my time with ye as much as I have any lass. But once ye've married my brother, I'll not be wanting ye anymore. There'll be another lass in my arms tonight. It's the way I am." His heart pounded off rhythm in his chest, painfully denying his lies. He expected her to match his hurtful words with some of her own, but as he watched her silently turn and walk out the door, he knew just how deep the wound was he'd caused.

He gripped the bedpost of Blaire's bed and slid himself onto the floor. Gripping his chest, he tried to stop the pain that built with each sob he held back, as he let the scars of his loss carve their way into his heart.

*I*t had been all she could do not to burst into tears. Never in her life had speech so utterly escaped her. With each additional word that Arran spoke, an icy winter spread through her core, making her completely defenseless against him.

She hated it. Hated how much she cared for him. How quickly her feelings had built and made her doubt everything she thought she'd known about herself.

Eoin had been nothing but kind and attentive since he'd returned from his trip. But he would never make her feel the way Arran did. She'd known deep down that it was Eoin she would have to marry, but she'd held on to the hope that she'd have Arran's affection as well.

With that gone, she didn't think herself capable of going through with her marriage to Eoin. It would be torture to be locked in a loveless marriage. To be so close to Arran, watching him with other girls, would be like throwing her heart onto a pile of burning coals.

If only convention allowed it, Blaire knew she would be happiest making her own way in the world, dependent on no one but herself. If it were acceptable, she would be pleased with taking lovers, remaining single, and taking in stray dogs instead of raising children. But things weren't different, and this marriage would be a prison. A prison filled with the expectations and ritualistic to-dos that would be required of the new lady of the castle.

The idea suffocated her. Each minute marked a minute closer to her wedding, and she could feel her spirit retreating farther and farther into itself. Her heart was breaking.

Stopping long enough to wipe the tears from her eyes, Blaire looked up and realized she had wandered into a part of the castle she'd never been before. She knew she was lost, but didn't care, and continued to flee down the dark steps, choosing her path at random.

When the stairs downward came to an abrupt stop, she lost her footing and stumbled through the castle's main basement and into the wall on the opposite side. When the wall gave way, she landed on her face with a thud on the cold stone floor.

The fall didn't hurt, but it was the pain in her heart that kept her from pushing herself up off the ground. She lay there crying until her eyes ran dry and her nose was sore, all the while wishing she could just disappear. She would rather be dead, would rather evaporate into nothing, than live her life trapped like a bird in a cage forced to sing whenever called upon.

She had no idea how long she lay there, but when she had cried all the tears she had to cry, she decided it was time to get up and face the miserable life before her.

Standing, she brushed the dirt off the side of her face and turned her head in the direction of the sunlight streaming in from the small window in the far corner. As she waited for her eyes to adjust to the lighting, she scanned the room and felt herself getting light-headed. Confused and frightened, she wondered if she had hit her head harder than she'd thought as she tried to make sense of what was in the chamber.

Hundreds of dusty old books, all circling a large oval desk in the center of the room, surrounded her. Books lay scattered and open on the desk, and as she lifted the page she felt a chill move down her spine as she began to read the words.

Spells. Some to bless, some to curse, some claimed to have the ability to move time itself. Fascinated, she rummaged through the pages, finding instructions on how to cast spells and cure various ailments.

Who could this belong to? Not Arran or Eoin. She glanced up from the dusty, yellowed page. Light reflecting off of something shiny at the back of the table caught her attention, and her blood ran cold.

There, propped up against the back wall, sat a round shiny plate with her likeness painted on the front.

Underneath were words scribbled in some unfamiliar language. With shaky fingers, she reached forward to touch the plaque. As she brushed her fingers over the shiny surface, some of the paint flaked off on her fingertips.

It was too old, she realized, to have been painted by Arran or Eoin. *Who could have done this then? Not Alasdair. This portrait resembles me now, and I was a small child the last time he saw me. Not my father. Who?*

Trying to form some sense, she sounded out the words written below her portrait. As she worked through the sounds, a strange energy began to build in the room. She could almost hear the walls humming, and despite something pulling at the edge of her brain, telling her to stop, curiosity piqued her interest and she continued to sound out the inscription.

Just as she finished sounding out the last syllable, an unbearable pain shot through her head. Gripping the edge of the table, she screamed out in agony. The entire world felt as if it were shaking, but when she looked around the room nothing seemed to be moving but her.

She spun around to the sound of someone's voice and found old Mary standing in the doorway with a horrified expression on her face.

"Miss! Miss! What's the matter? We've been looking everywhere for ye ..." She stopped speaking as Blaire cried out once more.

Blaire tried to focus on Mary's words, but the edges around the woman were blurring, and she saw the servant's face swirl in on itself.

It was the most excruciating pain, and she couldn't stop the agonizing screams that were escaping her lips. She was certain she was shattering into a million pieces.

When she looked down, she could no longer see the end of her dress, and she knew she was dying.

Her last conscious thought as she disappeared into the dust was that maybe she would get her wish after all.

CHAPTER 8

*S*cotland—*Present Day*

*I*t took less time than we had expected to get to the castle ruins, and as I rounded the last corner of the road, I could see my mother fidgeting with anticipation. She started giving instructions the second I turned the compact rental onto the rocky road leading to the site.

"Okay. Just pull over here. We'll walk the rest of the way. I'm going to go ahead and scan the area so I can decide how I want us to maneuver this. Meet me up there after you unload everything."

I pulled over to the side of the road and watched as mom jumped out of the car to make her way to the base of the ruins.

Okay. Sure thing, Mom. You go on ahead. I got it. Really. I'll have no problem carrying both of these backpacks. They're only filled with enough supplies to last us a week or two. I rolled my eyes and continued my mental, one-way conversation with her as I stepped out of the car and walked around to the trunk.

I heaved the two backpacks out of the car and, balancing as best I could, I hung one around my right shoulder and one around my left, wobbling to the top of the hill to meet up with Mom.

Looking out over the expansive area, I couldn't imagine how anyone could tell one area of the ruins from the next, but as I walked up behind Mom, I noticed she was already mapping out the site.

She pointed to the far right corner of the ruins. "See over there, honey, that was the laird's chambers, overlooking the sea. To the right was the grand dining hall, and where we are standing right now would have been the main entrance. Can't you see how beautiful it was?"

"I'm sure it was, but I have no idea how you are able to tell what room was what from staring at these piles of rocks."

"I've been studying this for years. I'm as familiar with these rocks as you are with your classroom, but I'm hoping I'm not quite as familiar as I think, otherwise there's no way another room actually exists in the basement. I think we should go straight down into the basement and start poking around there."

"I'm following your lead. But first, you have to take your backpack." I shrugged the heavy pack off my shoulder and dropped it at her feet.

"Let's get started." She quickly picked up the pack and, swinging it onto her back, took off toward the ruins, motioning for me to follow.

I stayed close behind as I followed her to a spot on the left-hand side of the ruins.

"Is this where the basement is?"

"Yes, it's right up here. It's been locked up to keep visitors out. Not completely safe, you see, but I have the key."

"It doesn't look as if it has been opened in a long time." I stared down at the metal door on the ground, closed with a lock that was covered in rust.

"I don't imagine anyone has been in since we stopped our excavation on the site. No other archaeologists have worked here, and now it's mainly tourists that come to look at the ruins."

In unison, we dropped to our knees. I grabbed the side of the heavy lock, holding it up in Mom's direction, so that she could insert the key.

"It's really stiff. I hope the key doesn't break off when I turn it." She paused nervously before turning the key to the left.

Luckily, it popped open with ease. Lifting the metal door open was another matter entirely.

Grass had grown up around the edges of the door, nearly burying it in the ground. Mom was already ahead of me, slipping on her yellow gloves and grabbing her shovel before I had a chance to swing my backpack off of my shoulders.

Half an hour later, with enough dirt dug up around the edges of the door, we were able to grab the large handle and pull it out of place, flipping it onto its other side on the ground.

I wrinkled my nose at the musty smell that rose out of the hole and motioned for Mom to lead the way.

When we reached the bottom of the stairwell, I watched as Mom pushed open the creaky, wooden door that must have originally been the entrance into the basement. Its hinges were worn and decaying, but as it creakily opened, we made our way inside.

The first room was empty, all contents cleared out during the original excavation of the site. At first glance, it seemed impossible that there would be any sort of secret room. How could they have missed it when such an extensive search and clean-out of the space had been conducted the first time around? But upon entering, both of our flashlights caught a glimmer of the same crack running down the back right corner of the space.

I watched as Mom hesitantly crept forward, obviously trying her best not to get her hopes up. As she approached the crack, she reached behind to grab a chisel and hammer out of the side of her backpack. Cautiously, she placed the thin edge up against the crack and tapped the end with the hammer. Dust and small pieces of debris floated into the air. Gaining confidence at her suspicions, she worked her way down the crack, tapping every few inches. About halfway down the wall, she hit a latch, and with one hard smack the door came swinging open.

Mom took off exploring the room with her flashlight, and I stood back to scan the room with my own. Stacks of books surrounded us, and one half of the room had collapsed in on itself, blocking any source of natural light. I slowly ventured further into the room, pulling up the V-neck of my shirt until it covered my mouth to block the dust that was invading my lungs.

I shined the light up and down the room, almost dropping my flashlight when the light beam reflected off a metal object sitting in the middle of the room and into my eyes. I blinked to adjust to the sudden flash of light and stepped forward to get a better look. When I caught sight of what was propped on the center of the table I actually did drop the flashlight, and I screamed as it bounced off the floor.

It hit the hard stone with a smash, and I was immediately engulfed in darkness until Mom shined her own light in my direction.

"What on earth's the matter? You scared me to death! Did you see a rat?"

My knees were shaking, and I couldn't seem to respond as thoughts raced through my mind. *Surely I saw that wrong. There was not a painting of me on that plaque!*

I reached to place my hands on the desk in front of me, and my hands landed in a pile of dust and cobwebs that painted every surface.

"Can you hand me my flashlight, Mom? I think it rolled over near your feet."

As soon as Mom located it and it was back in my hands, I banged on the end where the batteries were connected and managed to get the light to come back on. Slowly standing, I shined the light onto the center of the table again, and a chill ran down my spine as I looked at my own image peering back at me.

My fingers shook as I reached to grab the item. *How? Why? When?* A million questions swarmed through my mind as I tried to comprehend what I was seeing. The plaque was obviously centuries old. The metal was tarnished, the picture faded, and part of it had been chipped off, as if someone had inadvertently flaked part of it off many years after it had been painted.

Fear gripped my belly as I faced my mother.

"What is this? Is this some kind of joke, Mom? Have you been down here before?"

"What are you talking about?" She reached forward and grabbed the plaque out of my hands, letting out a low yelp as she looked down at the image.

"What's going on, Mom?"

"Umm . . . this is just a coincidence, darling. No, I haven't been down here before. I think it's been a very long time since anyone's been here. We do have Scottish ancestors, you know? You just look a lot like the woman in the painting."

She continued to mumble comforting words, but I could see fear spread across her face. I tugged the plaque out of her hands and blew the dust off the top, revealing etchings underneath the painting of my picture.

I didn't recognize the language, but slowly I began to sound out the words. From the moment I began to utter the strange syllables, I felt the room change.

The fear that had started in my belly moved up until it paralyzed me entirely. Small hairs on the back of my neck stood up on end.

Something pulled me toward the words, forcing me to utter them even as I tried to swallow the sounds coming from my mouth.

As I finished the string of sounds, I felt my body pull apart at the seams, spiraling me into agonizing pain. I cried out at the same time I heard my mother's horrified scream in front of me.

I dropped to my knees as the room trembled around me. My skin was on fire, and I felt as if someone was stabbing me repeatedly.

"Bri! Bri! Oh my God, Bri!"

I wished I could see my mom. I could hear her terrified screams not far from me, but my vision blurred as pain continued to course through my body.

Just when I thought I could bear no more pain, I heard what I thought was my spine snapping, and I gladly embraced unconsciousness.

CHAPTER 9

*S*cotland—1645

*V*ision slowly made its way back to me as I waited for the blurry images to clear. I reached to grip the edge of the table and struggled to pull myself to my feet. I moved my hands to grip the sides of my head, only briefly registering that my fingers didn't come away from the table's surface covered in dust. I could hear the blood pounding in my head, and I couldn't catch my breath. A voice from behind me started to penetrate my foggy brain.

On unsteady feet I spun toward the doorway, struggling to make out the form standing in front of me. I knew it had to be my mother, but it didn't look like her. This was a short, plump woman, while my mother was tall and slim.

I closed my eyes briefly and opened them once more, hoping it would help me clear my sight. It did nothing to increase my vision, but I could now make out the woman's words.

Why is Mom talking like that? I don't understand what she's saying. Am I injured? My head certainly feels like it. Did part of the ceiling collapse? What's happening? Thoughts coursed through my mind as I listened to the woman's ramblings.

"Oh God! Oh dear, sweet Mother O' God! The old laird was right. What is old Mary going to do now? And with the lass just hours away from her wedding! Lassies picked a grand time to be messing with magic, they did!"

That's definitely not Mom. Am I in the hospital or something? Wait! Wedding? What the hell is going on?

I struggled to process my surroundings as I felt the woman's hands grip my shoulders and shake them.

"Lass! Are ye all right? Old Mary needs ye to speak."

"Please, stop shaking me! It's killing my head!" I gasped and reached to grab my head once more, realizing I could finally see the woman clearly. The pain that had nearly ripped me in half only moments ago had slowly eased into a migraine.

"Oh dear heavens, lass! Where'd ye learn to speak in such a manner? Ye must be from far away, dearie. Old Mary's never heard any such speech in her life."

I felt the shaking stop and looked into the gray eyes that were studying me fiercely.

"Oh, by the Saints, lass! I never believed his stories, but ye do look remarkably similar; except Lady Blaire would never dress in such inappropriate attire. Why, ye look like the worse kind of tavern wench! I can see the shape of yer legs, lass! Not to mention . . ."

My head was throbbing too incessantly to concentrate. I scanned the room, while silently willing the woman to stop speaking.

I knew I wasn't in a hospital. The space looked old and somehow familiar. Slowly, I turned my head back to the table I was leaning against now and saw the portrait of myself.

Memories of what I'd been doing only moments before came rushing back, and panic burst forth as I shot out of the woman's reach.

"Where's my mother? What happened? What? What is that?" My voice and fingers were shaking as I pointed to the portrait and stared back at the old woman.

"Oh, ye poor thing. Ye look quite frightened to death."

I watched as the woman moved toward me once more and pulled me toward a stool in the corner of the room.

The woman was right. I was scared. Attempting to stifle my panic, I followed her urging and collapsed onto the smooth, wooden seat.

"Are ye all right now, lass? Allow me to explain to ye, Dearie."

I simply nodded as numbness replaced the sense of panic, and turned to watch the woman as she spoke.

"I'll not be sure about the where and when ye came from, dearie, but I can tell by yer manner of speech and dress, it is nowhere I've ever seen or heard about. Not that old Mary's been or seen very many places."

I watched as the woman paused and chuckled slightly. Then, seeing my confusion, she stopped laughing and pulled her face into a look of seriousness once again.

"But I can tell ye that today is the third day of November in the year sixteen hundred and forty-five. And it is yer wedding day."

I started to refute the woman's claims, only to find that my mouth was dry and my knees were shaking. I sat quietly instead.

"Ye are in Conall Castle, lass, and while old Mary knows ye won't be the Lady Blaire, the rest of the castle won't be able to tell the difference, and unless ye want to be locked up, I suggest ye doona let them find out the truth."

As I listened to the woman speak about my upcoming marriage to the castle laird, laughter threatened to bubble up out of my throat.

I definitely hit my head. The room collapsed, and I am in a coma. I'm in a coma, and I'm dreaming that I went back in time to marry a Scottish laird. That's what you get for daydreaming nonsense, Bri.

"And what was yer name before ye arrived here, lass? Ye canna be known by it from now on, but I'd like to know yer true name, all the same."

The woman's question seemed to throw me out of my thoughts, and I found myself answering automatically.

"I'm Brielle Montgomery. But call me Bri for short."

"Well, Briforshort, Old Mary's never heard of a name like that before. I'm pleased to meet ye, lass, but from now on, ye'll need to answer to the name Blaire, do ye understand?"

"Yes."

"Good. Now, I'm Mary, and ye'll be spending a lot of time with me. I'm the one to know around here, believe me. Now what's yer name again?"

I relaxed a little as I noticed that my knees were no longer shaking, and my breathing had returned to normal. I smiled at Mary as I replied, "Blaire."

"Verra good, lass! I could tell ye would be a quick learner by the looks of ye. Now, let's get ye up to yer room before anyone else sees ye dressed in such a manner."

Mary stood beside me and dusted off the bottom of her plain gray dress.

If I'm in a coma, I might as well try and have a little fun. It's probably a good sign that I'm dreaming, I'm assuming that means I'm not brain dead. Maybe this dream will allow my brain time to heal. In the meantime, I guess I'll just marry the Scottish laird I'd wished for.

I giggled inwardly at myself, deciding to enjoy the dream while it lasted. As I stood to follow Mary, I had to stop and steady myself on the wall to keep my head from spinning.

If only my head weren't hurting so much. But, I guess it probably should be hurting, since a 400-year-old solid stone ceiling collapsed on my head. Wait! Oh, my God! The ceiling collapsed! What about Mom? Is she injured?

I tried to calm my breathing once again and sat back down on the wooden stool. *No. I saw her when everything started to shake. The ceiling above her wasn't moving at all, and she was standing close to the entrance. She's fine. She's fine. She has to be fine.*

I continued to reassure myself until Mary's hands touched my shoulders once again.

"Come on, lass. We must start preparing ye for the wedding. I'll try and explain some more while we are getting ye washed up. Follow me."

The old woman took off toward a castle corridor, leaving me with little option other than to follow.

As I walked behind Mary, I rationalized my worries away by concentrating on two pieces of information that stuck out in my mind.

One, if both my mother and I had been hurt in the collapse, I figured there would have been no one there to get help. If Mom hadn't been able to get help, I would be dead rather than sitting in a hospital bed in the dreamlike coma I was in now. Mom was most likely fine. I just hadn't elected to let her into my dream yet, I supposed.

Two, regardless of what had happened, there was nothing that I could do about it now.

Unnecessary stress wasn't good for the healing process, so until I woke up and knew with certainty what had occurred, I was going to enjoy the surreal experience I was having now.

I looked up as Mary came to a halt in front of me and realized instantly that I had been paying little attention to the route we had taken to the door in front of which I was now standing.

It was a magnificent door. Strong yet feminine, the door was carved with precise detail that swirled in and around the wood with great craftsmanship. I thought it odd that I would be dreaming in such detail, but Mary interrupted me before I could explore the thought further.

"This is yer bedchamber, lass. Well, at least for a few hours anyway. After the wedding, ye will move to the laird's bedchamber for the wedding night." She paused to push the door open and gestured, nudging me inside. "I think ye'll find the room quite nice. The laird's mother used this as her own special sanctuary while she was living. Go on, dearie. Old Mary will be back shortly. I'll have a hot bath brought up for ye."

Before I could utter a reply, Mary was gone.

Alone, I stepped inside the doorway. My first thought was that it was far too large. My entire living room and kitchen could easily fit within this one room. Why did anyone need so much room to sleep? But as I continued to make my way through the space I realized the excess room made it easy to breathe.

The room exuded calm, and I allowed myself to fall onto the bed in the center of it. The bed was covered in the same shades of purple that were mirrored throughout the rest of the room. I was just snuggling deep down into the lush fabrics when the chamber door flew open and Mary rushed in.

"Come on, lass. Up ye go and into the tub." She grabbed me by the arm, hauling me up out of the bed.

My head swam once again as I stood, and I gripped the wooden bedpost to hold myself up as I watched several young men carry a large oval-shaped basin past the doorway. Several steaming buckets of water were poured into the tub, and the servants retreated, closing the door behind them.

As soon as everyone was gone, Mary reached forward, fumbling with my clothes.

"What are you doing?" I pushed the old woman's hands away from me.

"What does it look like I'm doing, lass? We doona have much time. Ye are to be at yer wedding promptly! Get yerself in that tub, dearie." Mary's voice was shrill and demanding as she placed her hands on her hips and glared straight at me.

"Ok. Alright." I held up a hand to Mary and self-consciously stripped down, hopping in the water as fast as I could. The heat of the water certainly felt real and it briefly crossed my mind that I couldn't remember ever having such a sense-filled dream before.

Mary's face seemed to soften as she watched me hiss at the touch of the steaming water. "Lass, I'm sorry everything is happening so fast for ye. I was hoping I would have time to explain, but I'm afraid that will have to wait."

I wondered what there was to explain in a dream. Dreams often made no sense. But as was becoming habit, I had no time to respond before Mary continued talking.

"Here's what ye will be needing to know today." Mary sank down onto the edge of the bed and crossed her arms with a look of exasperation. "Yer name is Blaire MacChristy. Yer father's name is

Donal, and it is yer duty to marry the laird, Eoin Conall, to help provide protection for yer father's territory."

I splashed water on my face, scrubbing my body with my hands as I listened to Mary's instructions. Yes, the water was definitely hot. My skin turned pink as I lifted my arm out of it to scrub myself clean.

"Ye look just like Blaire, so once we get ye in yer dress and pull yer hair up, there's not a soul in all of Scotland who would be able to say otherwise. That is, until ye speak, dearie. I've never heard anyone talk so plain. Old Mary's not so sure what to do about that."

Mary stood and paced back and forth around the room. The water seemed to help my aching head, and as I reached over the edge of the tub to grab a cloth and dry myself, I noticed my head didn't spin with the effort.

"Perhaps, I can try to mimic your accent." I began to dry myself, feeling refreshed and much more like myself.

"Accent? What do ye mean, lass?" Mary stopped pacing and pivoted to face me.

"I mean, that ye doona have to worry so much. I can try to mimic the way ye speak." I smiled as I tried to tilt my words into the best Scottish accent I could muster. Thank goodness for all the books I'd read aloud to my kindergarteners. They always loved it when I used voices, so over the years I'd developed quite the repertoire of accents.

"Ah! That's not bad, lass! Perhaps, ye can do it after all. That's always what the late Laird Alasdair said: that ye'd be a blessing to us all. But I never believed his stories until this day."

"What stories?" With my head no longer hurting, I found myself quite interested in what Mary was saying.

"Oh, I doona have time to talk to ye about that today, dear. Excuse me. I should have said, I doona have time to talk to ye about that today, miss. Old Mary has to start calling ye miss, if yer going to be lady of the castle." Mary paused and chuckled. "I never woulda believed that today would turn out as it has, lass. Oh my, it's been one turnip of a day for Mary. Not to mention yerself, dear. Ugh. I mean, miss. It's been a trying day for ye as well."

I laughed and listened to Mary ramble as I shrugged into the pale blue gown that she was holding up in my direction.

"Oh, Mary, it's stunning!" I looked down at the bodice, quite taken with the image below me. It was the most elegant piece of clothing I had ever worn, and I wondered why women didn't wear dresses more often. I couldn't even see myself yet, with the way Mary had me turned away from the mirror, but I felt beautiful inside the flowing fabric.

"Yes it is, lass. But ye canna look yet. Ye may only look when I've finished yer hair, and ye are all ready for yer wedding."

I smiled, deciding to enjoy my coma. "What does the laird look like, Mary?"

Mary chuckled, "Well, that's a fine question, miss. Look, I said it! I called ye 'miss,' miss!" She paused to laugh. "I doona believe ye could be more fortunate in a husband, miss. I love those two boys as if they are my own bairns, ornery as they are."

"Two?" I interrupted on reflex, and glanced backward at Mary, who was pinning pieces of my hair into place.

"Oh, yes. There are two Conall brothers. But ye are marrying the elder brother, Eoin. The younger brother is Arran. Most lasses would agree that there aren't two more handsome lads anywhere in Scotland. Even I would have to agree, and I'm far too old to unlace my corset over such things."

I let out a small yelp as Mary tugged especially hard on a tendril of my hair.

"Oh sorry, dearie. I mean, miss. Oh! Old Mary will fix her mind on it eventually. Doona be worried." She continued to arrange my hair as she spoke. "Both lads are handsome, but in my humble opinion, I believe ye will be finding yerself sharing a bed with the finer brother."

I should hope so. It is my coma, after all. Why would I decide to dream up a marriage with some ugly old fart?

"Wonderful!" I replied and was rewarded with a smack on the head.

"Ye keep slipping into yer strange way of speaking, lass. It's mighty important that ye doona do that anymore. If Old Mary can remember to call ye 'miss,' a young lass like yerself can remember to speak proper." Mary turned me around so that I was facing the mirror. "There. All done, miss."

I stared back at my reflection, unable to recall a time when I felt more radiant. The blue in the dress made my blue eyes sparkle, and the cut of the dress fit perfectly. "Thank you, Mary. I love it."

"I'm pleased to hear it, miss. Ye seem to be a smidge more accepting of the wedding than Blaire, so I'm glad ye're here. I can only hope Blaire is fairing well in . . . wherever ye came from."

"What do you mean?"

"Oh. I need to stop speaking of it. I already told ye, I canna explain it to ye today. I'll be speaking to ye in a few days, after the laird and ye have had some time alone together."

"I see." I didn't see at all, but I decided to let it go. Whatever it was couldn't be that important. This was all just a dream.

"Now." Mary gently pushed me toward the door. "It's time for yer wedding."

I smiled excitedly and followed Mary out the door, hoping that I wouldn't wake up before I got a chance to see my future husband and discover why I needed to change my name to someone else's to marry the man I'd dreamed up.

CHAPTER 10

resent Day

delle Montgomery screamed and reached behind her, grabbing for any sturdy surface to remind her of reality as the contents of the room swirled around her daughter, one minute picking her up into the chaos, the next minute sweeping her away into nothing. Her legs shook, and her ears ached at the sound of her own terrified screams. She reached up and smacked herself hard across the cheek, trying to wake herself from the twisted nightmare. When nothing changed, she forced her eyes to close and shook her head violently, hoping that the motion would clear the insanity from her head.

When she gathered the courage to open her eyes, she instantly relaxed against the back wall and breathed in deep, savoring the dusty, wet smell that filled her lungs. Bri was there, safe, and just where she'd been moments ago. It was her own head she was worried about. She'd make an appointment with a doctor as soon as she got home.

"Bri. Did I pass out? Fall and hit my head coming through the doorway? I was so sure . . ." She trailed off as she took in the horrified look on her daughter's face. Pins prickled down her back as her eyes took in the floor-length gown covering her daughter's body. "What? What's going on, Bri? I . . . I'm not feeling very well."

Adelle watched as her daughter's head quickly turned, scanning back and forth across the room.

"Where am I? And my name is not Bri? Who do ye think ye are?"

"Bri. What do you think you're doing? Seriously. Your accent is remarkable, but where did you get that dress? Is this some sort of weird joke I'm not getting? Do you think that lasagna was bad?" Adelle pushed herself off the wall and moved over to her daughter, grabbing the skirt of her dress to examine the gown more closely. "It's really remarkable actually. It doesn't look like a costume, but it's not an antique either. I think it's time you filled me in, sweetheart."

"Sweetheart? Why would ye address a stranger so? And why do ye keep calling me 'Bri'? My name is Blaire, and I doona understand why ye seem so fascinated with my dress. Have ye seen what ye are wearing? Do ye work for Mary? Did she send ye down here to get me?"

Adelle reached up to grab her forehead, her frustration growing at her lack of understanding. "Bri, what the hell are you talking about? It's really not funny. I seriously think I've lost my mind. We need to go back to the inn, maybe drive back to Edinburgh and check me into the hospital. Quit talking like that and let's go. Grab your real clothes on the way." She reached out to grab Bri by the arm, but the hold was broken as her daughter quickly jerked out of her grasp.

"Please, do not lay yer hands on me. I'll not marry Eoin. Ye'll have to send me back home."

"Bri." She reached out to grab her daughter once more. "We still have twelve days before we go back home. Surely you're not ready to go back to Texas?"

"Texas?" The woman's brows came together so quickly they almost bumped in between her eyes.

"Yes, Bri. Texas. Where you live and teach. I think we both need to have our heads examined. Maybe we breathed in some sort of hallucinogenic drug when we opened that doorway."

"I'm unfamiliar with this 'Texas' that ye speak of, miss. I live in the MacChristy keep, with my father, Donal. It's a three-day journey from here."

Adelle stopped trying to pull at her daughter's arm and turned to face her straight on. She *had* to be Bri. There was absolutely no question this was her daughter. But the accent? And the clothes? And she knew she'd tried to teach Bri some about the castle's history, but she found herself surprised that Bri was able to remember such names. Adelle stood there unmoving, trying to think of some sure way to confirm she was looking at her daughter, and that they were both on the receiving end of some powerful mind-altering drug. Whatever was going on, something was very wrong.

A sudden itch in her lower back caused her to jerk her arm around and scratch, and instantly she knew what she needed to look for.

Instinctively she crouched down low and began to lift up the young woman's dress, digging her way through the layers of fabric until she grabbed the bottom layer. The girl squirmed and protested, but Adelle kept her grip and, giving a hard tug, spun Bri around so that her back was facing her and she could lift the dress above her bottom.

"What do ye think ye are doing? Let go of me. I can undress myself if ye insist that I change my clothes."

"Just hold still. I need to check something." She hiked the bottom of the dress up until the skin of her lower back was clearly visible. "Sweet Mary, Moses, and Joseph! You don't have the tattoo. You're not Bri, are you?"

The girl stepped away so that the fabric fell loose from Adelle's grip and in frustration faced her. "That's what I've been tryin to tell ye, no? No, I'm not this Bri. And what is a 'tattoo'?"

"It's this." Adelle turned halfway and hiked up the back of her own shirt where the words *we shall never part* were delicately tattooed across her lower back. "Bri has one as well. We got them shortly after her eighteenth birthday."

Adelle watched as the stranger, whose face was so much like her daughter's, slowly turned ashen, obviously remembering something she hadn't thought of before.

"What's yer name, miss?"

"Adelle Montgomery. I'm an archaeologist working on the ruins of Conall Castle. What did you say your name was, since although I have no idea what the hell is going on, I know that you aren't Bri?"

"Ye may call me Blaire. The ruins of Conall Castle? What year is this?"

"What year is it? You really don't know the answer to that? Why, it's 2013."

Blaire slowly backed away until she steadied herself against the wall behind her. "I canna believe it. I knew they'd said she'd been a witch, but I'd never believed it was true. She left the portrait. It was her words I read."

At Blaire's mention of a witch, an inkling of her prior research on the Conalls nudged at the edge of her brain, but it stayed just out of reach as fear coursed through her.

"Slow down, sugar. I think it would be best if we made our way outside. Get some fresh air, maybe? I think we both need to figure out what's going on."

Color filled Blaire's face as the pitch of her voice rose. "I already know. It was the Conalls' aunt, Morna. She was a witch, and I stumbled upon her spell room by chance. I found it just moments ago, although I dinna understand what I was seeing. I read the words on the plaque, and then I ended up in front of ye."

"Okay." Adelle nodded obligingly. It was best to agree if she wanted the woman to help her find Bri, until she could remember what she needed so desperately to recall. "Well, why don't you tell me about where you were before you ended up here?"

"I was in this same room. But it was different, ye see? I was supposed to marry the laird of Conall Castle, Eoin, and I fled down here. I could not marry him. I'd only just been wishing I could disappear when I saw the portrait and sounded out the words."

Adelle's eyes widened, disbelieving but fascinated. "Eoin. As in Eoin Conall, son of Alasdair Conall? Laird after his father died in 1645, for only a few short months until the infamous massacre?" The research came back to her in snippets. Her mind started to grasp the facts one-by-one as they presented themselves.

Blaire's face drained of color once again, "massacre?"

"Yes. The entire Conall clan was murdered in late December of 1645. As to why, or who was responsible, no one has ever been able to find out. That's why my daughter and I were here actually. We were searching for documents or evidence that could help solve the mystery."

"That's why she did it, doona ye see?" Blaire moved forward suddenly, grabbing Adelle's arms and shaking them.

"Who? Did what?"

"Morna. Alasdair and Father told stories growing up about her. She could see things that were yet to happen. She must've known I would stumble into her spell room. She did her best to save them before her death. I'm meant to stop it, and ye can help me."

Something clicked in Adelle's brain, and the icy pinpricks rushed down her spine once more. "Are you telling me that this is for real? The old legend about the witch was true? You expect me to believe that you really came here from 1645?"

"Aye. I expect that's where yer daughter is now. Ye said that we look alike, did ye not? And where else do ye expect she'd be? We've switched places, we have. Did she read the words below the portrait as well?"

"Holy mother of Freddie! You're right. She did. Oh, my God! We have to get Bri back before the massacre . . ." Adelle's stomach turned over as the same icy grasp that had made its way down her spine gripped her around the middle; she wanted nothing more than to jump through whatever invisible void had taken her daughter and be there by her side.

Her logical brain had no advice on what steps she should take next, but she knew she'd be damned before she left her daughter to die as she knew the Conalls would in just a few short months. Adrenaline kicked in, pushing away all doubt and logic, replacing it with an eerily calm sense of determination. "Blaire. I know you are probably as scared as Bri is—*wherever* she is—but we have to help each other if we're going to get you two back where you belong. Let's go to the car and get the boxes and dollies. We need to gather up every book and piece of parchment in this place, and then get you back to the inn while Jerry and Gwendolyn are gone and get you changed into some of Bri's clothes."

Adelle turned, not waiting for a response, and only briefly registering Blaire's question as she made her way out of the basement room.

"Aye, but might I ask ye a question? What is a 'car'?"

CHAPTER 11

*S*cotland—*1645*

*E*oin stood at the edge of the rocky hillside that overlooked the ocean at the backside of the castle, waiting for his future bride. He scanned the crowd of townspeople all dressed in their finest, excitedly waiting for the wedding to begin.

He would gladly trade places with any one of them.

Any moment Blaire would arrive at the end of the aisle, dread simmering in her eyes as she glared up at him during her long march.

He would take her hand in marriage as his father bid, but he would live each day guilt-ridden for being the source of such great unhappiness for any lass, even one as miserable as Blaire.

He glanced toward his brother, who stood on his left-hand side. Arran looked as if he were having a hard time standing. His face was flushed and his eyes were bloodshot.

He'd been drinking again.

It hadn't escaped Eoin's attention that Arran hadn't stopped drinking since their return to the castle. What was bothering him? Had Arran taken their father's death harder than he'd realized?

Whatever it was, he vowed that he would talk to his brother as soon as this wedding was behind them.

A sharp intake of breath from Arran caused Eoin to jerk his head in the direction of Arran's stare.

His heart hammered wildly inside his chest, and his breath lodged in his throat as he locked eyes with Blaire.

Standing at the end of the aisle, she was beaming back at him with a smile so wide and bright he couldn't help but smile in return. It was the first genuine smile he'd seen from her, and it made him uneasy.

Has the lass been drinking also? She looks pleased. He wouldn't have blamed her if she had been. But no, the lass was too certain in her steps to be drunk, and her eyes shimmered with clarity as she neared him.

He stepped forward to take her hands in his as the ceremony began.

The entire ceremony had been a blur. I sat next to my new husband, watching the hordes of merry villagers dancing around the grassy expanse behind the castle. I knew I was dreaming; there was simply no other explanation for the whirlwind of confusion that had been the last two hours of my life.

The swirls of color and boisterous laughter—combined with music that I was vastly impressed with myself for dreaming up—had my head spinning yet again. I tried to stop the pounding in my temples by thinking back on what I could remember.

Meeting Mary; having not one, but two full-blown panic attacks; being tossed into a tub and dressed up like a Thanksgiving turkey; walking down the backside of the castle; laying eyes on the hunk now sitting beside me; walking up the aisle, grinning like an idiot. It seemed to me that I could recall everything that had happened since I woke up inside my coma. That is, until I had reached the end of the aisle. At that point, Coma Husband had taken it upon himself to grab my hands, and my brain short-circuited.

No surprise, really. My brain was obviously working overtime just to dream up Laird Eoin, not to mention that it was trying to heal itself out of a coma.

After he had taken my hands in his own, I could recall only two other things about the ceremony.

The first was his eyes. I had been immediately hypnotized by them. They reminded me of a black stone that used to sit in a bowl at my grandmother's house. When I was younger, I loved to hold it up to the light and examine all the different flecks of brown and gold that danced between the swirls of darkness. His eyes were like that stone. I wanted to examine every speckle of color that had stared back at me throughout the ceremony.

The second thing I recalled was the kiss at the end of the wedding. You would think that since I was staring at his eyes so intently, I would've seen it coming. I didn't.

The impact of his lips on mine startled me so much that I tried to jerk away from him on instinct, but I was prevented by his hand, which touched the smallest part of my back and pulled me close to his chest. His right hand cupped the left side of my face as he moved his lips confidently against my own.

Part of me felt I should have stopped the kiss; I was kissing a total stranger, after all. But this was *my* stranger, whom I'd created, and my body betrayed me as fire coursed through my core, sending heat down to the farthest ends of my fingertips and toes.

I couldn't breathe, and I parted my mouth to try and take in a breath, but his tongue deftly slipped inside, and instead of oxygen I breathed him in instead.

Had it not been for the roar of the guests, I think the kiss would have gone on much longer, but the noise from the crowd caused the laird to jerk away. As he did so, a look of utter frustration, almost anger, crossed his face. It confused me even more than I was already. His face hardly seemed to coincide with the kiss he'd just given me.

Thinking back on the kiss caused my temperature to rise, and my cheeks flushed as the sudden warmth of the memory washed over my body. I reached to lay my fingers against my cheek, hoping to cool them, when a voice to my left caused me to jump.

"Ye look beautiful, Blaire."

I started to correct him, but quickly remembered that my name while I was in a coma was Blaire, not Bri. Instead I turned to him as he gently lay his hand upon my thigh and smiled as sweetly as I could.

I expected a smile in return, but instead I was rewarded with the same irritated expression I had seen right after the wedding. He stared at me briefly, ice shooting from his eyes, and then stood abruptly, pulling me up with him.

"Are ye ready to retire, lass? I know ye must be tired."

I nodded as he quickly led me away from the dancing crowd.

I tried to keep pace with his stride, but the bottom of my dress kept getting in the way and instead I stumbled along, tripping with every other step. Each time I almost hit the ground, I found myself yanked up by his quick hands. *Couldn't a girl make herself graceful in her own coma?* Not that it was surprising, I didn't have much real-life experience when it came to grace, so I was certain my brain found it hard to dream up.

There was anger in the way he gripped me, which I couldn't understand. What could I have possibly done to upset him? This was surely not the best way to start out a marriage. Perhaps this Blaire had done something before I arrived for which I was about to receive the punishment.

He continued his relentless pace, and as I blundered along behind him I realized that this didn't seem like something I would dream. Scottish castle, yes. Scottish wedding, yes. Gorgeous husband, yes. Angry, Scottish brute . . . not so much.

The realization frightened me, and once I knew we were far enough away from the crowd to no longer be noticed, I jerked my hand away with all the force I could muster, causing him to release his grip.

"What are you doing?" I stopped walking and shook out my hand as I glared back at him, completely forgetting to speak in a Scottish accent. I didn't care. My wrist was hurting, and I was frightened by the look in his eyes.

I felt my back press into the stone wall of the castle behind me, and he was on me before I had a chance to protest. His hands gripped my shoulders, effectively pinning me to the wall, and his nose was but a hair's width from my own as he growled into my face.

"What am I doing? What about ye, Blaire? Ye have been moping about this castle since ye arrived, making no secret about how much ye detest me, and now ye show up at our wedding, smiling like a wee fool! Do ye think that ye can love me out of doors and then reject me when we're alone? I already told ye once, Blaire, I'll do right by ye, but I won't be toyed with, Do ye understand, lass?"

My head was pounding as I watched him rant. He was angry, but there was more than just anger in his eyes. Confusion? Frustration? I couldn't tell.

I didn't understand much of what he was saying, and Mary's story, the little she had explained, wasn't coming to mind as I stood there with the muscles beneath his clothes pressed against my chest. His breath was sweet and warm against my face, and when he stopped talking I unthinkingly leaned forward and pressed my lips against his.

His response was immediate. His hands moved from my shoulders to the sides of my face as he cupped my cheeks in an effort to get closer. He growled into my mouth as his tongue sought entry, and I willingly opened myself up to him. His teeth grazed my lips, and I got the feeling that he was struggling to control his anger.

The painfully exquisite tug of his teeth on my lower lip caused my legs to turn to jelly as I melted against him, moving my lips against his in a furious dance of give-and-take. I heard myself moan as I pushed my body more tightly against him.

Abruptly, he pulled away, leaving me wanting and confused. He slid his hands to my shoulders, effectively pinning me to the stone wall and holding me at arm's length away from him.

"Doona do that again, lass." He paused to catch his breath and removed his left hand to run it through his hair. "Next time ye do something like that to me, I willna be stopping myself, and ye have already made it clear ye want nothing to do with me."

The words escaped my mouth before I had time to rein them in. It was my dream after all. I could do what I wanted. "Don't then."

He stretched his arms out farther, locking his elbows into place and stared back at me. "What did ye just say, lass?"

Blood ran to my cheeks as embarrassment set in. I looked down and tried to remember the accent before I continued. It was too late to back down now. "Then, doona stop." The words came out breathlessly, and in an uncharacteristic show of courage I reached up to pull his hand from my shoulder as I placed it on my breast. I shyly glanced up at him, "Please."

He groaned and reached to grab my hand, pulling me swiftly along behind him once again.

---

*T*he stranger slowly set down his goblet, made his excuses to the villagers surrounding him and walked to the side of the castle, watching until he was sure the laird and his new wife had made their way up to their bedchamber.

He'd been given only two orders as he'd left Ramsay's quarters—not be found out as a stranger at the wedding and to wait until the appropriate time to set the fire.

Pivoting his head, the stranger made sure all eyes around him were diverted elsewhere as he worked one of the flaming rods from their post and turned the flame so that it lay on the ground, slowly scorching and taking root over the grass that sat underneath its light.

Once the ground slowly caught flame, the stranger turned and walked away, mounting the horse he'd tied far away from everyone's sight and rode as quickly as he could away from Conall Castle.

CHAPTER 12

I stumbled along as we entered the castle's main doors, cursing the length of my dress as I went. He was moving just as quickly as he had before, and taking the stairs at this pace proved impossible. I slipped, almost busting my lip against the cold stone steps.

I yelped, but before the impact his hands were around my waist, lifting me off the floor.

"Sorry, lass." He bent his head to plant a quick kiss on my lips as he carried me up the staircase.

Blushing once again, I allowed my head to fall against his chest. *God, he smells good. I have to remember to write every second of this down as soon as I wake up. I could live off of this dream for years.*

"Doona fall asleep on me yet, lass."

I threw my eyes open and squealed as he playfully pinched my bottom. This man was impossible to keep up with. His moods seemed to change rapidly, and this Blaire person had obviously done something to displease him greatly.

"We're here, lass." He carried me into the bedchamber, and I couldn't help but inwardly chuckle at the fact that I was now living one of the covers of the various romance novels sitting on the shelves at my home. My subconscious was clearly pulling at things from previous fantasies.

Coma Husband set me gently on my feet as he turned to close the chamber door.

I turned away from him to take in the room. Wood, stone, and furs surrounded me, all melding together to create the most sexy and masculine room I'd ever seen. I closed my eyes to breathe in the delicious scent of the room's luscious materials just as Eoin flattened himself against my back, wrapping his arms around my waist.

He nuzzled his mouth against my neck, and I could feel his hot breath on the exposed skin at the top of my dress. My heart was racing with anticipation as he touched his lips to my neck, trailing kisses from my collarbone up to my ear. He nibbled it gently, and I reached my hand up behind me so that I could run my fingers into his hair.

His hands left my waist, and he followed the length of my arms with tender, light touches that sent tremors down my spine and caused my nipples to harden beneath the dress.

He must have known the effect it would have, for he immediately dropped his hands to cover my breasts, and I gasped at the sensation.

Moaning, I relaxed my head against his chest, pushing my breasts deeper into his hands, encouraging the touch of his skilled fingers.

He quickly undid the laces at the back of my gown and pulled my arms through the sleeves so that my breasts fell free, and the dress hung at the curve of my hips.

His breath was shaky against the back of my neck as he filled his hands with my bare skin. Instantly my own breathing accelerated, the touch of his rough, calloused hands against my tender nipples sending me spiraling.

"Ye're beautiful, Blaire, and I apologize for leaving after ye arrived."

"What?" I started to interject on impulse but was silenced by a sharp bite on my neck.

"Shhh . . . I know I was wrong to leave, but by God, Blaire, ye have given me grief since ye arrived, and I intend to make ye pay for it now."

I squirmed underneath his tight grip, not enjoying the way his voice turned once again, but he tugged hard on my nipples and grazed the back of my neck with his teeth, and I couldn't help the groan of pleasure that escaped my lips.

"I have no idea what's caused such a change in ye, but I intend to make certain ye doona again decide I'm so displeasing."

Who could possibly find this man displeasing? I tried to make sense of his words. *What does he mean punish me? What's he going to do, sex me to death? If I'm going to die in a dream, that seems the way to go.*

He ran his hands up and down my waist, his cool hands sending hot shocks through my body. "I wanna feel ye squirm underneath my touch, Blaire, and have ye call out my name in answer to me. I'll be the only man to touch ye, lass, and when I do take ye as my own, it will be because ye beg me to do so."

I'd beg ya right now, if I thought I could form a coherent sentence.

I didn't have a chance to ponder the thought further as he slid his hands down to the gown gathered at my hips. I watched it fall to the ground and bunch at my feet as he worked it over my curves.

"Ye have the softest, smoothest skin, Blaire. I wanna fill my hands with ye while ye tremble beneath me."

Holy Mother of God. I let my head fall against his chest, losing any strength I had to hold myself up as I lost myself in the sensation of his hands thumbing my nipples. I moaned as one of his hands slipped in between my thighs.

"God, Blaire. I want ye. And ye want me, too, lass." He firmly cupped me in between my legs as if to emphasize this point.

His hot, ragged breath against my ear sent delicious pinpricks down my spine. I tightened my grip around his neck in an effort to hold myself up as he started to move his fingers in between my legs.

The breath left my body in a sudden rush as one of his arms tightened underneath my breasts, effectively lifting my feet so that they dragged along the floor as he backed himself up against the door. He held me there, so that I was prevented from placing any weight on the floor, with my back pressed flush against his front.

He continued to move his fingers quickly. Each flick sent shockwaves, causing me to gasp for air and arch my back. I was prevented from doing either as his arm underneath my breasts held me so tightly that I could hardly breathe. The lack of oxygen seemed to intensify the feeling building deep in my belly as he continued the relentless rhythm that pushed me closer and closer to shattering in his hands.

The room twisted itself into a swirl of colors, and heat washed over me as I briefly hoped that I wasn't making these noises in my sleep. I was having trouble thinking, everything pushed away by the exquisite feeling building between my thighs.

The lack of oxygen was too much, and just as I feared, I could take no more or I would lose consciousness once again, I exploded around his deft fingers. Every muscle in my body relaxed, and I went limp in his arms, trembling as the aftershocks rocked through my core.

He spun me around so that I faced him, and I swayed on my feet as he released me from his grip. Instinctively, I reached out to steady myself, placing my hands on his firm chest.

He leaned forward then, surprising me with his gentle kiss. The sweetness of it seemed odd following the aggressive way he had just explored my body, but once again I had no time to ponder the thought as he began to speak.

"Do ye still think I'm so displeasing?"

He stared at me, a look of teasing amusement playing in his eyes.

I still seemed incapable of forming an intelligible response, so I simply managed a sly smile as I struggled to regulate my breathing. Whatever drugs the hospital was pumping through my veins, I wanted to stay on them for life.

"Come on, lass, let's go to bed. Ye look as if ye might fall over."

I followed as he gently tugged on my hands, leading me to the bed across the chamber.

"Come, Blaire. I want to hold my new bride in my arms, satisfied that I know she doesna find me as abhorrent as she tried to make it seem."

He crawled into bed beneath the covers, and I looked down at him as he smiled. *That smile has probably found dozens of other women exactly where I am right now.* It both surprised and displeased me, so that the thought sent an unpleasant surge into my stomach. This man didn't actually exist, after all.

He gestured for me to join him, and I slowly crawled on top of the bed. I glanced down to see my breasts swaying to and fro and scrambled to cover myself.

"I . . . I forgot I was naked," I stuttered as I flailed my arms around wildly, trying to cover the most intimate parts of myself.

Eoin's hands caught mine, and I could hear him chuckling as he struggled to tug the blankets away from me.

"I've already seen ye, Blaire. Ye have the most beautiful breasts I've ever seen, and ye have no reason to worry. I'll not be touchin' ye again tonight. We've no rush, lass, and I'll see that I woo ye properly."

I stopped my senseless struggle as his words sank in. The time to be embarrassed had long since passed. I laughed at myself as I joined him beneath the covers and rolled into his arms.

*M*oments later, a fierce knock at the door caused us both to jerk upward in the bed. Just on the cusp of sleep, I found myself disoriented as I looked around the room to take in my surroundings, trying to remember where I was and what I was doing.

A hand on my naked back caused me to turn to my left, and the sight of Eoin beside me reminded me that I was still in a coma. I couldn't quite make sense of why I seemed to fall asleep while sleeping; the only answer that came to mind was different medications must be causing a different reaction. *At least my dream seems to be the same.*

Eoin's voice yelling toward the door caused me to jump, and he gently rubbed my back in response. "Who's there? Ye better have a damned good reason for waking my wife."

"My lord! Ye must come quickly. There has been a fire set outside. It's small, but we must contain it before it reaches the stables."

"What? I'm coming Kip. Get on with ye, and help the efforts."

I watched as Eoin, cursing, quickly dressed and headed for the door.

"I'm sorry to leave ye, lass, but I must go. Just go back to sleep, and I'll be back soon. I'm sure tis nothing to worry yerself over."

With that, he was gone. I stood and made my way to the window to watch the scene below. The fire was small, surely there'd been no injuries, but it would take the men awhile to properly put it out and clean up the mess. It seemed silly that I should stay and not offer help, but something told me that the offer wouldn't be appreciated. I didn't worry about Eoin. It was my dream. Surely, I wouldn't let anything like a fire take my Coma Husband from me.

Instead, I pulled one of the blankets from the top of the bed and wrapped it around my naked body as I curled up into the stone window seat that looked out over the back greens of the castle and out onto the sea.

CHAPTER 13

J'd just begun to drift, and I could feel my eyelids dropping further with each passing second when the door handle to my right started moving clumsily. Startled, I jerked upward and wrapped the blanket around my shoulders more tightly.

I glanced toward the bolt, which rattled noisily as the person opposite the door struggled to get into the room. At first I assumed it must be Eoin, but a quick glance out the window showed him still working away at the small remains of the fire. I scanned the room for my dress and spotted it still lying crumpled in front of the door where it had been so expertly removed.

I slipped myself off of the window seat and, leaving the blanket behind, watched my skin turn to goose flesh as my toes touched the cold stone below. I tip-toed as quickly as I could over to my dress and slipped it on as best I could. I didn't even attempt to tie up the back; the intricacy of the laces was impossible for me to maneuver on my own.

Twisting and turning, I worked the gown into place so that it fit snugly across the front. Perhaps now at least it wouldn't be quite so obvious that it was completely open in the back if I opened the door. As long as I kept my arms to my sides, I thought it would stay in place while I saw to whoever needed my attention.

The noise at the door had stopped by the time I went to open it, but I still made an effort to smush my hair into some semblance of order before I reached for the handle and opened it.

In a series of movements that came too quickly for me to process, I found myself knocked onto my bottom with a man lying in between my legs.

"Ooomph!" I shoved a foot into the ribs of my lap partner and pushed him away as I struggled to stand and keep my dress in place. "And you are?"

"God, lass! What are ye doing in my bedchamber? Eoin would be none too pleased to find ye here." The man stood with great effort, and I could tell from the glazed expression in his eyes that he'd been either unconscious or close to it when I opened the door.

"I know that I haven't been here long, but you are the one in the wrong room. You must be his brother?" I started to stick out my hand, but changed my mind as I felt the shoulder of my dress begin to slip.

"What the hell are ye talking about, Blaire? Ye know I'm his brother. Ye know me as well as ye know anyone else around here! God Blaire, I knew ye could be cruel, but I doona see why ye would punish me so! Ye have to know how hard it was for me to watch ye marry him! And why in the name o' God are ye talking like that? I know I've had too much to drink, but ye sound nothing like yerself!"

He swayed slightly and leaned back against the wall. His eyes were red, and I could tell it was more pain than drink that made them so. A hurt behind his reddened eyes went beyond his being drunk.

Something I'd said had upset him. This Blaire had hurt him, and once again I'd forgotten all about her. I'd also forgotten the accent Mary had been so insistent on. No wonder he thought Blaire sounded odd. I was making all this up as I went along. It couldn't be good for my brain to be dreaming up something this complicated.

As my current coma state crossed my mind, an uncomfortable flicker of a thought tugged at me, but I was too occupied with the situation in front of me to give it much thought.

I walked toward him and tried to remember the accent once again. "I'm sorry. I dinna mean to upset ye. Ye look as if ye are about to collapse. Let's get ye to yer room. Aye?"

He nodded somberly before responding. "Aye. That's where I thought I was when I fell over outside the door. I'm a fair mess, no? I'm sorry, lass. I doona like for ye to see me so."

"Oh, shhh. I'll help ye down the hall, and we'll forget all about it."

"Thank ye, Blaire, but I can make it on my own. I just missed by one door. I'm a bigger sot than I thought if I canna make it that far."

He pushed away from the wall and tripped with his first step but caught himself by placing his hand on my shoulder.

I snickered and placed my arm around his back, using his side to hold my dress in place as he wrapped his arm around my shoulder. I didn't see how I was going to get him to his room without my dress falling to my feet, but it was clear he wouldn't make it through the door without my assistance.

"Well, looks like ye are a bigger sot than ye thought, no? Let's go. Ye can use me for balance. But doona fall on me, or I'll be trapped under ye for a week."

"There's an idea, lass, and the kind I should keep to myself now that ye've married my brother."

He threw his arm sloppily around me as I started toward the door.

"Come on."

We waddled down the hallway, doing our best to help one another. He leaned on me to stay upright, and I leaned into him to keep from exposing myself in the hallway. This act was exactly the sort of self-deprecating comedy that I could see myself dreaming, and whatever unconscious thought had been nagging at me seemed to recede.

With each step, my dress slipped farther and farther off the shoulder that was underneath his hand, and I increased the pressure of my right side into his ribs.

It was a short distance to his room, but it seemed a mile, each of us struggling with every step. As we made it to his door, he removed his arm from around my shoulder and stepped away from my side.

I quickly made to squeeze my arms back against my own sides, but not before his first step away landed on the bottom of my dress, starting its descent to the floor.

Unable to catch the gown before it slipped off my shoulders, I threw myself against him to keep my chest from being exposed.

I glanced up at him to try and explain myself, but stopped as he backed me into the wall next to his chamber door.

"What do ye think ye are doing, Blaire? We canna do this! We shouldna have in the first place, but ye have married him now! We must stop."

"I . . . I," I had no idea how to respond. Obviously, Blaire had been involved with both brothers. Not that I could blame her, Arran was just as handsome as his brother. I couldn't imagine what their parents must have looked like to have two boys who appeared so different but were both equally breathtaking. He interrupted my thoughts before I could respond.

"God help me, Blaire! I've tried to stay away from ye. It felt like ye were ripping my heart out watching ye wed Eoin. I thought at the very least ye wouldna seem so pleased to be doing so. Ye have to know I dinna mean a word I spoke to ye this morning."

He bent down then, his hands on my hips to keep him steady. With his cheek pressed flushed to mine, he continued his plea.

"If I'm being a fool, Blaire, put me out o' my misery and tell me so. If I'm not, I doona think I can stay away from ye anymore."

I scrambled for a response. I didn't want to hurt him any more than he obviously was already, but I was afraid that in his state of intoxication whatever I said would do little to discourage him.

Part of me hoped that if I waited to answer he would simply pass out on my shoulder, and I could leave him snoring in the hallway and make a quick escape back down the hall.

Instead he seemed to take my silence as surrender.

"God, Blaire! I knew it was not only me. I want ye so badly. I'll burn in hell for it, I know, but I canna stop myself any longer."

His lips met mine with a heartbreaking sense of desperation. There was such an ardent sense of longing in the way he moved against me, I couldn't bring myself to stop him. It seemed too cruel to push him away. He wasn't assaulting me. He thought I was someone else, someone he loved. And he obviously believed Blaire would have matched his fervor with her own.

I found myself surrendering to him, responding and matching his affection with a sort of mind-body detachment that felt more dreamlike than the dream I was having now.

A roar to my right brought me back, just as a fist pulled Arran's lips from mine and sent him flying to the floor, unconscious.

Stunned, I let my dress slip below my breasts before I scrambled to put it back on.

Seeing that his brother was not to rise for some time, Eoin whirled on me, grabbing me around the middle as he threw me over his shoulder with far too little effort.

I assumed he was returning me to his bedchamber, but he took off in the other direction. He didn't say a word as my head jostled up and down against his back, and as he descended two different sets of stairs, dread settled in my gut.

I could tell he was angry. His face had been blood red when he'd spun on me, and I could feel his anger rising in the form of heat off his back.

I couldn't imagine what he would say or do. I'd seen him angry once before and that had been over nothing compared to this. And what could I say in defense of myself? *It wasn't me he was kissing.* I was sure that wouldn't cut it.

Dread turned to fear as the dank and dirty smell of some place far below ground reached my nostrils. I turned my head to see a row of dark cells, as empty and foreboding as the look on my husband's face. He carried me down to the last cell in the farthest corner of the room, which could only be described as a dungeon, and roughly threw me onto a stone seat that was part of the back wall. My back hit with a force that sent pain shooting up through my head, and tears unwillingly filled my eyes.

"Don't ye dare cry, ye wee bitch! Ye have no one to blame but yerself. What do ye expect me to do? Ye let me take you naked to my bed, and then the same night I find ye in my brother's arms! Ye are a liar and a whore, Blaire! I'll continue to protect yer father's territory for my own father's memory, but I will never lay eyes on ye again. I will not have a wretch like ye as lady of my keep!"

His hands were trembling and his face was deep red as he took in a deep, shaky breath and turned away. He threw the door shut and locked it in place, leaving me shaking and gasping as I tried to stop sobbing.

<hr />

*H*ours turned into days, and I started to fear that my placement here was not a temporary arrangement made out of his initial anger at finding me in Arran's embrace. By my count at least four days had passed. A total of eight meals, two a day, had been brought, as well as plenty of blankets. Someone had come to empty my chamber pot three times daily, and I always had plenty of water to drink.

It could have been much worse, and I was certain that for anyone else who had ever been placed here, it had been. Still, I was accustomed to central heating and air, at least three meals a day, and regular showers. Not to mention a daily dose of television . . . and toilet paper. As far as I was concerned, my pleasant, fantastical coma dream had turned to the worst kind of nightmare. A nightmare that I now firmly believed was not a dream at all, but a state of reality I couldn't begin to understand.

Always an over-thinker, I had learned through the years that it was best if I kept busy. Limiting my time spent analyzing and thinking about things too much helped me to stay content with work and a home life spent entirely alone.

Once the initial shock of being tossed into the dungeon had worn off and I realized that Eoin wasn't coming back to get me, I was left with nothing else to do but think. The dizzying emotional highs and lows, the elusive mentions of Blaire that I didn't understand, everything was far too complicated for me to dream up on my own.

These oddities alone should have been sufficient, but it was the events leading to my imprisonment that finally forced me to face the truth. More than once, I had been awakened from a light sleep, which means, I had been sleeping. The first time, I'd put it off to medication, but it seemed impossible that I would enter some sort of coma dream, dreaming the same thing, over and over again.

I truly was in 1645 Scotland. Truly in the castle and surrounded by the people my mother had spent her entire life studying. Every time I had felt panic begin to take over, every time some unpleasant thought had tugged at the back of my brain, it had been this realization trying to break through. I had given my greatest effort to push it away. Even the wildest imaginary scenarios seemed more favorable than this startling reality.

If I believed I was in a coma, there was hope of escape. Hope of returning to my life, my home, my students. Hope of seeing my mother again. Without that hope, I couldn't begin to comprehend what was happening, how I had ended up here, and what the rest of my life would look like.

However irrational, I was completely unwilling to give up that hope. Coma or no coma, I would escape from this prison and find a way to get back home. I knew it had something to do with the portrait I'd found when Mom and I were excavating the secret basement room. It had been my portrait, and the words below it must have been some sort of spell. If the contents of that room were powerful enough to pull me backward through time, surely there was something that could send me forward.

But first, I had to find a way out of this cell.

CHAPTER 14

"*L*eave it at the door, Mary. The same as I've been asking ye to do for days, now."

The knocking stopped, but the voice that came through the doorway had Eoin on his feet in an instant, fists trembling with the anger he'd been struggling to contain for days.

"Eoin! Ye know we must talk," Arran demanded. "What are ye doing to her? Ye canna keep her captive in yer bedchamber forever, and ye can not continue to ignore me either."

"Go away. I've no more use for either one of ye. Unless ye want me to beat yer head in, ye best get away from the door."

"What have ye done to her, Eoin? I swear if ye hurt her I'll kill ye myself, even if ye are my brother! Open the door!"

It had been four days. Four days locked up in his bedchamber, stewing over his anger and disappointment, trying to make everyone in the castle believe he was honeymooning with his new bride. Four days of imagining his brother touching and caressing Blaire, while she sank into him, moaning and moving in response.

The knocking turned to pounding as a large object made contact with the other side of the door. If Eoin didn't stop him, he was sure to draw attention from other parts of the castle, which was the last thing he wanted while his new bride was locked away.

"Stop it, ye fool!" He yanked the door open and stepped away as the post Arran was holding zoomed past his head.

Arran threw down the rod and pushed his way into the room. "Where is she, Eoin? No one has seen either one of ye since the wedding, which would be fine if I dinna know how angry ye are." He walked quickly through the room, looking behind curtains, turning over tables, looking for Blaire. "What have ye done with her?"

"She's not here, Arran." Eoin stood still in the doorway, watching as his brother tore through his room. "What the hell do ye think ye are doing? She's my wife, and an unfaithful whore at that, and ye dare ask me what I've done with her?"

"Where is she?" Arran pounded his fist against the wall and whirled toward Eoin. "It was my fault. I was drunk, Eoin. I thought that I was coming into my own room, and it turned out to be yers. She heard me outside the door and helped me back to my room. I could hardly stand up."

"Hardly stand? God Arran, ye were about to take her in the middle of the hallway. I doona care whose fault it is. I'll have nothing to do with the both of ye. Now get out of my chambers!" Eoin moved to place his hands on Arran's shoulders, but Arran quickly moved out of his way.

"I'm not going anywhere until ye tell me where she's gone. Did ye send her back home, Eoin? To disgrace her father and territory? Surely, ye could not be so cruel. Ye have already wed her."

"That didn't stop the two of ye from betraying me, did it? I willna listen to this from ye. Ye have to grow up, Arran, and stop taking everything ye want!"

"I wasn't trying to take her, Eoin. It was a mistake, and I'm sorry for it. She had little say in what happened."

"I don't care what ye have to say, Arran, the wee bitch is staying where I put her, and ye won't be seeing her again."

"Like hell I won't! I won't touch Blaire again. She's yer wife, and I'm sorry for what happened. But I will see her and make sure that ye have not harmed her."

"Do ye really think I'd harm her? I haven't even hurt ye, and ye deserve a beating far more than she does. How could ye do it? The one person that was forbidden to ye!"

"It was an accident. She was kind enough to help me to my room, and I took advantage of her. But to answer ye, I doona know what ye would do right now, brother! I've never seen ye so angry. If ye dinna harm her or send her away, then where is she?" Arran stepped forward and hesitantly placed a hand on his brother's shoulder.

Eoin flinched at the touch and tightened his fists to keep from striking his brother. "She's down below where she belongs. Where ye belong, too!" He stepped away so that he could better see Arran's face and gauge his reaction. He was looking for an excuse to hit him, and he hoped that his brother would give him the opportunity.

"Down below? Tell me ye dinna put her in the dungeon! No one has been kept there since before we were born."

"That's where I put her, and that's where she'll stay. If ye want to join her, ye are more than welcome."

In a flash Arran's fist hit the side of his face. It pushed his body sideways, but Eoin quickly recovered, charging toward his brother as Arran screamed at him between blows.

"What the hell is wrong with ye? I would not leave a dog down there. I will not let ye leave her down there to rot."

Pent-up rage erupted as Eoin slammed into his brother, sending them both to the floor in a whirl of kicking legs and surging fists.

"I doona think ye have much say in the matter, brother. Ye may be sleeping with her, but I'm laird. She's my wife. I'll do with the lass as I please."

The sudden sound of Mary's voice in the doorway caused both men to freeze in their entangled mess.

"Oh my God! What is the matter with the two of ye? Why, ye are both grown men and ye are acting like a couple of bairns, and in front of the new lady too! Why, I'm ashamed of the both of ye! And yer father would be, too!"

Both men guiltily untangled themselves and faced Mary, who stood in the doorway with both hands on her hips, no less formidable to them than she'd been when they were children.

Silence hung in the air, and both brothers knew Mary wouldn't budge until an explanation was given.

Arran broke the silence first. "We were not fighting in front of Blaire. She's not here. Eoin has her locked away in the dungeon."

Eoin and Arran watched as Mary's face turned ghostly white, only to be followed by a shade of scarlet rushing up into her cheeks.

"Forgive me? I know old Mary's hearing things now. Where did ye say the lass is?"

Arran turned to Eoin who continued to stare blankly ahead at Mary, anger flaring in his eyes.

"No, Mary. Ye heard me right. The bastard's locked her away. That's where she's been since the night of the wedding."

Mary leaned back against the doorway, fanning herself dramatically. "Oh, my God. Ye boys are going to be the death o' me! What in the blethering hell is he talking about, Eoin?"

"I caught the two of them kissing only hours after the wedding. I could not be near her, and I dinna want the entire castle learning what she'd done."

"Ach Eoin, if ye dinna stand several feet over me, I'd be knocking that pretty nose of yers back up into yer skull."

Eoin raised his eyebrows and Arran grinned slightly as Mary continued.

"I doona care if ye walked in on the lass lifting her skirts for the entire village. Ye know very well it is unacceptable for ye to leave her down there." She squinted her eyes at Eoin, each circle of gray saying more than her tongue ever could, and stepped to the right so that she was in front of Arran.

"And as for ye, boy! Ye better explain this situation to Mary right fast before I keel over at the stupidity of ye both!"

Arran cleared his throat and shifted uncomfortably on his feet before answering. "Well, truthfully, I canna say for sure what happened. I'm ashamed to say I was too drunk to properly tell which way was up or down, and I wound up at Eoin's bedchamber door, thinking it was my own."

"Eck hmm . . ." Mary cleared her throat disapprovingly and motioned with her hand for him to continue.

"Blaire must have heard me outside the door. She opened it, and I fell in on top of her. She could see I would not make it to my room without help. She helped me and I kissed her, I'm not too sure about the details."

Mary briefly rolled her eyes before shooting Arran another disapproving look, then slid back over to stand in front of Eoin once more.

"I'll not be letting that poor girl stay down there, Eoin. I doona care if ye never sleep in the same room, or if ye are never seen together except in public for the rest of yer life. Ye have to know she canna stay there!"

Properly beaten and ashamed, Eoin slowly nodded, trying to swallow his anger at the situation.

"I'll not be letting ye retrieve her from the dungeon either, Eoin. I'm sure the poor lass is scared to death of ye after being down there for days. I want ye to leave. Right now. Go for a ride, clear yer head, and only come back when ye are ready to apologize and make whatever peace ye want to with the lass. But there will be peace, do ye understand? I'll not have shouting day in and day out just because yer father is not here to keep the two of ye in line." She quickly marched around Eoin and gave him a hard shove in the back. "Get on with ye. Now. Ye can find the lass in the lavender room, later."

"What about him?" Eoin jerked his elbows in Arran's direction, suddenly feeling as if he was eight years old once again, and not understanding why his punishment differed from his brother's.

Mary shifted her gaze back and forth between both brothers before continuing. "I doona see why it's any concern of yers, but just so ye will both be satisfied, Arran is going to leave for a few days. Ride out with Kip to pick up a few more horses for the stables. He's leaving now, aren't ye, Arran?"

Arran lowered his head and made his way to the door, only pausing to address both Mary and Eoin. "Aye, Mary. I'll go. And

Eoin, I am sorry, brother. Doona take it out on Blaire. The blame is mine."

Eoin turned, intent on making it to the stables before his brother left to meet Kip. "Aye. I'm sure ye put the lass in a difficult position, but she should not have behaved as she did. I'll speak to ye when ye return, Arran. Safe travels."

With that, he turned and was gone. Arran and Mary following silently behind him.

*familiar voice caused me to stir from the restless and— thankfully—dreamless sleep I'd fallen into after hours of unsuccessfully trying to figure a way out of this hellhole.

Exhausted, filthy, and most of all frightened, it took me a moment to realize that the voice belonged to Mary. I swallowed a hard lump that rose in the back of my throat, bringing with it tears of joy, which came from the almost certain knowledge that she would not let them leave me down here.

"Ach, lassie! Ye sure have managed to upset the men around here. One's yearning for ye so much he has not stayed sober in days, and the other's calling ye a whore, and that's the nicest of it! Now, stand up! I've sent both of the boys away for a bit. I'll bring ye back up and place ye in his late mother's chambers, and ye can get yerself cleaned up. I expect ye'll have some time alone. It will take the lads a wee bit o' time to calm down and realize how foolish they've both been."

I stood a little more shakily than was warranted. Physically, I was fine. Mentally, I was so confused and pissed off that the effort it took to stand seemed almost too much. My voice cracked when I spoke. "Mary, I need to know exactly what's going on here. You have to tell me what you know."

"What did ye say, dearie? Wait until we get ye settled in yer new room, and the two of us will have a nice, long talk." Mary motioned to the guard standing at the end of the passageway, who obviously knew better than to question her. He retrieved the cell key from his belt before he made his way to the door and obediently opened the lock.

Now released from my cell, I gladly followed her into a beautiful bedroom directly across from Eoin's. Mary left after depositing me in the room, but within minutes she returned with a trail of servants carrying steaming pitchers of water to fill the tub. After laying out some fresh clothes, she sat down on the edge of the bed and crossed her arms, resting them on the fullness of her stomach. She waited until the tub was filled with steaming water and the servants had retreated before she spoke.

"Alright, dearie. I know ye must be scared to death after the last few days ye've had here. I apologize for not explaining what I knew before the wedding, but there just was no time. And believe me, dear, I dinna know where Eoin had placed ye. If I had, I would've retrieved ye immediately."

I smiled gently and stood watching her intently. "I know, Mary. Thank you. But, please, tell me what's going on. How did I end up here?"

Mary uncomfortably crossed her arms, only to cross them once again as I watched her struggle to find the right words.

"Well, the truth of it is, dearie, that I doona know all that much. Before Alasdair's death, he told me a long story, but at the time I put most of it up to his injuries. But then, I saw ye, strange as ye could be, and as ignorant as a wee lamb, and I knew everything he'd said was true."

"What did he say?"

"He said that his sister—she was a witch, ye see—placed a spell and someday soon a young lass in the likeness of Blaire would be brought into our lives. He begged me to watch over ye and to help ye in any way that I could. He said that ye would save us all from something horrible. What he meant by that, I'll never know. I expect more answers could be found in Morna's basement, but I canna read myself and never thought to look."

"Morna's basement? Where is that, Mary? I need to go and look immediately. I have to find a way home."

"Ach, dearie. I doona expect ye'd find anything to help ye do that. There was a reason Morna wanted ye here. I doubt she would make it easy for ye to leave. If ye want to look, I'll help ye anyway I can. But not tonight, lass. Right now, ye are to get yerself into that tub immediately and relax until Old Mary brings ye something to eat, do ye understand? Come morning, I'll show ye to Morna's room."

She gave me no opportunity to argue, and as I watched the steam rise from the tub I found myself less anxious to explore Morna's spell room. I could smell myself, even standing still, and knew I was in desperate need of a bath.

Once stripped, I sunk gratefully into the tub, bending my knees so that the water came up to my chin and only my head and kneecaps breached the surface of the water. The water had clearly just been taken off the fire. It was almost too hot, but I was too tired and dirty to care.

It seemed odd to go from watched prisoner to complete solitude so quickly. It occurred to me briefly that I should jump out of the tub and flee the castle immediately, but I knew there was nowhere better for me to go. I wasn't likely to find any answers outside of these walls, and at least Mary seemed to know where I might find them, even if she did a lousy job of explaining it.

I hadn't realized how tense I was until the heat from the water slowly worked its way over my body, forcing my muscles to relinquish their tight grip. I breathed deeply, relishing the feeling of my nails against my skin as I scrubbed away the dirt on my ankles and arms.

With the tips of my fingers and toes wrinkled to prunes and my skin red from both the heat of the water and the thorough scrub-down I'd just given myself, I lay my head against the back of the tub and threw my hair over the side, allowing it to dry.

The steam from the water quickly receded, and as my skin tightened in response to the cooling water I turned my head toward the fireplace and stared into the flames. The brilliant amber beams danced over the wood, and as I followed their movement the cooling water seemed warm once more.

The tub was close enough to the fireplace that some of the heat from the flames warmed my left arm, which hung over the side of the tub. The light emitting from the fireplace mixed with the darkness, which had slowly flooded the room as the sun dropped lower into the horizon. The combination of light and dark was soothing, and my mind drifted closer to sleep with each flicker of the flames.

Just as I was at the edge of slumber the bedroom door opened and closed, causing me to nearly jump out of the water. Suddenly being jarred from my daze made me realize how cold I had actually become. My entire body was wrinkled from being in the water too long, and my nipples were pointed into hard beads. I assumed it was Mary with some food, but then I heard the deep voice. I moved quickly to cross my legs and cover my chest with my arms as I heard Eoin's footsteps behind me.

"I'm not sure what to say to ye, lass. I behaved badly by locking ye away, but I was so angry it was all that came to mind."

He stopped right next to the tub, but his head and eyes were turned away from my body as he bent and touched the surface of the water with his fingertips, quickly jerking them away.

"Ach, lass! Ye'll get yerself sick sitting in water that cold. How long have ye been in there?"

"I . . . I don't know. Since Mary brought me up here. I might have fallen asleep." I pulled my knees up toward my chest and wrapped my arms around my legs. It was warmer, and it seemed to cover a little more of my intimate parts.

I watched as Eoin reached toward the bed to grab a blanket off the top. He stretched it out and held it open for me, still looking away. "Here, lass, stand up and go sit by the fire."

He could sense my hesitation, and I could see the corner of his left brow crease in frustration. "I'm not looking at ye, lass. I just want to talk to ye, but if ye doona get yerself out of that tub I'll lift ye out of it myself."

Even through the little time I'd spent with him, I knew he wouldn't make an idle threat. I reached out and snatched the blanket, wrapping it around myself as I stepped out of the large basin.

Silently I walked closer to the fire, sitting as close to the flames as I could on the stone floor. Keeping my hands, arms, and legs inside the blanket, I hugged myself, enjoying the feeling of hiding every part except my head underneath the blanket. It helped conceal the fact that my legs were shaking. I was so nervous for whatever he was going to say, I felt like I could vomit. Thankfully, he didn't force me to wait too long before he spoke.

"Blaire. I canna pretend that I'm not any less angry at ye than I was before. I know that Arran puts the blame on himself, but from what I saw, ye are guilty as well. I know I must allow ye to live in the castle and act as my wife on certain occasions, but as far as I'm concerned, our marriage is invalid. I'll not be unkind to ye, but I'll not treat ye as I would a loving companion either."

He paused, obviously waiting for a response, which I didn't have. After waiting a few moments, he gave up and continued.

"No one outside of the castle will know the truth about our marriage, but we will live for the most part separately, only joining when it is time to produce an heir. Regardless, ye are never to be alone with Arran again. And we will be spending quite a lot of time together for the sake of appearances, aye? It is my hope that we can both learn to live in peace with one another."

He stared intently, his dark eyes blacker than usual, as he awaited my response. I was so filled with relief at learning that I would be staying in a separate room and living separately that I was unsure of what to say. As far as producing an heir, I had no intention of hanging around long enough for that to be an issue.

I could tell he was still furious and it was all he could do to speak to me politely. If I showed him just how glad I was to hear every word he'd just said, I knew it might crack his calm façade. Remorse was the best way to soothe a man's wounded ego.

"I am sorry for what happened, Eoin. I have no good explanation. I understand the reasons for yer requests and, aye, I accept them. Ye have my word that I will not make the same mistake again. Thank ye for not leaving me in that prison." I tried to look as apologetic as I could. I truly was sorry for upsetting him, but I knew the situation was really caused by someone other than myself.

Eoin's eyes softened at my words and he walked toward me, gently placing a hand on the top of my head. "Aye. I know ye are, lass. I'm sorry that it must be this way, too. I'll leave ye to rest now. We all gather for breakfast in the grand dining hall every morning. Ye will be expected at my side."

I glanced up at him, and he jerked his hand away, his eyes hardening as he turned and left, leaving me alone in the room once more.

CHAPTER 15

"*D*oona worry so much, dearie. Ye've done fine so far, and it's unlikely that Eoin would press ye with such a question, but it's important that ye know it if ye are here long enough to have to meet Blaire's father. Now, which ear is it that he canna hear from?"

"It's his left ear. He was born that way and can't hear anything unless you speak loudly or into his right ear."

"Yes, dear. So doona be alarmed if he screams at ye. It's only that he canna know how loud he can sometimes be."

I watched as Mary laughed, her entire belly moving with each chuckle, causing me to smile in return.

It had been two weeks since I'd been released from the dungeon and, while the first few days after my imprisonment found me under Eoin's constant watch, Mary quickly picked up on the problem and suggested that I ask Eoin if I could spend my afternoons with her so that she could teach me how to cook. While it was highly unusual for the laird's wife to spend her time in the kitchen, I knew he was tired of babysitting me, and he consented easily. Since then, I'd spent a large portion of every day either training with Mary so that I could learn family history and cultural customs, or digging through the mountains of books in Morna's spell room.

While I was enjoying my lessons with Mary immensely, the search to find a spell that would get me home was an entirely different story. The small room was crowded with books, journals, records, most of which had absolutely nothing to do with spells. Morna's records and diaries I could read, but the majority of her spell books were in Gaelic, which I did not know. I was slowly having to search through everything written in English first, all while sorting through the things in Gaelic that looked relevant and setting them aside to deal with later.

I was busy thinking of my game plan for the next few hours, which I would spend sifting through the rooms' contents, when Mary stopped chuckling and spoke once more.

"Ye have noticed that he doesna seem as angry anymore, haven't ye? He's slowly warming to ye, a little more each day."

Her words surprised me. Sure, Eoin no longer seemed angry in the way in which he carried himself when he was around me, and his eyes didn't look as dark, but 'warming'? I hadn't seen anything to make me think that. "What do you mean, 'warming'? I wouldn't say that exactly."

"Oh, that's because ye doona know him the way I do, dearie. He doesna warm to people as easily as his brother does. He guards himself closely, he knows that ye have the power to break his heart. But, Old Mary's known him his entire life, and I see the way he looks at ye. He cares for ye, even if he willna let himself know it."

"I think you're wrong, Mary. He's never done a thing to make me think he's anything but repulsed by me. But even if you're right, it's best that he doesn't let himself start to care. I'll be gone from here before too long."

Knowing that today's family history lesson was at an end, I stepped inside the doorway and made my way over to the pile of my modern clothes, which I'd hidden away to put on only while I worked in the spell room. I looked forward to those hours every day, so that I could put on a bra to strap the girls in place and put on my favorite pair of jeans. It was heaven, or as close as I was going to get to it here.

Seeing that I was preparing to work on the books, Mary stood to leave. "Well, dearie, I see that ye are about to slip on those awful shreds of cloth ye seem to care so much about, so I'll leave ye to yer work and come back to get ye before the evening meal. But, I'll not lie to ye, Eoin's already allowed himself to care. If ye open yer eyes up, ye will be able to see it as well."

With that she turned and left the basement, and I sat down to get to work.

*E*oin made his way down to the dining hall for the evening meal and stopped abruptly when he caught a glimpse of his reflection in a piece of armory which hung on the wall. He was surprised to see that the corners of his mouth were pulled up, so that they resembled something of a smile. He tried to relax his face, so that his mouth fell back into where it usually stayed, but he found that his lips didn't want to stay put.

Confused, he turned away from the reflection and continued to make his way down the hall, all the while wondering why he was so pleased and excited at the idea of eating. It hit him when he walked into the dining hall to see Blaire seated in her usual place.

It wasn't the prospect of food that excited him. After spending the entire afternoon alone, he was going to get to see Blaire.

He'd done his best to stay angry at her and resolve himself to the fact that their marriage was always going to be one of convenience, but he knew he wouldn't be able to stay angry at her forever. It was getting harder each day for him to ignore his feelings.

When he'd walked in on Arran kissing her in the hallway, he thought he'd seen two lovers stealing a precious moment alone when he wasn't around. But after spending a fortnight watching the two of them around each other, he thought that perhaps Arran had been telling him the truth. Every meal, he watched as the two of them sat across from each other, but there were no knowing glances, no palpable tension that he could pick up on. In fact, they never spoke to each other. All conversations took place entirely between Blaire and himself.

And what great conversations they were! He'd never been around a lass that seemed so interested in his stories. She asked questions and listened eagerly, as if savoring everything new she learned about him. Oftentimes he would say something and a look of pure surprise or slight confusion would cross her face, and he immediately saw a glimpse of the ornery child he'd known growing up.

But, she was no longer that child. She was a woman, no denying that, and looked to him more beautiful each time he saw her.

He loved the odd way in which she spoke. Sometimes she said strange words, and her accent often slipped into an odd mixture of Scottish and something he'd never heard. He wondered if she'd spent a lot of time around a foreign nurse growing up, whose influence had shaped the way she said her words. He loved the disjointed sound of it and found himself wanting to listen to it all day.

As he sat down diagonally from her at the large table and looked up at her bright, dimpled smile, he decided it was pointless to remain angry for the sake of his wounded pride. Tonight, he would take the lass somewhere special. Mayhap they both could take a step toward shaping their marriage into what a marriage should be.

CHAPTER 16

*M*aybe Mary was right. The thought crossed my mind several times throughout the evening meal. Halfway through whatever strange meat sat before me—I'd stopped asking after about three days—I'd glanced up to see him staring at me in a way that sent an unfamiliar shiver down the back of my neck. At one point, he'd even reached over and squeezed my hand in the middle of one of his stories. The touch was so unexpected, I nearly spit up my food.

He seemed to be in an especially good mood, and it wasn't until he stopped talking, as if waiting for me to answer a question, that I realized I hadn't been listening at all.

"I'm sorry. What did ye ask me?" My cheeks suddenly warmed.

"Would ye allow me to take ye somewhere this evening? I'd like to show ye something." He smiled kindly, and it was shocking to me how his eyes changed depending on his mood. I smiled, unable to hide my flattery at the question. Regardless of how much I wanted to get home, I loved talking to him, and I couldn't repress the pleasant hum that settled in my stomach at the thought of being alone with him. "I would love to."

"Aye?" He asked the question as if surprised by my response, but smiled as he stood and offered me his hand.

"Aye." I extended my hand in his direction, and as he took it I saw Arran rise from the other side of the table and quickly leave the room.

---

*I*t didn't matter that he was drunk. Arran had stayed that way for weeks. He still knew something odd was happening with Blaire. Something had changed between them, and it had nothing to do with the fact that Eoin had caught them in the hallway.

Arran knew she wasn't avoiding him out of guilt or remorse. In fact, it seemed as if she wasn't intentionally avoiding him at all. She was behaving as if nothing had ever happened between them, that no love had been shared, no kind words exchanged.

He could tell that Eoin was starting to fall for Blaire, and he couldn't blame him. She was his wife, after all, and ever since the night he'd released her from the dungeon, she'd been nothing less than kind, enthusiastic, and alive around him.

If Arran wasn't completely sure that he knew exactly who Blaire really was, he would have found himself charmed by this new 'Blaire' himself and been happy that his brother had found himself such a wonderful wife. But, what his brother failed to see was just how different this Blaire was from the one he'd married only a few short weeks ago.

Blaire's personality seemed to have changed overnight. She was quieter, less feisty, and entirely likeable. One of the things Arran loved most about Blaire was that not everyone found her likeable. But he couldn't like her more.

Even her voice was different. She said words that had no meaning and mispronounced others that he'd heard her say correctly many times before. She looked at every meal as if she was afraid to eat it, and she'd never seen such fare in front of her before.

But all of those things were nothing compared to what really bothered him about her behavior lately. He knew he'd broken her heart the morning of the wedding. He saw it in her eyes the moment it happened, and he'd felt her pain through every inch of his own heart.

Her behavior was not that of someone who'd just suffered heartbreak. It was the opposite entirely. She smiled and laughed and asked questions like someone who is just at the thrilling beginning of a newfound love.

Perhaps it was all an act. It must be. Arran was sure of it. For, how could she have healed so quickly from the pain that still rendered him senseless? Perhaps she thought to build Eoin's hopes, only to hurt him as some form of revenge for the hurt that he himself had caused her.

If that was the case, Arran would not let his brother be hurt by the pain he'd caused. Whatever was going on with Blaire, he intended to find out as quickly as possible.

*W*e made our way to a corner of the castle I'd yet to see in my few weeks here. He stopped at a small door and reached for a lantern before opening the door and moving us into a small winding stairwell.

It was totally dark except for the small flame that flickered each time we moved up the steps together. Eoin didn't let go of my hand as we moved, and with each step upward our bodies would touch, spreading delicious shocks over my skin.

I couldn't see the top landing, so when Eoin stopped and faced me I continued to try and walk up the next step. As I rose, I bumped our chests together and whacked the top of my head hard against the bottom of his chin. I yelped at the impact and nearly teetered off the top landing, but was gathered in close by Eoin's quick hands.

"Ach, lass. Ye've got a hard head. Do ye see any of my teeth lying around? I think ye might have rattled some loose."

He removed his left hand from my lower back and reached up to rub his chin. I laughed and bent my head in shame, my forehead delicately touching his chest. He surprised me by pulling me closer to him and wrapping both arms around me. He gently kissed the top of my head, right on the spot I'd whacked against his chin.

"But, I'm sure my chin wasna so pleasant a feeling on the top of yer head, now was it? Come, lass. Crawl out onto the wall with me."

He raised a wooden panel at the top of the landing, revealing a small window-like space through which he crawled. Once on the other side, he reached his hand through the opening to assist me. I grabbed his hand and, with my free one, hiked up the back of my dress and rather ungracefully made my way out onto the wall.

"Come and sit out on the ledge, I willna let ye fall." I watched as he made his way over to the edge of the wall that surrounded the back side of the castle. Deftly, he jumped up onto the stone wall and sat, letting his legs hang freely off the edge.

Seeing that his eyes were turned away as he stared out at the ocean, I quickly hiked up the bottom of my dress so that I could leap up onto the edge, and sit down beside him before he turned back to see how unladylike I really was.

"Well, I'd meant for ye to see the stars, lass, but as ye can see, there's not so much to look at tonight. Looks like a storm's headed this way."

The sky was black, and there were storm clouds rolling, as if following the waves that crashed up onto the shore below us.

The wind was blowing hard, and the sound of the wind mixed with the harsh sound of water smashing against the rocks was oddly beautiful.

We sat there silently for some time. The wind chilled me so that I shivered beneath the thick dress that covered all of my body, but I was unwilling to say anything, not wanting to shatter the moment. A closeness between us hung heavy as we shared the long silence, listening to the water crash on the rocks and the distant sound of thunder over the horizon. I felt as if I'd known him for a long time, rather than the few short weeks I'd spent here at the castle.

The touch of his fingers as he laced his own with mine caused me to cautiously glance toward him out of the corner of my eye. He held my hand gently, drawing small circles along the base of my thumb with his, but he didn't look in my direction as he kept his gaze straight ahead, seemingly distracted by the water down below.

I closed my eyes briefly and inhaled the cold wet air, savoring the sensation of his rough fingers against my hand. A loud boom of thunder brought large drops of water, soaking us both in seconds.

I cringed inwardly as the rain hit my hair. I was having enough trouble keeping my mane tamed without the use of a straightener.

Eoin swung off the ledge, extending both hands out to me. "Come, lass. Ye will catch a cold, standing out in this rain. Let's go inside."

He stood back, allowing me to crawl through the window-space first. As I stood in the dark stairwell once more, I brushed the wet strands of hair out of my face, swinging drops of water in every direction.

I knew Eoin had made his way back into the stairwell, but the candle in our lantern had burned out while we'd been out on the ledge. Once he closed the hatch that covered the window, the stairwell descended into pitch darkness.

"Doona worry, lass. I know my way down these stairs well. We will make our way down them together, aye?"

Blindly I reached forward, palming the air, expecting to make contact with his hand. Instead, my palm rested on his chest as he stepped closer. Slowly, he backed me into the wall and my breathing accelerated as the evening whiskers from his cheek scratched against the side of my face.

His hands moved so that he held onto both of mine as he gently placed his lips against my own.

It was surprisingly gentle and sweet, and it was over far too quickly as he moved his lips right next to my ear and whispered, "Ach, lass, if tis alright with ye, I doona think I can stay angry at ye any longer."

And with that, he turned and led me down the dark stairwell, the heavy thumping of my heart beating in my ears.

CHAPTER 17

*E*oin stroked the mare's mane as he worked to prepare her for their ride into the village. His own horse sat ready, tied at the end of the stables, glancing impatiently in Eoin's direction.

Eoin smiled at the old, gray stallion, his trusted horse and companion since childhood. "Ah, Griffin, doona look at me so. We will be leaving soon enough. But ye see, Sheila will be joining us today. Blaire will be riding her, and I expect ye to be on yer very best behavior. Do ye understand?"

The old horse neighed as Eoin walked toward him, offering him an apple to placate him until they rode out for the village.

Footsteps from behind caused Eoin to spin around toward the west entrance of the stables. Expecting to see Blaire, he couldn't repress the look of disappointment on his face at seeing Kip make his way over to Sheila.

"Looks like ye did a fine job with Sheila. Her coat hasna shined so brightly in years. But I still doona understand why ye won't let Blaire ride Angus. She's good with horses; she will think that Sheila is too tame." The old man shook his head as he loosened Sheila's reins and went to tie her up by Griffin.

"Angus is only fit for racing through the countryside, not a trip to the village, and ye know it, Kip. Now, I know Blaire dinna treat ye well her first night here, but I wish ye'd ease up on the lass."

"I'll not be having ye tell me what I should do, laddie, laird of this keep, or not. But it doesna matter, my thoughts on her. She's yer wife. Ye are the one that has to bed the ungrateful . . ." He was cut off by a cheery 'hello' at the end of the stables.

Eoin turned to see Blaire making her way toward him. She looked beautiful with her bright eyes and smile and her hair pulled up in a delicate knot at the base of her neck.

He watched as she bid Kip a good morning and was rewarded with a huff as he retreated from the stables.

"Doona let him bother ye, lass. He's only hard on the outside."

"Oh, it's alright. Where are ye taking me?" She reached up and touched his shoulder, and he had to restrain himself from pulling her against him.

"To the village. There's just a few things that need attending." He walked over to where both horses were tied and gestured toward Sheila with his head. "Ye can take the brown one. Her name's Sheila. Ye will have no problems with her, I'm sure."

Blaire cautiously approached the mare, hesitantly reaching out her hand to touch the horse's throat. Eoin watched, curious as to why she seemed so unsure. He'd always known her to be a fine rider.

"What's wrong, lass? She's got more fire in her than she looks. She'll be a fine ride for ye."

"How do I get on her?"

The question surprised him, but he ignored it as he bent to offer her his assistance in mounting the horse. No sooner had Blaire situated herself on the mare than the mare started whining and trying to pull at the reins that kept her fastened to the edge of the stables.

"What do I do with her, Eoin?"

"Just stroke her, lean forward and whisper in her ear, calm her as ye would yer own horse." He turned and climbed onto Griffin, leaning forward to untie the reins of both horses so that they could set off toward the village.

He rode ahead a short distance, waiting for Blaire and the mare to join him, but when he heard no hooves he turned to see Blaire and the mare sitting at the side of the stables where he'd left them.

Clicking, he steered Griffin back toward the stables. "What's the matter with ye, lass? Do ye no longer want to go?"

"No, I do want to. I just don't know how to do this."

Eoin frowned as he pulled back on Griffin's reins, stopping him next to Sheila. He knew Blaire could ride. He'd seen her do it many times, with many different horses. Why was she feigning ignorance now? Perhaps, she was afraid that he'd be angry with her for not wanting to accompany him. Or mayhap she wanted a reason to ride with him on the same horse.

While he wasn't sure of the reason, he enjoyed the second possibility much more. "Would ye like to ride with me, lass? Griffin may be old, but he can carry ye and me together, easily."

"Aye, I think that would be best."

Ah, so she did want to ride next to him. He smiled inwardly at himself, pleased at the notion, as he lifted her from Sheila's back and placed her snugly in between his legs astride Griffin.

I rode with my rear pressed firmly against him as we made our way down into the village. That had almost been an unimaginable disaster. I'd never ridden a horse in my life, and I had no idea what I'd been thinking when Eoin asked if I would like to go with him and to meet him in the stables.

I'd ignorantly pictured some fancy horse-drawn coach taking us into town, like a scene out of *Pride and Prejudice*; I was obviously not taking into account that things of that nature were from an entirely different century that was yet to come.

Still, I much preferred this method of transportation over any sort of pulled wagon, and I relished the feeling of his chiseled muscles pressing against my back. He rode with his hands around my waist, and the strength in his legs and arms as they surrounded me made me hope it was hours until we reached the village.

Instead, it took us less than an hour before Eoin stopped the horse and dismounted, quickly reaching his arms toward me to help me off of the horse. He smiled at me as I reached behind to rub my sore bottom. He gestured for me to follow him as he made his way to a small cluster of cottages in front of us.

Eoin turned his head to tell me something, but he was interrupted by a loud voice coming from one of the doorways.

"Well, if it isn't Laird Conall! Why, it's been too long since we have seen ye here, son!"

Eoin's face lit up as he moved away from me and embraced the large, red-faced man. "Aye, it has, Bran! How's yer wife and children?"

"Fine. Fine. Dona is in bed, nursing our sixth bairn. She gave birth only two nights ago." The man's eyes gleamed with pride as he spoke of his family.

"Six, my God, man! Do ye not ever let the lass rest? How have ye been managing the others on yer own, the last few days?"

"I havena." The man let out a loud, deep chuckle before continuing. "They've had free run o' the place while their mother has been in bed. I'm sure she'll be not too pleased with me once she's up. Come inside. Let us have a drink for old time's sake, aye?"

Eoin reached his hand behind him, and I instinctively took hold.

"Let me introduce ye to my wife, Bran. This is Blaire."

I smiled as the man quickly looked me up and down. "How did this old sot get such a beautiful lass like ye to marry him? Oh, never mind. What's done is done, aye? I shouldna try to talk ye out of it now. Come. Ye shall have a drink with us as well."

I followed the two men through the small entranceway into a one-roomed first floor where all five children, minus the newborn, were running around, creating chaos. All children were under the age of seven, and a few days without strict structure from their mother had put them in a tailspin.

I knew that the noise level in the home could in no way be

conducive to their mother's rest, and my teacher drive immediately kicked in.

"Alright, stop where ye are!" And I quickly held my hands up as I stared them down. "My name is Blaire, and ye are all going to follow me outside so that we can allow yer mother some rest time. Aye?"

I watched as the three oldest children glanced up to take in the shocked look on their father's face. When he stood silently, they looked up at me and seemed to consent, slowly marching out the front door together. I yanked up the two youngest—year-and-a-half-old twin boys—and placed one on each hip.

I turned to address the two men before following the children outside. "Go ahead and enjoy a drink. I'll keep the children busy so that the two of ye can visit and yer wife can rest with the baby."

Leaving them both open-mouthed, I made my way outside with the two squirming toddlers.

CHAPTER 18

Scotland—1645—Kinnaird Castle

"The fire served no purpose! The lad is too foolish to see when he's been warned and to be afraid. He thinks the fire happened by chance, set by a drunkard at the wedding." Ramsay Kinnaird sat at the end of a long table, staring down the two servants unfortunate enough to be called to his service.

"What will ye do, sire? Attack them at once?"

The servant's words were rewarded with a large bang as Ramsay threw his fist down on the table hard. "No, ye fool! To attack by surprise would be too easy! I want Eoin and his brother Arran to sense the darkness coming for them. I want them to feel afraid for their home and their loved ones and know that there is nothing they can do to stop them from losing everything." He stood from the table and walked toward the servants until his own face was but inches from theirs. "The first attack was too simple. We must take something that is precious to them."

"What would be best? Would ye like us to slaughter their sheep?"

Ramsay contemplated the servant's suggestion. A wicked grin contorted his face as his next plan came into full view in his mind.

"No, the Conalls have no real connection to their sheep, but they've always loved their horses. Conall Castle is known for them, all cared for by that pathetic stable master. The loss of horses will hurt them. Send the two lads that work the stables out tomorrow midday. Take their mother, should they need motivation. Tell them to take the head of every last horse, and leave behind the pieces to be found."

"*N*o, Arran. I'm telling ye the truth. I dinna ask her to take the children out of the house. She offered to do it all on her own. I was surprised as well, and ye should've seen Bran's face."

Arran ran his hands through his hair as he paced back and forth in front of his brother. He'd spent days trying to make some sense of Blaire's strange behavior, and the only thing he could come up with was that this lass wasn't actually Blaire. That conclusion made no sense to him at all.

"It just doesna make sense, Eoin. Blaire hates children. If ye left her alone in a room with them, she'd be more likely to eat them than offer to care for them."

"Aye, I know the Blaire we knew as children was that way, but perhaps she's changed."

"She hasna. Because the lass ye have married isn't Blaire." Arran could sense Eoin's temper flaring as he finished his sentence, and he marched over in front of his brother to stop him from pacing back and forth.

"What the hell are ye talking about, Arran? Ye are making no goddamned sense, and ye havena been for some time. I know that ye are still grieving for our father, but ye have to stop drinking so much. It's beginning to addle yer thoughts."

"I've not been drinking today, Eoin. I know what I'm saying sounds foolish, and I canna make sense of it myself, but this lass is not Blaire."

"Just because she spent part of a day around children doesna mean a stranger has replaced Blaire. God, listen to what ye are saying, Arran. Ye've gone and lost yer mind."

"I havena. Kip also told me that ye dinna even end up taking Sheila to the village, because Blaire could not ride her. Ye know Blaire can ride well, Eoin."

"Aye, we left her at the stables, but only because she wanted to share a horse with me."

Arran rolled his eyes as he crossed his arms and leaned back against the wall behind him. "Did she tell ye that?"

"No, but ye are not the only one who can sense what a lass wants, Arran. Doona mention this conversation to me again, aye? I'm worried for ye, brother. Perhaps ye need to go away for a few days. I believe Kip is about to make another trip to bring back another horse or two for the stables. Go with him, and doona drink while ye are gone."

"Aye, I'll go. I canna stand to be around ye when ye refuse to see what's right in front of ye. All I ask is that ye watch her. She doesna talk like Blaire either. If ye'd only pull yer head out of yer arse! Test her. Take her to do something ye know Blaire was good at as a child, and see if she succeeds."

With that he turned and left, leaving Eoin to think about all that he'd said.

CHAPTER 19

$\mathcal{I}$ was going to throw up. There was no doubt about it whatsoever. I was about to be expected to string, or whatever the crap you do, a bow and arrow and shoot the damn thing right in the middle of the target.

When Eoin knocked on my door this morning shortly after breakfast, I'd been excited. It was unusual for me to see him after breakfast, and with progress moving so slowly in the spell room, I was happy for any excuse to keep me from my work. That is, until he asked me to go shooting with him and proceeded to tell me over and over how wonderful I'd been at it as a child, and how he and Arran never wanted go shooting with me because they knew I would beat them ruthlessly.

The gig was definitely up. The shit had certainly hit the fan. And by tonight, I was absolutely positive I would be locked away again where I'd been a few weeks ago.

It's not that I was in bad shape. I did try to drag myself to the gym, one, sometimes two whole times a week. But jogging a mile had nothing to do with maneuvering this huge wooden contraption in such a way that it would send an arrow soaring through the air. I seriously doubted I could even pick the thing up off of the ground.

"Well, that was a fairly good shot, but I have no doubt ye can beat it."

He flashed one of those smiles that made my muscles feel weak—exactly what I didn't need at the moment—as he stepped out of the way to let me take my place in front of the target. "Here ye go, Blaire."

I gripped the bow unsurely, sighing with relief when I found it wasn't as heavy as I'd first expected. My hands shook as I fumbled with the arrow, trying my best to mimic Eoin's movements exactly.

Pulling back, I released the arrow high into the air. Two seconds later, it unceremoniously landed three feet in front of me. I shut my eyes in defeat, only to hear Eoin's laughter from behind me.

"Ach, lass. Has it been a long while then since ye went shooting?" He came up behind me and gave my shoulders a gentle squeeze. "Perhaps my memories are wrong about how good ye used to be at this."

"I suppose they probably were. Best if I just watch ye shoot." I tried to back away, but his hands on my shoulders held me in place.

"Nay, lass, I wasna wrong. It's just nerves is all. Give it another go, aye?"

Reluctantly and, with the most unpleasant look on my face that I could manage, I reached for another arrow and went about shooting it off once more.

It hit the target right in the middle.

"What? Yes! No freakin way!" I jumped, tossing the bow to the side as I shot my hands up in the air, realizing too late that I'd let my language slip and that I must have looked like a buffoon as I leapt gleefully up in the air.

Eoin cocked his head and looked at me with a confused expression. "What did ye just say lass? 'Freakin'?"

I fumbled for an explanation. "No, I just made a noise, a happy noise for hitting the target. I'm surprised is all."

"Why would ye be surprised, lass? Ye have always been good at this. Here, let's take turns shooting a few more. Aye?"

*T*hey continued to take turns shooting arrows until all that they'd brought stuck out of the target. After the first one, Blaire had hit every single one right in the center.

Eoin had expected her to excel. That's why he'd asked her to go shooting, so that he could prove Arran's ridiculous theory wrong. But why did he feel so surprised?

He knew all that Arran had suggested was impossible, but just to humor him, shouldn't he test her in some other way as well? A fair number of lasses in the Highlands could shoot a bow and arrow decently, and he knew there were always a few people who could succeed at anything at their first try. Perhaps Blaire was one of those naturally gifted people?

As they gathered up their mess and began the half-mile trek back to the castle grounds, Eoin thought of a few questions that he knew would help put his own mind at ease, and hopefully put an end to his brother's ridiculous notions.

"Blaire, do ye remember the time ye shot me in the arse? Did ye really think it necessary? All I did was tell ye that you could not come down to the village with me and Arran." He turned to watch her closely, hoping she would correct him. He knew why she'd really shot him. His father had spent what seemed like half a day explaining to him why he was never to speak to a lady in such a hurtful way ever again.

"Nay, Eoin. That isn't why I shot ye, that day. I shot ye because ye told me I was the ugliest lass that ye'd ever seen, and ye'd rather kiss Griffin's arse than be married to me someday. It was the summer we walked in on our fathers discussing the betrothal."

"Aye. That's right. I do apologize, Blaire. I was young and foolish. At that age, I'd rather have kissed Griffin's arse than any lass." He laughed, thinking himself foolish for giving Arran's notion any thought.

As they reached the castle grounds and Eoin stashed their equipment away, he thought of one last question as Bri turned to make her way up to her room in the castle. "I canna remember which ear it is that yer father canna hear from. Which is it?"

"It's his right."

As she turned and walked inside the castle, Eoin felt his heart drop into the deepest depths of his stomach.

He knew it had always been her father's left ear.

CHAPTER 20

S cotland—1645

W as it his right ear or his left? Dammit! I couldn't remember, and I second-guessed myself a thousand times as I made my way back to my bedchamber. Why did Eoin ask the question in the first place? Was it really that he just couldn't remember, or did he suspect something?

It had to be the first. What on earth could he suspect? Surely, even if he found my behavior different than Blaire's, he wouldn't immediately jump to the conclusion that I was someone else. From everything Mary had told me, I looked exactly like her.

It didn't matter at this point. If he asked, surely he wouldn't know whether or not what I told him was true. He wasn't testing me; although, the way he went on and on about how great Blaire was with a bow and arrow, it did sort of seem that way. Luckily, I'd had a knack for it. Who knew? I'd never been coordinated at anything, and all of a sudden I was an expert archer. The entire situation was just too odd for words, and it made me even more anxious to get back to work in the spell room. I'd spent far too long here, and with each passing day I found myself more reluctant to spend hours searching through spell books. I'd much rather spend my time exploring the castle, visiting with Eoin, or actually cooking with Mary like Eoin thought I was.

And while I missed my mother, homesickness wasn't settling in like I thought it should have. I loved it here—the lack of cars and modern technology, the way you didn't hear car horns and sirens every time you stepped outside, the way everything was quieter and, as a result, more simple as well. People had to work so much harder for everything that there was an overwhelming sense of pride and work ethic that just radiated from every person I'd met while here.

I was also beginning to love everyone at the castle: Mary, Eoin, even Kip and Arran—both of whom seemed dead set against getting to know me. It was okay. I still felt more at home here than I did in my newly remodeled former bachelor pad of a home, where I'd spent so many nights alone. It was comforting to know that there were people just down the hall. It somehow made every second feel less lonely.

Yeah, it was definitely time to get back to work in the spell room. As nice as it was to escape reality here for a few weeks, this was not where I was meant to be. If that was the case, I would've been born here, hundreds of years ago. I was an unnatural imposter, and it was vital that I find the spell that would get me back home.

Estimating that I still had a couple of hours before everyone gathered for the evening meal, I made my way down into the kitchens to let Mary know where I'd be. Her hands were busy, pulling away at some nameless animal I was certain would be staring up at me from a plate come dinner, and as she nodded in acknowledgement that she'd heard me, I made my way into the secret spell room in the back of the basement.

Walking to the side, I scooted past a pile of books I'd already gone through, which were now serving as a secret hiding nook for my beloved normal clothes. Now an expert at laces, I whipped myself out of the heavy gown I was wearing and quickly slid on my jeans, bra, t-shirt, socks, and tennis shoes, smiling as I instantly felt more like me.

I'd methodically sorted out every book in the spell room and had separated them into piles according to language, age, and probable relevance. I was now on my last pile of books written in English, and I hoped with everything I had that what I needed would be in this pile. If nothing turned up, I was going to be forced to enlist someone who could read Gaelic to help me with the rest of the book. I knew that doing that would significantly increase the risk of Eoin discovering the truth.

I let my head fall loosely toward my chest and rolled it around in both directions, trying to release some tension and get myself into work mode. Crawling onto the old wooden bench that sat in front of the desk, I pulled both of my legs toward me, turning them in so that I sat crisscross on the bench.

The ability to move my legs freely after being trapped under heavy layers of fabric was so refreshing that I found myself sitting in odd positions every time I came down to the spell room to work. Throwing my arms high above me to stretch before reaching for the top book on the large stack, I felt the back of my shirt rise with the movement of my arms, exposing the lower half of my back. It stayed bunched there as I reached for the top book and opened it on the desk, bending to begin my examination of its contents.

I knew Mary would have keeled over at the sight of such skin exposure, but the coolness of the room felt nice on my back, and what did I care anyway?

I was alone in the room; and would be until dinner.

---

*H*e was certain she hadn't seen him peeking out from behind his own door as she exited her own and made her way down into the kitchens. He knew he was making a mistake by following her. What did he expect to find her doing? She was on her way to help Mary in the kitchens; the same as she did everyday around this time.

Still, she'd misspoken about her father's ear, and it caused a sense of dread and unease to build in his stomach. Eoin couldn't do anything, or think about anything else, with the last three words she'd said to him churning in his mind.

He knew Arran was wrong. He was married to Blaire, not a different-but-similar-looking lass. But he did now see what Arran had been trying to tell him the other day, something was different about her. She was keeping something from him and everyone else in the castle.

He paused and sat down in the small hallway outside the entrance to the kitchen, content to listen to their conversations as Mary and Blaire worked side by side. Perhaps she'd been more open with Mary, and listening to them speak would give him a better sense of what was happening with her.

But the lass didn't go all the way into the kitchen, and as he heard her stop at the doorway to tell Mary she was going below to work, his blood ran cold.

Mary's belated "Aye, lass. I'll come and warn ye when the food is nearly prepared" did nothing to calm his growing sense of unease.

He waited until he was sure she was far enough ahead of him not to hear his footsteps. From the direction in which Blaire went, he knew there was only one set of steps that led below the castle.

Hesitantly, he made his way into the one-roomed basement. He hoped to see her working on some task for Mary, but when he saw the light flickering from the doorway at the back of the room, he knew he would find nothing good beyond that door.

There could be no good explanation for why Blaire was in his late aunt's spell room. She shouldn't even have known the room existed. Besides their late father, Arran, Mary, and himself, no one else on the castle grounds had ever seen the inside of that room.

Slowly he crept toward the doorway, barely pulling at the crack so that it opened only slightly, allowing him to see inside. Confusion filled his mind as his gaze poured over the lass sitting, rather twisted, in front of his aunt's old desk. The clothes that the woman had on were completely senseless. Why, the lass had fabric that went up in between the length of her legs! For a moment, he assumed the lass wasn't Blaire but a lunatic that had made her way into the castle tunnels.

Then he caught a glimpse of something black and odd spread across a bare space on the lass's back. Swirling and dark, the shapes seemed to spell out something, permanently etched into her skin. Surely something like that could only be accomplished with witchcraft.

When he heard the strange lass speak, as if trying to sound out something written within the book she was staring so intently into, he couldn't help but swing the door open with a crash, the shock of all he'd seen reverberating through his veins.

"Christ, Blaire! Ye are a damned witch!"

CHAPTER 21

The first book I'd pulled off the top of the stack was one of Alasdair's old journals, and while the majority of entries held nothing of great relevance, there was an entry at the end of the volume that had me leaning far over the desk in anticipation.

In it, Alasdair referenced his last conversation with Morna. And while most of it left out details of their conversations, he did say that it was vital to ensure that Eoin marry Blaire. He wrote of the spell his sister had cast and how Blaire and, I could only assume I, would switch places in time, and that I would help save them.

From what exactly, I wasn't sure. And while I could feel a thought tugging at some part of my brain, I couldn't think of any real reason for my presence here. Besides, I didn't intend to stay long enough to find out and the further I got into the entry, the more excited I became. At the end of the journal entry he had spelled out the title of a book, three words written in Gaelic, prefaced with the words, "Morna said to remember this, if the time comes that it is needed."

It had to be the name of one of the Gaelic books stacked on the other side of the room, and it had to have something to do with the spell. I just knew it. I stared at the three words. They sounded completely foreign as I worked to pronounce them as best I could.

I was just rounding the end of the last word when a crash from behind me caused me to whip around to see Eoin's angry presence in the doorway, his thunderous voice screaming something about me being a witch.

Before I could get out a word in protest, he jerked me up by both arms and roughly dragged me away from the small room. He trembled with anger. I could feel it in the grip with which he held onto my arms. I would unquestionably be bruised tomorrow. As he dragged me up the stairs toward his bedchamber, screaming in Gaelic every step of the way, I found myself hoping that Mary would hear him. Perhaps, she could at least help me explain the situation. Not that I was very optimistic about him giving me the opportunity to do so.

He flung open the door and nearly threw me across his bedroom as he let go of his hold and slammed the door shut behind him.

He came toward me, seeming larger than he actually was, and stopped in front of my hunkered-down figure. I stood shakily, refusing to let him bully me until I'd told him all that I knew.

"Let me explain, Eoin. I'm not a witch. I . . ."

He immediately interrupted me with more words in Gaelic that I didn't understand before he turned and walked over to the window seat to stare outside.

"What do ye expect me to do with ye now, lass? I should've left ye down in the dungeon to rot, but I expect ye spelled me so that I would relent and release ye, aye? What did ye plan to do, Blaire, place spells on us to do yer bidding and torture me for having married ye? I canna believe Arran was right! What a wicked bitch ye are!"

Anger flared within me, and I made no effort to continue the accent I'd tried so hard to use over the past weeks. "Are you crazy? Have I done or said anything to anyone since I've been here that would make you think that I wanted to hurt you? If you'd just stop all of your insane ranting and listen to me, I could explain what I was doing in the spell room."

"How did ye even know about the room, Blaire? Ye had no business being in that part of the castle at all!"

"Mary showed me. It's where she found me when I showed up here."

"Ye are a damned liar, Blaire! Do ye not remember the day ye arrived? Ye insulted just about everyone in the castle, and ye nearly broke poor Kip's back with the inconsiderate load ye piled onto him!"

"No!" I was no longer afraid, but I was so angry I was on the verge of tears. Each breath seemed painful in my chest. "I don't remember the day Blaire arrived because I'm not Blaire! I don't understand why or how I got here, but I've spent almost every minute since I showed up in this godforsaken place trying to get back home to Texas."

"Not Blaire? Texas? God, Arran was right! How could I have been so blind? Well, I'll no more be fooled by ye, and I'll not have ye causing havoc here anymore."

He reached as if to grab for my arm, but I evaded him, jumping quickly to the left and chunking the nearest object I could reach at his head. It hit him square on the nose. With a ferocious growl, he leapt in my direction once more.

If Mary didn't get up here soon, I was seriously screwed.

*D*usk descended over the castle, slowly covering every inch of the grounds, creating the perfect shade from which the two servants could hide. They stopped their horses nearly a mile away from the stables, tying them securely to trees far enough away so that they wouldn't hear the sounds of the horses dying. It wouldn't do for them to spook their own. They needed them to get back quickly to Kinnaird Castle.

"I thought ye said there would be over a dozen here. There's only nine. The three stables at the end are empty."

"Aye. There should be, but we only take what's here. We doona have much time to begin with. We must do it quick, do ye understand? They'll not be without someone in the stables for long. We must come while they are all at dinner. The old stable master eats with his wife in the kitchens, while the laird, wife, and brother dine in the grand hall. We shall only have a few short moments to accomplish the task."

The youngest servant, a lad of no more than sixteen, reached to wipe the sweat from his brow. It was a chilly evening, but he felt strangled by the heat rising from his own body and breathed in deeply to try and still the frantic thumping of his heart. It was the worst kind of crime for which he was about to be responsible. The animals would not be used for food. They were not killing them out of mercy. These horses were some of the finest he'd ever seen, healthy and strong. It broke his heart to know they would be ending the horses' lives for no great purpose.

As he watched his older brother raise his blade high above the first horse's head, he reached forward to stop the swing downward, latching onto his brother's hand. "Swing true and hard. Doona let the blade stop halfway through. I know we must do this to save Mother, but I willna have them suffer more than they must."

As his brother nodded, the younger released his grip and turned quickly to shield his eyes, choking down the bile that rose in his throat as a spray of warm blood splattered across his back.

With tears streaming down both their faces, the brothers moved quickly, trying to finish their horrid task as mercifully as they could.

When the last horse's head had been severed, and the stable floors were covered with a sticky sickness, and the walls dripped with fresh blood, the two boys fled into the night with their souls and minds heavy and their hearts filled with hate for Ramsay Kinnaird.

CHAPTER 22

*T*he trip to get the horses had been shorter than expected, but Eoin had been right. He needed to calm down, and getting away from the castle for a day or so with Kip helped tremendously. He had been drinking too much, and he was certain it had impacted his feelings about Blaire. She wasn't someone else, someone trying to harm his brother. She was simply as lost as he was, trying to deal with her new marriage in the best way that she knew how.

It was time that he do the same, and with his mind set on doing just that, he smiled and pointed so that Kip would look out over the horizon where they could see Conall Castle off in the distance, bathed in moonlight.

He was feeling better than he had in ages, and he knew the last time he felt this good was before his father's tragic death. Perhaps Blaire's hold on him was not as strong as he thought. He only needed time to heal from the changes of the last few months.

The stables were only a short distance away, and it startled him that instead of picking up their pace in their anticipation of getting home, both horses reared up on their hind legs and tried to turn in the other direction. Both men steadied their horses, and Arran reached down to soothe Sheila as Kip did the same to Griffin.

Arran scanned the distance between themselves and the stables, looking for something that would have caused the horses to start. Suddenly, out of the corner of his eye, he saw what could only be Angus, charging in their direction.

"Ach. Angus! I doona know how else to keep him in the stables. If he knows we've taken other horses out, he willna stay put. I expect he's been loose since we left."

"Kip, he looks frightened. I know he's wild, but I've never seen him behave so."

Angus didn't slow his pace as he reached the two men, instead charging in wide circles around them, whinnying and making noise.

"It's not too far to the stables from here. Let's leave the horses here and take a look first. Aye?"

Kip was already dismounting Griffin and walking him over to the nearest tree to secure him as Arran nodded in agreement, easily swinging himself down from Sheila as he patted the side of her neck. "It's alright, sweetheart. Ye stay here with Griffin and Angus, and I'll come back for ye shortly."

Fear lodged securely in Arran's gut. With each step closer, his fear grew. "Something isna right, Kip. I fear someone's been in the stables." He turned to see the old man slowing his pace, his face still and pale.

"Aye, I believe ye are right, son. I smell blood, lots of it. I doona know if I can make myself see. Would ye mind going on yer own? I'll stay right here."

Kip's words did nothing to soothe Arran's fear. He'd never known the old man to back away from anything, but as he saw the distraught expression on his old friend's face, he knew that whatever he was about to see was terrible. Kip loved nothing in the world more than his horses, except perhaps Mary, and Arran could feel it in his bones that it would be best to spare Kip from whatever awaited him beyond the stable doors. He reached out and placed both hands on Kip's shoulders.

"Aye. O' course. I'm sure tis fine, but I'll go and see by myself. Ye stay here and keep an eye on the others." He nudged his head toward the top of the hill where Sheila, Griffin, and Angus, along with the other four horses they'd acquired, stayed tied to the trunk of a tree.

He turned and made his way to the side entrance of the stable. With each step the smell of blood became stronger, causing his stomach to churn uncomfortably.

Arran stepped inside the dark center walkway of the stables, grabbing the lighted flame from outside the entrance to set light to the first lantern in a long row that hung outside each stall door. An awful squishing sound echoed as his feet made contact with the cold, wet liquid that covered the ground. Hesitantly he walked from lantern to lantern, slowly illuminating the horror that filled each stall.

Every horse was dead. He knew it even before he gathered the courage to peek over into one of the stalls. It was too quiet, and there was too much blood for that not to be the case. Once he did look, he had to grab onto the blood-soaked post to his right just to keep himself steady. The sight of the decapitated horse, its head lying separate but close to the rest of its body, sent the contents of his stomach retching out onto the wooden floor.

He didn't need to see the others right now. He knew it was all the same, and he would be forced to view the massacre later when he cleaned up the remains. He would do it himself to ensure that Kip didn't make his way into the stable. It would be hard enough for the old stable master to deal with the death of his horses. There was no reason that he should ever have to see what had become of his beloved animals.

Somberly he made his way back to Kip, his face showing what he could hardly bring his voice to say. "I'm so verra sorry, Kip."

"Ye canna mean it. What happened to them? I need to see, Arran. Perhaps ye are wrong." The old man staggered forward, trying to force himself to make his way toward the stables.

"Nay, I'm not wrong. They were slaughtered, Kip. All of them. Now, we must clean up the mess and then find who did it. But, I willna be letting ye lay yer eyes upon a bit of it."

Kip sobbed as he took another step toward the stables. "I doona want to see it, Arran, but I must. I've cared for all of those horses since they were born, and I willna disrespect them by leaving someone else to care for the mess of their death." Tears rolled down the old man's cheeks as he dragged his feet toward the side entrance of the stables.

Arran quickly moved to block Kip from taking another step, and doing the only thing he could think of to stop him, punched him square in the face. "Aye, Kip, ye can let someone else care for them. I'll be the one to do it now." Swinging the unconscious stable master over his shoulders, he turned to make his way up to the castle.

I had no idea how long we'd been screaming at one another. Half of the words he was screeching in my direction I had no meaning for, and I was equally sure the same could be said for the things I was saying to him.

I was holding nothing back now, screaming in my normal accent, using modern words for which I knew he had no context. I did everything I could just to talk and talk, hoping that he would eventually stop screaming long enough to listen to what I had to say.

It didn't work.

And as we continued to yell at each other, he continued to try and forcibly remove me from the room. We played an odd sort of cat-and-mouse game: me dancing out of the path of his reaching hands, him bobbing out of the way so that whatever object I hurled in his direction didn't bludgeon him in the eye.

He now stood in front of the door, blocking my path to any exit, while I stood on top of his bed reaching for some sort of metal object that sat beside it and chunked it across the room. He swiftly moved out of the way just as the door opened. The projectile flew through the open door just above Mary's head.

"What in God's name do ye think the two of ye are doing? Bri, get down from that bed this instant, and for God's sake, stop throwing things! Eoin, stop ranting in Gaelic. The lass has no idea what ye are saying. It's time we had a talk, all three of us, but I will have no part in it while the two of ye are acting like ye have gone and lost yer minds." Mary stared us down from the doorway, an uncomfortable hush settling over the room.

Embarrassed, I slid off the top of the bed and moved to stand beside her. "I'm sorry Mary. He walked in on me while I was working in the spell room. I was trying to sound out the name of one of the books, and he saw me in my normal clothes. I'm pretty sure he saw my tattoo as well. Then he yanked me up and accused me of being a witch. He won't listen to me."

Eoin moved out from behind the door and, with both fists on his hips, looked at me and Mary. "Tattoo? Mark of the devil, ye mean. Why, I've never seen such markings in my life. And Mary, did ye just call her Bri? Do ye mean to tell me that ye knew that we were being fooled by this witch?"

Mary left my side as she moved in front of Eoin and slapped him right across the face. I couldn't stop a grin from spreading across mine, and a giggle escaped my lips at the sight of his reddened face.

"Have ye forgotten just who ye are talking too, Eoin? Aye, I did call her Bri, because that's the poor lassie's name. But she's no witch. And the only fool around here is ye, ye thick-headed, stubborn arse! Now ye are going to sit down and not say a word until the lass has finished telling ye everything she knows. Aye?"

Silently he nodded and sat down on the edge of his rumpled bed. I was definitely going to have to take lessons from Mary. She would've made one hell of a teacher.

A breathless voice screaming "Mary" from out in the hallway caused us all to file out of the bedchamber. Arran was struggling down the hall, carrying a seemingly unconscious Kip over his shoulders.

"What's happened?" Mary ran toward Arran, grasping her husband's arm as it hung limply down Arran's back.

"It's alright, Mary. He's fine. I hit him to keep him from going into the stables. I'll lay him in my room. Stay with him until I return. No matter what he tells ye, doona let him out of the room. He doesna need to see what's down there, no matter how much he thinks he needs to."

Eoin spoke now. "What's happened in the stables?"

"The horses. They're dead, brother. All but Griffin, Sheila, and Angus. Someone decapitated them shortly before we arrived back at the keep."

"I'll come with you."

Everyone scattered very quickly. Arran and Eoin moved together to deposit Kip into Arran's room with Mary following along behind them. Once they'd laid him on the bed to rest they quickly took off toward the stables, leaving me alone in the hallway.

My skin was clammy, and I reached out a hand to fan myself as the full realization of what was going on came to me. I remembered Mom pointing out a special site for horse burials down away from the ruins where she'd said the Conalls had buried a group of their animals that had been slaughtered. She believed it had been done to serve as a warning for the darker trouble that was still to come to the Conall clan.

That was why I found myself in seventeenth-century Scotland. I'd spent all this time around the people my mother had spent years trying to learn more about, and it hadn't crossed my mind until this very moment that I knew how it would end for all of them.

The fire at the wedding had been the first warning, the horses the second.

I'd been sent back in time to help change their fate, and if Mom's research was correct, everyone I'd come to care about here was set to be dead within a month.

CHAPTER 23

J'd fallen asleep in a cushioned chair situated close to the fireplace in Eoin's bedchamber, only waking when I heard the door open and close and his voice speak behind me.

"Alright, lass, I'm far too tired to scream at ye. Mayhap, now would be a good time for ye to tell me what's going on."

I sat up and reached backward to squeeze my neck, sore and stiff from sleeping in an odd position for far too long. They must have spent the entire night cleaning the stables and burying the horses, as light was already beginning to stream through the window on the other side of the room.

"Is everything all right?"

"Aye, at least for now. This will be a major loss for Kip, but Mary will help him through it. If only I could see some reason for such an act, but I can think of nothing that would cause someone to act so upon innocent animals."

"I think I know why it happened," I said cautiously, half expecting another outburst like I'd witnessed earlier. But he was far too tired for it now. I could tell by his eyes that it was all he could do to stay sitting upright.

"Do ye, lass? Did ye use one of yer spells to give ye the answer?"

I rolled my eyes as I leaned forward in my seat, staring at him straight on. The door swung open once more as Arran came to sit on the floor next to Eoin's side.

"If ye doona mind, lass, I'd like to hear what ye have to say as well. Mary tried to explain a little, but I found I could not make sense from what she said."

"It's fine, Arran. I already told you. I'm not a witch. But it was one of your late aunt's spells that brought me here."

"And how exactly do ye expect she could've done that? She's been dead for nearly thirty years."

"I have no idea how she did it. All I know is that she did. Now, please, just listen to me. I guarantee you, I'm just as confused as you are about to be, so let me explain the best I can."

"Aye. Go on." He leaned back in the chair opposite mine, seemingly settling in for what he expected to be a long explanation. Truth was, I knew far less than he assumed I did.

"I'm not Blaire. I've never met or seen her in my life, but from what Mary tells me, we look very similar."

"That ye do, lass. Exactly."

"Right. Well, anyways. My name is Brielle Montgomery. Most everyone I know calls me Bri. I was born in the year nineteen hundred and eighty-five. I'm a kindergarten teacher in Austin, Texas. My mother is an archaeologist, someone who studies and tries to find objects from historical sites. She asked me to accompany her to Scotland, to help her with a dig on the ruins of this castle, nearly three weeks ago, in the middle of October 2013. Are you following me?"

"Nay, lass. I canna understand half of what ye say. What is 'kindergarten' and 'Texas'?"

"Kindergarten is just a school for very small children. I teach five-year-olds how to read, count, and write. Texas is the name of a state in North America. It doesn't exist yet."

"Aye?" Eoin briefly scratched his forehead before exhaling loudly and leaning up into his seat so that our body positions mimicked one another.

I glanced quickly at Arran, who'd said nothing since entering the room and looked far more confused than Eoin. He saw me staring and nudged his head forward as if wanting me to continue.

"Yes. So anyway, we were digging at the ruins and found access into the old spell room. It held all of its original contents, unharmed by the fire and undiscovered during previous digs. We walked into the room, and I saw a portrait of myself, the same one that sits on the table there today. It frightened me terribly, and when I started to sound out the inscription written beneath it, something started to happen. I felt as if I was being torn apart and then everything went black. Shortly after, I woke up back here, with Mary looking at me as if I was an alien from outer space. She gave no real explanation at the time, and quickly rushed me upstairs to prepare for our wedding. Until you threw me in the dungeon, I thought perhaps I was dreaming."

Both men sat unmoving, staring at me as if I'd sprouted three heads. "That's all I know. I've been sneaking away to the spell room to try and find a spell that could get me back home. And get Blaire back here."

Eoin was the first to speak. "If Mary dinna seem to believe ye, I'd think ye were the craziest lass I'd ever laid eyes on. Still, she seems certain that she saw ye appear here, and ye do speak verra strange."

"Yeah, well, I can't help it. Sorry."

"Ach, lass. I'm sorry, too. I should not have screamed at ye so. I still doona understand, but perhaps we can all work together now to get ye home."

"Please. And maybe I can help you as well."

"What did ye mean when ye said ye knew why the horses were killed?"

"You remember that I said my mother studies things that happened in the past? She works to find objects that will help people understand things that have happened. She's spent years working on the ruins of this castle, trying to find answers to who killed you all." The words lodged in my throat, and I could barely get them out as I finished the sentence. It alarmed me how much the thought of that happening caused my insides to hurt and tears to fill my eyes.

"Killed, lass?" Eoin lifted his chin out of the palm of his hand and sat up to look at me more alertly. "The castle in ruins?"

"Yes. Your entire clan was destroyed at the end of December, this year. I think your aunt knew that and that's why she cast the spell. Maybe we can stop it from happening. All we have to do is figure out who's going to do it. They left no clues. It's still a mystery even in my own time."

"I assure ye that we will do all that we can to prevent it. But what do the horses have to do with this?"

"I think they were a warning or an omen of what's to come. As terrible as it is, it's nothing compared to what will happen to everyone else, unless we stop them. The fire at the wedding was the first warning, the horses the second, I don't know if there will be a third."

Eoin stood and grasped my forearms, lifting me so that I stood in front of him. He gently wrapped his arms around me in apology. "Thank ye for telling me all ye know, lass. I doona see how I have any choice but to believe ye, and I'm glad ye are not a witch. We shall work together to find whoever poses a threat, aye? And then once our safety is secured, we'll find a way to send ye back to yer own time. Though, I must say, I will miss . . ." He said no more, letting his words span the distance now growing between us.

I allowed myself to fall into him, letting my head lie firmly against his chest as I wrapped my arms around his waist. "Deal. I'm sorry for not telling you sooner. I'd forgotten about the ruins, forgotten about everything but trying to get home."

He placed one of his large hands on my head, calming me as you would a small child. "Hush, lass. I doona think I would've believed ye, unless I'd walked in on ye in these awful rags. The truth has come out as it was meant to. Now, we have no choice but to make the best of it. We are all too tired to speak more of this now. Let's all find our way to our own beds and sleep a while. We can discuss this more at the evening meal. Today shall be a day of little activity around the castle, I expect. We've all had a day of it. Aye?"

I nodded against his chest and pulled out of his embrace as Arran stood from his place on the ground, coming alive for the first time since I'd stopped talking.

"Does this mean Blaire is in the time and place that ye came from?" The pain and fear on his face was evident, and I finally understood why Arran had seemed so displeased with me over the past few weeks. He loved Blaire, and it had hurt him to see me so pleased in Eoin's company when he thought her heart was his.

"I assume so. I expect she's with my mother. If that's the case, you have no reason to worry about her. She will be working just as hard as we are to get us switched back. I'm sure my mother's also thrilled to speak to someone she's devoted her life to learning about."

"Forgive me, lass, if that does nothing to ease my mind." As he turned and walked out of the room, I said a silent prayer that Blaire was safe and in the overbearing arms of my mother.

*P*resent Day

"*I*s it really true what ye say about women reading and writing in this time? Can most of them really do it? I can, but only because I begged Father until he agreed to let me learn. Very few women are allowed to do so."

Adelle grinned at what must have been at least Blaire's one thousandth question of the day. Over the past weeks, they'd spent every day working through the contents of the old spell room, and while they'd learned that a spell had caused the switch, they'd yet to find one that would switch the two girls back. "Yes, all children are taught to read now, and they all go to school from the age of five until they're eighteen. A woman doesn't have to be married to find success in this time. I divorced my husband nearly twenty-five years ago, and haven't been married a day since, and I think I'm doing just fine."

"Aye, I believe that ye are."

"I think we are both about to be doing even better, Blaire! I think that this might be the right spell." Adelle stared down at the faded, aging page, double-checking to make sure she was translating the Gaelic inscriptions correctly.

"Do ye think so? What will we have to do?"

"Yes, this is it. She even wrote notes in the margins about what she intended to use the spell for. It's amazing really. She knew that Bri would be born, and that the two of you would look identical. She hoped that by switching the two of you, Bri could help stop the tragedy that befell everyone at Conall castle all those years ago."

"Do ye think that she can?"

"I don't know. I hope she's listened to me speak of this enough to know that she's approaching the time of the tragedy. But I don't intend to wait and see if she stops it. We are switching the two of you back as soon as we can gather the materials." Adelle didn't miss how Blaire's smile shifted into a rather uncomfortable position at the mention of returning home. The girl's heart was hurting from something recent, and although Adelle didn't know the cause of her pain, she'd seen the same expression on her own daughter's face enough times to recognize it.

"What do we need?" Blaire moved about the small room, trying to look as helpful as possible.

"Most of the items shouldn't be too difficult to find. Herbs and things grown locally, which I'm sure Gwendolyn will have no problem helping us locate. We also need the portrait, which we already have. The only thing that we don't have is Alasdair's ring. Morna says here that she gave it to him, and that he would've passed it down to Eoin. We didn't find any such item in our original dig, so we better hope that it's down here in this room somewhere, or we may have a problem."

"Oh, doona worry yet. We've spent our time looking through the books that could hold the location of the ring."

Adelle leaned to the left as Blaire approached her right-hand side, giving the girl a better view of the spell.

"Adelle, did ye see this? It looks as if the spell may only work for a short time."

"What?" Adelle leaned forward to stare down at the page once more, her veins suddenly flooded with panic. Sure enough, scribbled in tiny Gaelic letters, the paper stated that once the original spell had been set into motion, it could only be reversed until midnight of the night before the anniversary of the massacre.

One month from today.

---

1 645

*J*ust passing through on his way back to Kinnaird Castle, the stranger sat silently in the back of the tavern. He watched as Arran Conall downed one goblet of whiskey after another, until he couldn't begin to contemplate how the lad was still conscious, let alone rambling on as he was doing.

"I doona think I should give ye another, lad. Ye are far enough gone into the cup as it is, aye?"

The stranger listened in as the tavern master tried to discourage the lad from drinking more.

"Nay, not nearly far gone enough," Arran argued. "We shall all be dead within the month, according to my brother's wife, and I dare say I've not had nearly enough to drink to let me forget that."

The stranger stood and slipped quietly outside into the cold night air. It was time he finished his journey with haste.

He had very interesting news to share with his master.

CHAPTER 24

*M*orning brought particular success down in the spell room and we'd only been working for a short amount of time. We'd finally found the spell book with the title that matched the one I'd been trying to sound out when Eoin walked in on me a few days earlier.

The process of searching through the Gaelic books in the spell room moved much more quickly once Eoin knew the truth. Since our heart-to-heart a few days prior, our days were spent either in the spell room sifting through books or meeting with Arran to discuss the best way to find out who was to be responsible for the upcoming tragedy.

It was nice to live openly among them and to finally be able to behave normally. It seemed to me that the friendship I shared with Eoin grew stronger with each passing day. I enjoyed every moment I spent with him, and the realization made me even more anxious to return home before I surrendered my heart completely.

I hovered uncomfortably around the spell room while Eoin read each page, searching for whatever spell might be helpful. I was unsure of how to help, most of the books already having been gone through, and found myself staring at him while he worked.

God, he really was beautiful. I'd never in my twenty-eight years in the twenty-first century seen a man that looked so much like a man. He oozed masculinity, but not in a way that seemed to diminish his intelligence. He was smart as a whip, no doubt, and his eyes displayed a sort of hidden kindness; the kind that, while hard to get to, would change your world if you were able to get him to open up and show you his true self.

He must have felt me staring at him, and he turned to catch me red-faced as I scrambled to look as if I were doing something productive.

"Come here, lass. This is it."

I walked over to his side, surprised when he turned toward me, opening his arms and prompting me to sit on his knee. Hesitantly, I took a seat, trying to think of spilled finger paint, runny noses, and sticky fingers—anything to keep me from concentrating on the hard chiseled body I now found wrapped around my own.

"What does it say?"

"This is the spell she used. See, her own notes are written along here." He grabbed my hand from my lap and, using his hand, guided my fingers along the side of the page. Tingles swam over every inch of my body. *Cheetos in the carpet, boogers on the chair backs, pink eye outbreak.* No thought helped.

"I see. Will it work to switch us back?"

"Aye. I think it will." He didn't let go of my hand as he continued. "We need a few items. Mary can locate most of them. But it speaks of my father's ring, and I doona know where that is. I believe he always meant to leave it to me, but his death was sudden, and I doona think it crossed his mind."

"Well, we can find it, right?"

"Ach, lass. I suppose we shall have to. But it says something else as well."

I looked up into his eyes, waiting for him to continue.

"The spell will only work until midnight on the twenty-eighth of December, then ye canna return home."

"Well, we have to find it by then anyway. That's right around when they think the massacre happens."

"Aye, we shall. Doona worry. Knowledge is the best defense we could have. It willna come to that."

His left hand laid casually upon my knee while his right wrapped around my back, his palm now resting just above my hip on the curve of my waist. He squeezed me in closer to him, drawing his right hand up to my shoulder so that it brought the side of my face closer to his lips.

"I know I've given ye no more than trouble, lass, but I shall be sorry to see ye go." With that he leaned in as if to kiss the side of my cheek, and I nearly turned us both onto the floor with my quick leap out of his lap.

"Yes. I'll be a little sad too. I think of you, and Mary, and Arran as friends, and it will be odd to no longer get to see you." I awkwardly patted him on the shoulder and turned abruptly to make my way out of the spell room, cursing my heated cheeks with each step. I knew they'd given me away.

*K*innaird Castle

"*W*hy would the lass have told him such a thing? She has no way of knowing they will be attacked."

"I doona know, sir. I'm only telling ye what I heard. Arran said that Eoin's new bride believed they'd be dead within the month."

"Perhaps she's got more brains about her than I would've expected, being Donal's daughter. The old sot is the silliest fool in the shire. She must've known that the fire and horses were to serve as warnings."

"Aye. I suppose she must've, though Arran dinna seem to know what the lass meant. He was quite drunk. I could not understand how he was still conscious."

"Aye? Well ye did right by making haste to come tell me. Now go, and keep in mind what will happen to ye and yer family if word of our conversation spreads."

Ramsay watched as the man turned and made his way out of the room. He'd intended to warn them, to make them fear what was coming, but now that he knew the Conalls were suspicious, he found himself less comfortable with the idea of a straightforward attack.

"Gregory, find yer way in here at once!"

Quickly the man burst through the doorway and stood before Ramsay, awaiting his instructions.

"Ye are the most cunning lad I have in my command. Ye know how to surprise an enemy, how to throw them off course of yer plan. I need ye to advise me on a matter."

"Of course, sire."

"We will soon be planning an on against Conall Castle. It is my intention to destroy all who reside under the castle's protection. It seems Eoin and his brother have heard news of a possible attack, and I doona want them to suspect us in any way."

Ramsay watched as the young lad took in the news with a look of shock. An attack on Conall Castle would be a surprise to all who served him. The two clans had been allies for decades.

"Give them cause to suspect another clan. Send me to Conall Castle, but dress me in the tartan of a distant clan. I will say I am a runaway criminal, seeking refuge with the clan for the information I bring to them. I will tell them that my laird is planning to attack them."

Ramsay clasped the boy on the shoulders. "Aye, perfect. Ride out come morning."

CHAPTER 25

"Where's Arran? I haven't seen him all day." I sat down in my usual place as we gathered for the evening meal. I'd spent the day with Mary, gathering the herbs needed for the spell, while Eoin had searched through Alasdair's things looking for the ring. Although I'd finished the day with an armload of needed herbs, Eoin's hunt had been less successful.

"I sent him to the village to see if any travelers or townspeople might have heard anything about a possible attack. He was also going to meet with some men to discuss our defenses. It will be important to let the villagers know so that we can be as prepared as possible."

"Good idea, but we will figure out who's planning the attack and stop it before it gets to that point." I gave him a reassuring smile across the table, quickly averting my eyes when his smile turned upward at the corner, his eyes staring flirtatiously.

I simply couldn't allow myself to get any more attached to him than I already was. If someone had told me six months ago I would be doing everything I could to "friend zone" a man this good looking, I would have thought they were out of their mind, but that was exactly what I was dead set on doing until I made it back home. He was making it incredibly difficult.

Just as Mary exited the kitchen to set out supper, Arran burst through the back doors, dragging another man roughly along behind him.

"I found him trying to climb over the castle gate. I started to throw him in the dungeon before I came to get ye, but he swears he has news that we will both want to hear." He released his grip on the man, who stood upright and brushed his arm where Arran had gripped him with his hand.

The man threw a very unpleased look in Arran's direction. "Aye, sir. I come to ye seeking refuge in return for news."

Eoin stood from his place at the stable, briefly holding a palm up in my direction as if asking me to stay seated. Naturally, it did nothing but encourage me to stand and join him in front of Arran and the stranger.

"Refuge from what? Are ye a criminal? Ye will not find refuge here, if that be the case."

"Nay, sir. I was held a criminal, but the only crime I was guilty of was loving the laird's daughter. He caught us tupping in her bedchamber and locked me away."

"As right he should."

"Ach, Eoin! Doona be so noble. If tupping were a crime, there's not a lad over the age of fifteen who wouldna be locked away!" Arran chuckled slightly before stopping when he glanced at Eoin's face.

"Aye, sir. I wanted to wed her, but he wouldna consent. I was too lowly for the old bastard." The stranger reached up to grab his heart as if in pain.

"Ach, well yer crime may not have been so bad, but I've yet to hear the news that ye think is worthy of a place here for ye."

"Aye, sir. Laird MacLyrron is staging an attack on ye."

Both Arran and Eoin's faces shifted into a look of shock, and I was sure mine was no different.

"I've never even met Laird MacLyrron. His territory is far to the south of here. Why would he attack us?" Eoin stared at the man suspiciously.

"He's a foolish bastard. He wants to expand his land, and yers is one of the most beautiful parts of the country."

"How can we know if ye tell us the truth?"

The stranger shook his head as he looked down at the floor. "Ye doona know. I canna give ye more than my word. Allow me to stay here, and perhaps with time ye will see that what I've told ye is true."

A long silence stretched out as the stranger, Arran, and myself watched and waited for Eoin to give his decision. I could see with every twitch of his hand or pull of his eyebrow that he was trying hard to make the best possible decision. He knew that, if correct, the information the man had just given him was vital. If wrong, the man was too dangerous to have in the village. Finally he cleared his throat before speaking.

"Ye will stay on castle grounds, and ye will work with Kip on the new horses until ye have earned our trust. Then ye may choose to move to the village if ye wish. If Kip is dissatisfied with ye or yer work, ye will be returned to MacLyrron at once. Do ye consent?"

"Aye. Thank ye. I canna begin to express my gratitude for yer kindness."

Eoin shot the man a hard look, his eyes cold. "Doona make me regret my decision, lad. It will not end well for ye." He paused and turned to look at Arran. "Introduce him to Kip, will ye? And get him situated in the hut near the stables."

Arran nodded and grabbed hold of the man's arm once more as they started to leave the dining hall.

"And Arran," Eoin raised his voice so that he would hear him before he made his way out the door, "will ye meet me in my chambers after ye have seen him put away for the evening?"

"Aye. O' course." As Arran left with the still nameless man, Eoin motioned for us to return to our places at the table.

We passed dinner in silence, only glancing up at one another occasionally by accident.

I could see how distracted Eoin was, and it was evident in the way his facial expressions seemed to continually shift throughout the meal that he was still wrestling with his decision.

While I understood his decision, I wasn't sure if I would've made the same one myself. Granted, it was the most promising piece of information we'd received, and it would be much easier to reach out for help in preparing a defense if we knew where the attack would be coming from.

But there was something about the stranger that made me uneasy. Something queer about the delivery of his story planted seeds of doubt deep in my stomach, seeds that were starting to take root.

*E*oin turned his gaze away from the fire as he heard his brother enter into his chamber. "What did Kip say about the lad?"

"Well, he was not too pleased to be tasked as caretaker, but I expect twill be good for him to keep busy. He's still taking the loss of the horses quite hard."

"Aye, I doona blame him. Arran, do ye think the lad was telling us the truth?" He watched Arran's face, trying to read his expressions as his brother sat down in the seat across from him.

"I doona know, brother, but I'd have made the same decision. What do ye think we should do now?"

"We canna confront MacLyrron. For if they've planned no attack, that's a fine way to start a war, no? I think we must reach out to our most trusted allies, ask them to bring their forces here to help us mount a defense a few days before the expected attack. That way, regardless of who is planning it, twill be more than us alone to defend ourselves."

"I think ye are right. What clans will ye call on?"

"Blaire's father, o'course. And although he's a wretched old arse, Ramsay Kinnaird. Our father considered him a friend and ally, and I know that both of them would be willing to come to our aid." Eoin waited cautiously for his brother's reaction, still unsure of his place as laird.

"Aye, tis the finest chance we have. Do ye want me to make a trip to both Donal and Ramsay?"

Eoin shook his head. "Nay, I need ye to stay here and train the men in the village, strengthen our defenses, and work with Mary to help prepare the castle for so many guests. Bri and I will travel to both territories. Donal will be anxious to see his daughter, and Ramsay may not yet know that I am married."

"But ye doona have Donal's daughter. He will be able to tell the difference!"

"I doona think that he will. Bri was able to fool the whole castle for weeks, surely she can fool Blaire's father for only a few days. The two lasses are identical."

"They're not so identical as ye seem to think, brother, but ye do whatever ye must. I'm happy to stay and work here. I'll keep an eye on the runaway as well."

"Aye, please do. I'm not so sure if I made the right choice, but I'm glad ye think so. Bri and I will leave in the morning."

Eoin watched as Arran stood to leave. "Aye, brother, I do. But ye should tell Bri tonight. Lassies like to know things ahead of time."

Eoin chuckled and stood to stretch as his brother walked out the door. "Ye are right o' course. I'll go and tell her now."

CHAPTER 26

$\mathcal{M}$y skill with horses had not improved since our last little journey away from the castle, and so with no other alternative we rode together on Griffin for our journey to MacChristy Keep and Kinnaird Castle.

The proximity of our bodies was doing nothing to help my "friend zone." In fact, he was increasingly getting more fresh with his hands. Every hour further into our journey, the reins seemed to move closer to the point in between my legs.

The nerves caused by my ever-tingling insides, the soreness of my ass from riding a horse all day long, and the fear of not being able to pull off 'Blaire' in front of Donal MacChristy had me on the verge of a nervous breakdown.

I nearly spooked the horse with my erratic jerk at the sound of Eoin's voice in my ear. "What's the matter with ye, lass?"

"Nothing is the matter. Why would you think something was the matter?" I exhaled rather loudly.

"Because, I've been listening to ye breathe like that for some time now. Ye sound like Griffin."

"Right. Sorry."

"Ye doona need to be sorry. Ye need to tell me what's bothering ye so. I'd like to help if I can."

"You can't help. My ass is sore from riding, and I'm about to have a freaking panic attack at the thought of fooling a man who has known Blaire her entire life into thinking I'm her."

He did nothing to help my mood as he laughed at me. "Lass, ye say 'arse' rather strangely. Not that ye doona say a lot of things rather strangely. But ye doona need to worry about Donal. He canna hear well, and ye look just like Blaire. He willna be able to tell the difference."

"I hope you're right." I exhaled loudly once more just for good measure.

"I am, lass, so ye doona need to worry about that. And as for yer sore 'ass,' I'd be more than pleased to help ye with that." He moved the reins so that he held them in one hand and deftly slid his other up under my thigh to squeeze the inside of my leg and buttocks.

I yelped and jerked my bottom upward, this time successfully spooking Griffin. As the horse reared on his back legs, Eoin was forced to relinquish his grip on my thigh so as to get the horse under control again.

"No, thank you," I screeched. "My bottom is just fine, all on its own."

He laughed heartily in my ear. "Whatever ye wish, lass. But I've no doubt ye'd feel much better after a good rub."

"I'll rub it myself when we get to the castle."

For some reason, this made him laugh harder, and I crossed my arms in a sign of annoyance as we continued our journey to MacChristy Castle.

It was just after dusk when Eoin spotted MacChristy Castle off in the distance. With luck they'd arrive just in time to dine with his father's old friend.

He couldn't wait to dismount Griffin and stretch his tired, aching muscles. He'd no doubt the lass did have a sore arse; his was sore as well, and he was much more accustomed to riding. He'd most likely have to help the poor lass out of bed in the morning, a torturous task to be charged, he was sure. He smiled at the thought as he quickly squeezed his arms around the lass to get her attention.

"Ye see that just on the other side of the hill? We are almost there. Would ye like to stop for a moment so we can relieve ourselves and make ready?"

Her response was immediate. He'd expected no less. "Yes, please. I'm about to pee myself."

He smiled widely into her hair. The lass said the most peculiar and wonderful things. He led Griffin over to the base of a large tree and dismounted before helping Bri get off as well. He scooted closer to Griffin than was really necessary, so that the front of Bri's body slid down his chest as he lifted her off the horse.

She rewarded him with a knowing glare, and he let out a small laugh before walking away to find his own tree behind which he could relieve himself.

He was back at Griffin's side before Bri, and after a few moments of waiting for her to appear from behind a tree he hollered after her. "Bri! Where are ye lass? Are ye alright?"

A loud "Shit! Gosh damnit! Ow!" came from behind the tree.

"Lass, what the hell's happened? Are ye covered? I'm coming yer way!"

"No! Don't! I just . . . I wiped myself with the first leaf I could find, but it was prickly, and now there's a sticker poking out of my rear!"

The sound of his own laughter rippled through the trees surrounding them. "Come on out, lass. Do ye need my help?"

He did his best to keep his composure as Bri made her way from behind the tree. Carrying the back of her dress with both hands, she hobbled slowly until she stood in front of him.

"I can't get ahold of it. I think it's in pretty deep. I need you to grab it."

He couldn't keep the corners of his mouth from twitching upward.

"But I swear to God, Eoin. If you look at anything but that sticker,

I'm going to give you a swift kick in the balls. Do you understand me?"

"Aye, lass. I give ye my word! Now turn around and bend over."

As soon as she turned away from him, he let go of the tight rein he'd been trying to keep on the corners of his mouth and gladly let them slide upward as he grinned at her white rear end, beaming in the moonlight.

The sticker was easily visible and, with one swift pull, he dislodged it, flinging it onto the ground.

"Alright, lass, ye can let yer dress down now, even though I'll be sorry to see ye do it. Now, let's get back on Griffin and make our way to see yer da!"

I'd never been more humiliated in my entire life. Not only did I get a giant sticker stuck in my ass crack while peeing in the middle of a forest, I had to have the most beautiful man I'd ever seen pluck it out.

At least, it would be easier to keep him in the friend zone now.

We'd just arrived at the castle, and Eoin was handing Griffin off to the stable master, when what I could only assume was my 'dad' burst through the large main doors of the castle.

"Blaire! Ach, I'm so pleased to see ye, lass! I doona like not having ye here by my side." Mary was right about his screaming, and as he picked me up around the middle and swung me in a circle, I was sure my eardrums would burst.

When he set me down and stepped toward Eoin, I nearly choked on my own spit when I got a good look at his face. No wonder Blaire and I resembled one another so strongly. He looked exactly like my own father. Same dark hair, same blue eyes, same small, circular patch of gray which stood out among his otherwise ebony-colored hair.

I had to blink quickly, swallowing hard to fight back the tears that threatened to break loose at the sense of overwhelming nostalgia. While my parents had divorced when I was young, I'd stayed incredibly close to my Dad up until his death only three years ago.

It turned out that I'd no real reason to worry about fooling Donal. He gave me little time to speak or respond to him in any way, immediately jumping into a conversation with Eoin and ushering us inside for supper.

As we sat down at the grand dining room table, I sat sipping on the glass of ale I'd been given and listened to the two men converse.

---

*A*s he'd expected, Donal had immediately consented to bring all of his men to Conall Castle to help with their defense on December twenty-sixth, two days before the expected attack. In fact the agreement had been made before the first course was laid out, and the rest of the evening passed easily as the two men reminisced about his father and years past.

Eoin had known Bri had no reason to worry. Donal did not converse easily with women, and he'd have little to say to his daughter, despite his claims of how much he'd missed her.

Worry about Bri filled him. As Eoin glanced in her direction, he tried to cast a frown at the servant who was silently refilling her goblet for at least the sixth time. Bri's eyes were visibly glazed, and she looked unsteady as she rested her chin against the hand she'd propped on top of the table. She'd said nothing throughout the meal, and with the amount she'd now drunk he greatly hoped she would continue to stay silent now.

He'd never seen her drink more than one cup-full during meals, but then again, Mary never allowed any of them more than that. Mary always said that Arran did a fine job of finding drink on his own. She wasn't going to aid him in his task.

A large belch from Bri's end of the table was enough to make him certain it was time for him to make his excuses and take her away to their shared bedchamber. He could only hope no one else had heard the location of the unladylike sound.

Raising his voice so that Donal would hear, Eoin stood from the table. "I find myself weary from the long day's travel, Donal. If it pleases ye, I believe I will take my wife upstairs so that we may retire for the evening."

His old friend stood and clasped him on the shoulders. "Aye, o' course! It was wrong of me to keep ye so late after the long ride. We will talk more tomorrow. Would ye accompany me on a hunt?"

Eoin smiled and nodded as he walked to Bri's side. "Aye! I shall look forward to it."

He bent to place his hand under her arm and help steady her as he pulled her up out of her seat.

"Goodnight, daughter. I'm glad to have ye home, if only for a short time." Donal stood waiting for Bri's response, and Eoin bent to whisper in Bri's ear.

"Tell him, goodnight. Doona say anything else."

"Goodnight." She smiled sloppily, and Eoin found himself glad that the old man's sight wasn't much better than his hearing as he watched him turn and leave the room.

"God, lass! What the hell do ye think ye're doing? I've not had that much to drink since I was a young lad." He took one step away from her, but quickly reached to grab her once more as she swayed on her feet.

"What are you talking . . . ?"

She left off the end of her sentence, but Eoin understood her meaning well enough. "Ye are mighty drunk, Bri. Ye have not stopped drinking since we sat down to eat!"

"I am not! I've only been sipping. What was I supposed to do while y'all were visiting?"

"Well, not drink them dry, Bri! If ye're not drunk, why doona ye walk a few steps and show me, aye?" He stepped out of her way while she grasped onto the edge of the table to support herself.

"Fine."

He watched as she took three or four wobbly steps in his

direction before swaying widely and falling into his side. "Ye are not drunk, ye say?"

"Ok, fine. But I didn't mean to. They just kept refilling it, over and over again, and this hasn't been my most favorite day."

"Aye, I saw them, lass, and I doona suppose that it has." He bent to scoop her up around her knees, cradling her against his chest as they made their way up the stairs to their guest bedchamber.

She was asleep by the time he lay her on the bed, and gently tucking the covers around her, he moved to find himself a spot on the floor.

As much as he wanted to cradle her in his arms all night long, he wouldn't share her bed until she asked.

CHAPTER 27

*P*utting aside my monumental hangover, the trip to visit Donal MacChristy was an undisputable success. Over the two days that we'd spent there, Eoin had kept Donal so busy that I hardly ever saw either of them. I spent my time lounging around the castle, tenderly caring for my wicked bad headache.

We were now on our last day of riding to visit Ramsay Kinnaird, an ally according to Eoin, but a man I knew very little about from either Mary or history. It was a longer journey from MacChristy's to Kinnaird's, and we'd been forced to camp two nights along the way.

Eoin was slowly-but-surely chipping away at the rock wall fortress of my friend zone. The first night the weather had been warm enough for us to sleep on opposite sides of a fire he'd built in a small clearing.

On the second night, the wind blew too roughly through the trees to start a fire, and we were forced to snuggle together to stay warm. It had started out as a necessity, with both of us covered by the same blankets and me curling into the nook of his arm with my head against his chest. But as the night progressed he turned his body so that our fronts were flush against each other, his warm breath wafting against my face, his breath shaky as he pressed himself against me, hard and ready, inviting me to accept him.

I'd feigned sleep, refusing to open my eyes and give myself away. Always a gentleman, he only tried a moment before giving up and kissing me lightly on the forehead, quickly rolling onto his back, shifting me into the crook of his arm once more.

I slept maybe half an hour the entire night.

*T*he next day, I couldn't keep from squirming in the saddle. Eion seemed concerned. "We are almost there, lass. Do ye need me to stop?"

"If it's alright with you, I'd rather not. Don't want to risk getting another sticker stuck in my bum."

"Aye, it's fine. I'm anxious to finish the ride, as well."

When we arrived at Kinnaird Castle, we weren't greeted by Ramsay at the entrance as we were Donal. Instead, we were escorted into a long study, and expected to wait until Ramsay chose to bless us with his presence. I'd never met the man, but I was already sure I wouldn't like him.

After nearly two hours, he burst through the doors. "Ah, Eoin! What an unexpected surprise. I was verra sorry to hear about yer father's death, but I'm sure ye will make a fine laird yerself."

Eoin stepped almost protectively in front of me, and it did nothing to make me like the man more. "Thank ye, Ramsay. It's been too long. I'd like ye to meet my wife. This is Blaire, Donal MacChristy's daughter."

"Aye, I'd heard that ye'd married, but I never imagined she'd be so beautiful. I bet it is lovely to have her warm yer bed at night. Would ye mind if I borrow her for a night, while ye are here?"

Surprising me, Eoin reached out and laced his hand with mine. If I'd been in reach of anything heavy and solid, I would've chunked it at the ugly bastard's head.

"Ach, Eoin, doona fash yerself, I'm only fooling with ye. Come, join me for food and drink, and ye can tell me what has brought ye here. Sylva here will escort Blaire up to yer bedchamber and will have food brought to her." Ramsay didn't give Eoin a chance to reply before charging through the doors from which he'd come.

I whirled on him, jerking my hand free. "What? You don't seriously expect me to eat dinner in my room like a punished child, right?"

He reached forward and grasped both of my hands and brought them to his lips. "I'm sorry, lass. Ramsay's an arse, but we are guests. We must do as he bids. I need his men if we are to have adequate protection against the attack."

"Fine." I pulled my hands free of his grasp and started moving toward the door. "Show me to my room, please. I'm a woman. I'm sure it's too hard for me to find on my own."

He laughed and rolled his eyes as he moved past me to direct me upstairs.

---

*A*t first, Ramsay assumed that Eoin had found him out. Perhaps the man he'd sent to fool them had betrayed him, revealing the truth of his murderous plan to Eoin and his brother. But no, as he sat across from Eoin over their evening meal listening to what he requested of him, he knew his secret was safe.

Actually, it couldn't have been better. Eoin inviting him to come and help protect them from an outside attack made his own plan even more easily accomplished. He wouldn't have to gain entry to the castle; he'd already have it. And it would be that much more rewarding to see the look of shock at his betrayal as he plunged his sword through Eoin's heart.

"Aye, ye know that you needn't ask. The Conalls and Kinnairds have been allies for years. Ye have my word that we shall march to help defend ye."

The young, foolish laird had just sealed his own fate.

*T*hankfully Eoin and Ramsay's conversation was much shorter than Eoin and Donal's, and I'd just finished my own food when I heard the bedchamber door open and close as Eoin walked in.

"How'd it go? Will he come?"

Eoin walked up behind me as I sat in a chair close to the room's fireplace and placed both of his hands on my shoulders as he squeezed gently.

"Aye. He'll come, but I'm not so glad that we have to ask him. He's a wretched man. And I'll never understand why my father kept him so close." He continued to massage my shoulders, working his way up and down my back, as I released my neck and allowed my head to fall forward, relishing the feeling of his strong hands on my sore and tired muscles. Travelling in this century was hard work.

I unintentionally let out a small moan of delight, and I caught my slip as his hands stilled at the base of my throat.

Taking it as a sign of my enjoyment, he slid his hands lower so that they dipped into the cleavage of my gown. He only left them there for a moment, quickly pulling them upward, swirling his hands over my neckline with light touches that sent tremors down my body and caused my breathing to speed up.

There was no chance I could pretend to be asleep now, and I was quickly losing any willpower I had to keep him away.

"Do ye like that, lass? I love the way yer skin feels."

I didn't answer him. Instead I leaned my head back so that my neck was elongated, allowing him more space from which to move his fingers.

He stopped abruptly and came around to kneel in front of me, taking both of my hands in his.

"I know that ye must return home once we find the ring, Bri. But would ye mind so much if we behaved as husband and wife just for now? I willna ask ye again, but it's been too long since I've had the company of a woman, lass, and I want ye badly."

It was much easier to be brave with him when I thought I was dreaming. Now, as his words sent my heart racing, I had a difficult time choking out any sort of response.

"Alright."

I didn't have to say more as his lips found mine instantly, his arms wrapping around my waist, lifting me out of the chair with ease.

We moved to the bed until he sat on its edge, holding me out in front of him as he gazed at the front of my gown.

"Turn around."

I obeyed, and his hands instantly moved against the laces, loosening them with only a few quick strokes. As the dress fell to my feet I faced him, only to be pulled against him once more as he brought my breast toward him, sucking one of my nipples deep into his mouth.

I moaned loudly as the sensation caused my knees to weaken and the entry between my legs to grow slick.

As he continued to kiss and suckle on my breasts, one hand moved to my lower back, holding me in place as the fingers on his opposite hand sought entry in between my legs.

I gasped as he slipped two fingers inside me, my wetness giving away just how badly I wanted him, and he groaned as his fingers glided easily in and out of my center.

"Ach, Bri! Are ye ready for me, lass? 'Cause I doona believe I can keep myself out of ye much longer."

"Yes." I moved away from him to climb atop the bed, lying backward and spreading my legs to welcome him to me.

He grinned and quickly removed his own clothing, and I was sure my eyes widened at the sight of him. My legs involuntarily closed, and he let out a deep chuckle.

"Doona worry, lass. I'll be gentle with ye."

He spread himself on top of me, his mouth meeting mine with a desperate hunger that I returned. He placed his fingers in between my legs once again, slowly readying me for entry with his fingers.

Just as I was on the brink of shattering beneath him, he would slow his rhythm, easing the torturous longing in between my thighs by nipping me gently at the base of my neck or drawing his tongue up from my navel and chest.

He continued his playful torture, bringing me to the cusp of release and then stopping until I could take no more. Finally I reached down to stop his hand from trailing upward and pleaded breathlessly in his ear, "Please. Please, don't stop."

He kissed me roughly and moved his fingers once more. "As ye wish, lass." And I went flying over the edge, moaning and squirming underneath his hands as I trembled from the sensation.

Just as the shockwaves of pleasure subsided, he pulled back and positioned himself for entry, plunging into me at my nod of approval.

I screamed as he filled me, my insides shifting and stretching to make room for him as he began another devastating assault on my senses. With each thrust, I struggled to pull him closer, feeling empty each time he slid himself partially out of me. He was a selfless lover, and as each rock of his hips brought him closer to his own release, he worked hard to ensure that I climbed the peak with him.

It was instantaneous, the thrust that sent us both spiraling back down to earth together, and as we shuddered in each other's arms, our lips met once more, silently worshiping one another.

CHAPTER 28

$\mathscr{H}$e needed to find the ring. It was his only chance at getting Blaire back, and he wasn't going to let the time window close before they tried the spell.

Arran knew Bri had been searching for the ring since they'd learned it was needed for the spell. And while Eoin claimed to be helping in the search, Arran knew a part of his brother hoped they would never find it.

If the spell did work and Blaire returned to him, he wasn't going to give her up again. She wasn't actually married to Eoin. It was Bri who'd said the vows, and he'd be damned before he let her go again.

If he located the ring before Eoin and Bri returned from their trip, perhaps she would have no reason to stay any longer.

He'd searched everywhere: each bedchamber, each study, even Morna's spell room he'd turned upside down in his desperate search for the ring.

The ring was buried with his father. He'd known it all along but had wished ardently that he was wrong, that perhaps his father had removed the ring from his finger before death.

He couldn't do this himself. He knew he wasn't that strong. Even going to the gravesite seemed impossible to him, but the ring had to be found.

His stomach rolling uncomfortably, he made his way down to the stables to enlist help from the runaway, now under Kip's command. He hadn't bothered to learn the lad's name. He didn't trust something about the fellow and didn't expect him to stay long enough for it to be worth learning.

When Arran entered the stables, Kip was leaning back against the doorway, looking pleased as he watched his new worker shovel out manure.

"Kip, may I speak with ye a moment?" Arran didn't approach the stable. He wasn't ready to enter after the gruesome mess he'd been forced to clean.

"Aye, o'course ye can." The old man pushed himself off of the doorway and made his way to Arran.

"Kip, do ye mind if I borrow the stable lad for the rest of the day? I have an unpleasant task that I'd rather not do myself if I can have someone do it for me."

"Aye, there's not much for the lad to do here anyway. We've fewer horses now, and I managed just fine on my own. Ye are welcome to use him as long as ye wish."

"Thank ye, Kip. Send him to the graveyard."

Arran turned before he could see the questioning look on Kip's face as he solemnly marched toward his father's grave.

They dug for hours, each shovel of dirt opening the poorly sealed wound of grief that crossed right through the center of Arran's heart. When they finally hit the wooden box set low beneath the ground, Arran dropped his shovel and faced the man beside him.

"Ye are to get inside the box and get the ring on his right hand. Doona disturb anything else that ye find inside the coffin. Once ye have it, make sure that the box is closed before ye ask me to come help ye fill in the hole. I doona want to see anything inside it."

"What makes ye think I do? I doona want to upset a man's resting place."

Arran grabbed the man roughly, shoving him against the side of the deep hole. "I doona care what ye want to be doing. Ye can either do as I've asked ye, or we can send ye back where ye came from."

Arran didn't wait for the man's response as he crawled out of the hole and sat on the grassy patch next to his mother's grave, covering his eyes to push away the memories each thrust of his shovel had dug up.

---

*E*ven Laird Kinnaird wouldn't have asked him to dig up a man once he'd been buried. It was mighty bad luck.

But as he pushed away the heavy lid on top of the box, he saw an opportunity that pushed all of his guilt away. For upon the decaying remnants of Alasdair Conall's right hand were two rings.

The first was a thin band topped with a wide oval. Noting the feminine look to its setting, he determined that this was most assuredly the ring that Arran sought. The second was larger and held the seal of the Conall clan, a signet which Alasdair most likely used to seal and sign letters. It was this ring that caught the man's interest. Such an item would be of great use to Laird Kinnaird, a way to swing the odds of the upcoming battle even further into his master's favor.

Turning his head, he reached and removed the rings as quickly as possible, holding the first in the palm of his hand and silently slipping the second away, out of sight.

CHAPTER 29

*P*resent Day

"*I* don't know where else to look, but we have to find that damned ring. It's only two more weeks until the anniversary, and I will not let her be left there." Adelle sat down. Dirty, exhausted, and on the verge of panic, she placed her head in her hands to cry.

She was surprised to feel Blaire's arm come around her shoulder to offer her comfort. "Doona worry, we will find it."

"Yes, we will. I can't allow myself to consider that we won't. She's my only child, Blaire. She's all I have, all I've ever had. She's the only person I've ever known that could put up with my flakiness and still love me. I was never the mother I should've been to her, and I won't fail her now."

"Oh, ye should not say such things. I doona believe that Bri thinks that ye were a terrible mother. Why, ye have treated me with more kindness and allowed me more freedom than anyone I've ever known."

Adelle lifted her head and patted Blaire on the knee. "Thank you for that. I'm so glad that you've been here to help. And you've handled everything beautifully. You're a wonderful girl. Now, we have to think about where else the ring could be. Everything else on site has already been excavated and is in the Edinburgh museum, and the collection of items does not include the ring."

"We know that the spell book is powerful. 'Tis what brought me here and sent Bri back in my place. Do ye think tis possible that we could convey a message to yer daughter through it?"

Adelle stood, shaking her head. "I doubt it. I didn't read a spell for anything like that."

"I think ye should give it a go, anyhow. Why not write a note to her in the margins of the spell we are working on? Perhaps, she will see it, when she looks at it."

It was too much to hope for, and Adelle didn't want to get her hopes up over such a ridiculous possibility. Blaire was trying to help, and it wouldn't hurt to humor the girl, pointless as the act would be.

"Alright, why not give it a try? I'll just tell her that we are working on the spell, but we haven't been able to find the ring." Adelle opened the spell book and obligingly flipped to the appropriate page.

---

*B*laire didn't believe her own suggestion would work any more than Adelle did, but it bothered her to see her new friend so distressed. She couldn't imagine the pain the woman must be feeling after having her daughter ripped away from her so inexplicably.

She desperately wanted Adelle to get her daughter back. But—just as desperately—she never wanted to return home. She couldn't bear the thought of it: being married to Eoin and living in the same place as Arran. Every glimpse of him would break her heart all over again.

If Arran didn't want to be with her, she'd rather stay here in this strange and foreign time, where at the very least it was acceptable to live independently. She would be free to live her life without putting her heart in the hands of someone else. She could live a guarded, simple life all alone. And, with her heart and soul broken, she couldn't think of anything she wanted more.

Even if they found the ring, she wasn't going to go back. They'd simply have to find a way to bring Bri forward without making a switch.

1 645

I was deliciously sore and as happy as I'd ever been when we set out on our return journey early the next morning. I'd fallen asleep wrapped in his arms, only to be awakened a few hours later by his lips kissing the side of my cheek and trailing down my neck.

I smiled into his lips and faced him, wrapping my arms around his neck. "I don't have the energy to do it again tonight, Eoin. I'm a bit out of practice."

He kissed the tip of my nose before pulling back to prop himself up on his elbow. "Aye, that may be so. But ye were not a virgin, aye?"

At first I was a bit taken aback by his question. At my age, it seemed odd that he would assume that I was. At second thought, I realized just how surprising it most likely was to him to find that I wasn't. While most men in this time found themselves in the bed of another far before marriage, any respectable woman would never have let herself be "ruined" before reaching her marriage bed.

"No. I wasn't. It's different where I come from. People often have sex before marriage."

He frowned at my answer. "I see, lass."

"Does it bother you that I wasn't?"

"Nay, I canna fault ye for the life that ye lived before ye came into

179

my life. But, I'll not say it pleases me. Thinking of another man holding ye and touching ye as I just have stirs a rather dreadful feeling in my chest. I'd like to bludgeon the lad that did so."

I smiled, pleased at his jealousy. "All three of them?"

He sat completely upright in the bed. "Three! My God, Bri! Tell me, lass, were ye a harlot in the time ye came from?"

It was my turn to frown. "No, I was not! I can assure you that for someone my age that is a very respectable number! Just ask Mitsy! She's got me beat for sure!"

"What's a Mitsy, lass?"

"Mitsy is a person. A friend. Who, come to think of it, is probably worried sick about me."

He lay back down and draped an arm over me as he snuggled in closely. "I'm sorry, lass. I suspect there are a good many things that I doona know about ye that would surprise me."

"Yes, I'm sure there are. We are from different worlds, Eoin."

"Aye, lass. But for now, they are the same world, and that's all I can bear to think of now."

I thought back on those words as I rode in front of him, now only a short distance from arriving back at Conall Castle, as we could see it in the distance. It surprised me how much I could relate to what he'd said. I found it hard to think of our worlds separating, as well.

Thankfully Eoin pulled on Griffin's reins, slowing him to a stop before I could allow my thoughts to descend so negatively. He said nothing as he dismounted, turning to lift me off of the horse.

He dragged me until my back was against the side of a tree and his mouth was on mine.

After kissing me ruthlessly, he pulled back, his eyes hungry. "When we get back to the castle, we shall all be busy with preparations. I doona want to end this constant companionship with ye, and I must take ye once more before we arrive at the castle.

I reached forward to pull him toward me, gladly fulfilling his desire.

---

*G*od, he wished he could spend his life buried deep inside her. He leaned forward, deeply breathing in the smell of her hair as the breeze lightly lifted it toward him. Each time he made love to her, he found himself wanting to go deeper, to claim every inch of her, to melt her with himself so that she would stay his forever.

In past experience he'd found that once he slept with a lass his fascination was gone, that having her for one night was enough. Not with Bri. She'd captured a part of him he'd never lent to anyone, and if he let her go, he knew that she would take that part of him with her when she returned home.

He squeezed her tightly around the middle as they pulled reins at the stables where Kip was waiting for them, ready to care for the travel-worn Griffin.

As they made their way up to the castle, hand-in-hand, Eoin caught sight of Mary waiting at the entrance. Mary glared at him as she saw him and quickly called Bri to join her, for there was something she wanted to discuss with her.

Knowing better than to deny Mary, Eoin squeezed Bri's hand, encouraging her to leave him. As the two women entered the castle, worry started to build. Whatever Mary was going to tell Bri, he had a feeling it wasn't going to mean anything good for himself.

CHAPTER 30

J was definitely about to get into trouble. For what, I had
no idea. But from the look on Mary's face I could tell she
was not overjoyed to see us back at the castle.

She didn't let go of my hand, nor did she stop moving until we
reached Morna's spell room deep below the castle. Once inside, she
released my hand and pointed to the wooden stool in the corner.

"Sit."

I finally understood how my kindergarteners felt when they had
to sit out during recess. "Is everything all right, Mary?"

"Nay, lass. What exactly do ye think yer doing?"

I couldn't for the life of me figure out what she was talking about.
"I don't think I'm doing anything. What's the matter with you?"

"What's the matter with me, lass? What's the matter with ye? Ye
and Eoin were up to no good while ye were away, and doona try to
tell me that ye were not."

I couldn't repress a smile. "Define 'no good.'"

"Ach! Why, ye have been tupping, and enjoying every bit of it,
have ye not?"

There was no reason I should've felt guilty for my recent
activities with my sort-of husband, but Mary was quickly succeeding

in making me feel so. It instantly made me defensive. "I don't believe that's any of your business, Mary."

"Oh, ye doona think that it is, do ye? Well, pardon me, but while ye've been away, the whole castle has been running ragged trying to find the ring for the spell so that ye can return home, and ye go off and act like ye doona want to go."

"I do want to go home," I paused, unsure if I believed my own words. "I think."

"Aye, there ye go, lass. That's the first truth ye've spoken. Ye doona know if ye want to go home. And would ye like me to tell ye why that is, lass?"

"I feel quite sure you're going to anyway." I smiled, but she seemed unamused.

"Aye, that I will, lass. Ye doona know if ye want to go home because ye have let yerself fall in love with Eoin. How could ye be so foolish? Ye know that it canna be so."

I stood, feeling angry and inexplicably on the verge of tears. "It's not like I meant to fall in love with him, Mary. Have you seen him? I don't think I had much say in the matter at all. And why can't it be so? If I look just like Blaire, what's the problem with me staying?"

"Ach, lass, I doona know the lass well, but I expect that Blaire is ready to return home. I'm sure she's right scared out o' her mind being trapped in yer strange time, where she's most likely been forced to dress with cloth that rises up between her legs! Not to mention that yer own mother is desperate to have ye back!"

I was sure that my heart nearly stopped at the mention of my mother. "Wait! Why would you say that about my mother?"

Mary reached for the spell book, which still lay open on the table, and thrust it in my direction.

"She wrote to ye. Look around the edges of the spell. I noticed it when I was down here looking for the damned ring. A handwriting I dinna recognize caught my eye. I could not read it, o' course, but I had Arran come and look, and he told me what she said. She's working on the spell too, Bri. And she needs the ring as well. She's worried sick that ye might not be safe."

I held it before me, reading my mother's words over and over, a mixture of emotions flooding me. I was thrilled to know that she was safe and that she'd figured out that the spell was the key to switching Blaire and me back. I was also horrified to know how worried she must be for me, and I was certain she'd spent every waking second trying to get me back.

"How do you think she was able to do this, Mary?"

"I doona know, lass. Perhaps, the book's magic allowed the writing to show through."

"Do you think it would work both ways? I need to let her know that I'm safe and that I'm looking for the ring, as well." I held the book tightly to my chest as if by cradling it I was holding on to a piece of my mother.

"I doona see why not. It willna hurt for ye to try. But do ye mean it, lass? Are ye truly looking for the ring?"

I understood her meaning well enough. She seemed to have a better understanding of my feelings than I did, and she knew that part of me didn't want to return home.

"Yes, Mary. I am looking. I know that we have to find the ring. I can't deny the feelings I have for Eoin, but I won't share them with him. It's too selfish for me to stay here. My mom deserves to have me back. Blaire deserves the chance to be able to return to her home. And besides, I doubt Eoin feels the same way."

Mary reached forward and rubbed the side of her thumb down the side of my cheek in a motherly fashion. "Ach, lass. I believe he does care for ye as ye do him. That's why it troubled me so to see ye walking toward the castle so happy with one another. I doona want this to hurt both of ye."

"It's too late for that, Mary. It hurts me now just to think of it."

Mary smiled as she turned to leave me alone in the spell room. "I know it does, lass. It hurts me to think of ye leaving as well. I've come to love ye like I would a daughter. Write to yer mother. It will do her good to know that ye are safe."

"I will. Thank you, Mary."

Once she was gone and I could no longer hear her footsteps on the stairs leading out of the basement, I placed the spell book back on the desk and crawled on top of the stool, pulling my knees in toward me as I buried my head and cried.

I wasn't accustomed to allowing my emotions to affect me so drastically. Living alone for so long, I'd made it a habit of pushing away anyone who dared interrupt my set routines and the comfortable, albeit lonely, life I'd created for myself. If I allowed myself to feel too much, I made myself vulnerable, and that was a feeling that my control-freak personality absolutely rebelled against. Hence why none of the countless men Mitsy had set me up with ever made it past date three.

So, how was it that Eoin had been able to slip inside the confines of my heart so easily? I didn't know, but I loved him. I knew it without question. But I also knew that it didn't matter. This decision affected the lives of too many others, and I couldn't be so selfish as to only consider my own heart.

If no one else were involved—not my mother, not Blaire, not Arran and his love for Blaire—I would gladly cease searching for the ring and stay here forever. But that wasn't the case, and no number of tears was going to change that.

Drying my eyes on the sleeve of my dress, I unfolded my legs and stood to go and look for a pen and inkwell with which to write a message back to my mother.

I found them quickly and, leaving as much room around the edges of the spell as I could so that we could communicate further if the message worked, I scribbled simply, *"I'm safe, Mom. We haven't found the ring yet, but we are searching. Take care of Blaire. I know she must be ready to return home. I love you. Write back if you get this."*

Inhaling deeply to push back the remnants of unshed tears, I turned and walked out of the room, leaving the message for my mother to see.

It was time to find that freaking ring. Or, apparently, we would all die trying.

CHAPTER 31

"Come in." The knock startled him. He'd expected to be left alone until morning. When Arran walked through the doorway, Eoin was sure his face showed his disappointment. Part of him had hoped Bri would seek him out before bed.

"May I talk to ye a moment, brother?" Arran walked through the room, stopping to sit in one of the two chairs situated in front of the room's fireplace.

Eoin joined him, sitting opposite. "O'course. How did the meetings and training go while we were away?"

"All went well. Everyone in the village has been informed, and they are working together to strengthen defenses. All people outside castle grounds will come to stay at the castle the same night as Kinnaird and MacChristy's men. We will leave the village empty so that they have no one to attack there."

"Good. With both clans coming, I'm not so worried about the upcoming attack. How's the runaway lad been? Is he working well for Kip?" Eoin leaned over the side of the chair and, grabbing a poker, stoked the dulling fire.

"Aye. Kip said he's caused him no trouble, but there's little to keep them both busy. I borrowed him for a task once while ye were away. That's actually why I came to speak with ye."

The fire now burning full flame once again, Eoin returned the poker to its home and sat back in his seat to look his brother in the eye. "Aye?"

"I spent some time looking for the ring that ye need for the spell. I found it. It was buried with father." Arran reached out and placed it in Eoin's hand.

"Arran . . . tell me ye dinna do it?"

Arran stood defensively. "Aye, I could not bring myself to do it, so I had the lad retrieve the ring once we unearthed Father. Ye had to know that's where the ring was. It was the only place we had yet to look."

"Aye, I'll not lie and say I dinna know it was a possibility. But I doona think we need it anymore."

"Doona need it? Christ, Eoin, have ye gone mad? The lass canna stay here."

Eoin cringed as the thought of her leaving caused an uncomfortable pain to hit him right below his ribs. "Aye, she can. She's my wife, Arran, whether I knew it was her that I married or not. If ye hadna gone and pried the ring off of our father's dead finger, then she wouldna had a choice. I canna lose her, Arran. I'm not going to give her the ring."

Arran paced the room as if shocked by Eoin's words. "Ye doona have a choice, Eoin! I know that ye care for the lass, but it is not fair to leave Blaire there. I willna let ye do it."

"Ye have no say in it, Arran. And why do ye care about leaving Blaire where she is? She's a wretched lass." Eoin watched Arran prowl the room, struggling to rein in his anger. Arran's passion on the subject confused him greatly.

"Blaire's not so bad, Eoin. What makes ye think that Bri no longer wants to go home? Has she told ye that?"

The question threw him. It hadn't until that moment crossed his mind that she wouldn't want to stay. He knew he'd tried to make it sound as if he knew she was planning on leaving once they found the ring, but deep down he thought she'd choose not to go.

But Arran was right. She'd never said anything to him about

staying here. Still, she'd shown him with her affection how much she cared for him.

"No, but I doona think she's too concerned with finding the ring now. She will not mind having to stay."

"Do ye really think so? Go and see where she is right now, Eoin. Ye will find her in the spell room, looking desperately for the ring that ye hold in yer hand. She will never forgive ye if ye keep it from her. She must at least be given the choice."

Eoin stared down at the ring, not looking up as his bedchamber door slammed shut at Arran's abrupt departure.

Surely Arran was wrong. After the long journey back from Kinnaird Castle, the lass would be too tired to search for the ring tonight. And after the way she'd cried out in his arms, letting him hold her through the night, would she even want to?

It didn't really matter. Even if she still did want to return home, he knew he couldn't bring himself to let her go. She'd captured his heart completely and he didn't want to spend his life with any other. If she didn't love him already, he could make her love him with time.

He just had to make sure she didn't find out that Arran had found the ring.

With re-hiding the ring set as his task, he left his bedchamber to head for the outer wall of the castle, intent on chunking it into the ocean. He paused briefly at Bri's bedchamber door, hoping to catch a sound of her moving about the room.

When he heard nothing, he quietly lifted the handle to peek inside, hoping to catch a glimpse of her sleeping soundly in the large bed. She wasn't there. His heart sank as he took in the vacant room. Changing his path of direction, he turned to make his way to the spell room in search of her.

As he descended into the castle's basement, he found himself hoping that she wouldn't be there either. He desperately wanted Arran to be wrong.

He heard her moving about the room before he saw her. Frantically lifting books and shifting through shelves, she jumped when he spoke to her. "Ye should be in bed asleep, lass. It's been a long day."

"Eoin. Gosh, you scared the crap out of me. What are you doing down here?"

"I looked in on ye in yer bedchamber, but ye were not there."

"Oh. Yeah. I'm about to go to bed. Here, wait and I'll follow you up." She blew out the candle and reached out for his hand in the dark.

He took it as he walked toward the staircase on the other side of the basement. "What were ye doing, lass?"

"Just going through the things in the spell room, looking for the ring."

The words cut through him, just as if she'd run a dagger straight through his heart. He couldn't keep the lass here against her will. Arran was right. He knew he had to give her a choice.

He stopped and pulled her close to him just before they entered the staircase. He wrapped his arms around her, kissing the top of her head as she murmured into his chest.

"Is everything alright, Eoin?"

"Aye, lass, all is well. Tomorrow evening, would ye accompany me somewhere? I'd like to surprise ye with something."

He felt her grin against his chest. "Of course. I love surprises."

Tomorrow he would tell her everything; tell her that he found the ring, tell her that he loved her, tell her that he didn't want her to leave. He would place his heart in her hands. And the choice would be hers.

CHAPTER 32

J woke early the next morning, anxious to get to the spell room to see if the message had worked and Mom had replied. I did my best not to get my hopes up, but it didn't work well as I threw on the simplest dress I had and hurried down into the basement.

Carrying the lantern from my room, I shared the flame with the candles scattered around the work table and waited for the room to light up as I nervously glanced down at the parchment.

It had worked, and I smiled and dragged my finger over her markings as I read the words aloud to myself:

"Sweet Mother of God, I'm glad to know that you are safe, baby. I'm sure one of us will find the ring, and we will have the two of you switched back soon. Now that I know you're safe, I can tell you how jealous I am that you're there, getting to meet and live with the very people I've spent my life trying to learn about. I can't wait to hear all of the wonderful stories you must have. I miss you, darling and I love you more than you will ever know."

No doubt that was Mom. She wrote just like she spoke, and it relieved some of my anxiety to know that she would no longer be as worried for my safety. I was reaching to grab the ink and pen and write back when handwriting different from the others on the page caught my eye.

Scribbled in fine lettering beside my first message to Mom, the words were so tiny that I'd almost missed them. I was sure Blaire had scribbled them, and the words caused my breath to catch in my throat.

Right next to my own mention of how much I knew Blaire must be ready to return home, she had written,

"I cannot go back. I want to stay here."

I sat down on the bench in front of the table and read her words once more for good measure. An uncontrollable excitement spread throughout me as I took in her words a fourth and fifth time. If Blaire didn't want to come back here, was there really any reason why I had to leave?

I already knew deep down that I didn't want to return home. Strangely enough, I fit here in this time, with these people, with Eoin. But I couldn't bring myself to make that decision for the others involved. I couldn't deny Blaire the right to return to her home, I couldn't deny Arran the chance to see the woman he loved again, and I couldn't deny my mother the knowledge that I was okay.

Now that I was able to communicate with Mom, no matter how small the form, she would at least know that I was safe and happy. That's all she wanted for me anyway, and if she knew that I'd found happiness here, she would be able to make her peace with that in time.

It would be hard for Arran to accept Blaire's absence, but if her writing was any indication, it didn't seem to me that she reciprocated his feelings. Perhaps it would be easier for him to move on believing she still loved him but couldn't return home, rather than have her returned to him and find he was unwanted.

I'd left the spell room the night before heartsick, knowing that each time I went to sleep, I would wake up with one less day that I would get to spend here. Today, the possibility of being able to spend all of my days here had me on the edge of pure elation.

But there was still one factor I wasn't taking into account. I was assuming, most likely foolishly, that Eoin wanted me to stay. He was kind, attentive, loving, and seemingly sad when the topic of my leaving came up in conversation. That being said, I knew that knowing he would miss me and him wanting me to stay beside him forever were two very different things.

I wasn't the woman he'd agreed to or thought he had married. And he'd yet to verbally express his feelings for me. Was I willing to make myself so vulnerable to him by telling him how much I loved him, how desperately I didn't want to leave him, with the hope that he would match my own feelings?

The thought terrified me, but I didn't see how I had any choice. I knew myself well enough to know that the regret I would have over not taking the risk would be far more painful than the heartbreak I would feel if he didn't want me in his life.

I loved him too much to leave him. Whether we had years to love or just days left, I would treasure my time with him forever.

I was unsure of where he was taking me tonight, but it would allow me the perfect opportunity to tell him I no longer wanted to go home.

With my mind set, I nervously made my way out of the spell room and went in search of Mary. I was going to be an anxious wreck all day, and I knew she would keep me busy. Plus, maybe she could help me find a sexier dress. I was going to need whatever I could manage to help me keep my cool.

*rran was already past his boiling point, and his anger over Eoin's selfishness had him ready to spring on the first bastard unlucky enough to cross paths with him. Unfortunately for himself, it was Kip who he decided to unleash his anger on. He couldn't have made a worse decision.

It was early afternoon when Arran stormed out of the castle, planning to get some fresh air. As he walked toward the stables, he saw Kip's runaway walking casually in the direction of the village. It was the only excuse he needed.

Making as much noise as he could manage, he walked into the side door of the stables, knowing it would draw Kip's attention. Kip held a pitchfork and was working on maneuvering hay around to the different stalls.

"Where the hell did ye let him go, Kip?"

He was rewarded with a smack right in the middle of his forehead as Kip brought the end of the wooden stick forward, slamming it into his face.

"Now, what did ye say, Arran? I do believe ye thought ye were talking to someone else for a moment."

Rubbing the now red and tender spot in between his brows, Arran blushed with embarrassment at his behavior. "I'm sorry, Kip. I'm not in the best humor. Now, where is the lad off to? Do ye not need him today?"

"He said he had some errands he needed to attend to in the village, and I saw no harm in letting him go. I doona ever need him, I do a fine job running the stable all on my own."

Arran poked his head around the stable door to make sure he could still see him off in the distance. "Do ye trust him, Kip?"

The old man stopped fussing with the hay and leaned against the stall door as he spoke to Arran. "The lad has given me no reason not to, and I think it's best to let people prove ye wrong before ye go about mistrusting everybody."

"Do ye? Well, I'm not as good a man as ye, Kip." Arran turned and followed along on the path leading to the village. The runaway was up to nothing good. Arran could feel it, and he intended to find out what it was.

CHAPTER 33

"*J*'m not gonna cut the neckline any further. Do ye not want them to stay in the dress at all?"

I rolled my eyes as I glanced down at the very modest v-cut I'd spent the better half of the afternoon talking Mary into cutting into the gown. "It's not even that low, Mary, but to answer your question, I'm not all that concerned with them staying in the dress very long."

"Oh, hush, lass. Ye will make an old lady blush with such talk. I'm glad that ye have decided to stay, but ye doona need these alterations to entice Eoin into wanting ye around."

"I'm not trying to entice him. I'm trying to make myself feel as pretty as I can so I feel confident before I tell him what I have to say. With no make-up or hair straightener, a girl's got to do what a girl's got to do around here."

"Fine, lass, but please tell me ye decided not to wear that strange object ye wear under yer shirt when in the spell room."

I smiled and reached over to grab my bra off the top of the bed. "No, Mary. I'm definitely still going to wear my bra. He knows I'm not from here now, so it won't be a huge surprise for him to see something odd on me. Besides, it lifts the girls up, and they'll look better in the dress. Watch."

I turned so that my back faced Mary, discreetly scooting the dress down off my shoulders so that my breasts sprang free and I could rope them into place with the bra. Reluctantly, Mary had washed all of my modern clothes for me. They'd started to get pretty ripe after weeks of not seeing a washing machine.

Slipping the dress back on, I faced her, triumphantly. My breasts filled in the new v-cut in the dress perfectly, and the cleavage was just enough to draw attention, without completely giving away the farm. "What do you think?"

Even Mary couldn't hide her amazement at the difference it made. "Aye, lass. I regret what I said before. Do ye think we could make me one? I believe I underestimated the size of yer breasts, lass. They're a good deal higher now."

"I told you. And I bet you could fashion something that would work the same way. Just look at what you've done with this dress!" I spun, feeling dainty and beautiful, and my nerves subsided slightly until I heard a knock on the door.

"Ach, lass, there he is." She paused and came to place a hand on each of my shoulders. "Doona worry, lass. If he tells ye anything other than what ye want to hear, then I doona know the lad as well as I think I do." She gave me a brief hug and surprised me by giving me a quick swat on my bottom. "And ye look beautiful. Have a good time."

With that I opened the door to him, and as he took my hand, I followed him outside.

---

*A*ch, the lass looked beautiful! But what had she done to the top of her dress? Did she want him to take her right in the middle of the hallway? Nay, he would not allow himself to have her until he'd told her all that he needed to, and she'd chosen him as her own.

If she rejected him, he would take her to do the spell tonight. He didn't think he could bear to have her stay here even a moment longer if he knew she didn't want him in the same way he longed to have her.

It was a long walk to the cave at the base of the shoreline, and he was anxious to get her there quickly. Each second of wondering was more torturous than the last. It was a chilly evening, but the small cave blocked the wind and provided a perfect place from which to watch the waves as the tide rolled.

As he led her onto the sand, he smiled as she paused to hike up her dress, gathering it in her arms and revealing the pale skin of her legs. He didn't know of another lass who would so unashamedly expose her legs while walking, but he'd expect no less from his strange lass, and he loved every odd thing about her.

He could only hope she loved him in return. As he led her into the candlelit cave, he breathed in a deep ocean-filled breath for courage. It was time for the truth to be known.

*E*oin said nothing as we walked away from the castle, and while I knew we were headed to the shore, he gave no clues as to where he was taking me.

He seemed nervous, and it did nothing to help my nerves. Part of me wondered if he was dragging me away to tell me privately just how ready he was for me to return home. It was easy for my mind to always drift to the worst scenario.

When we reached the sand I jerked loose from his grip, apologizing as I kicked off my shoes and gathered the bottom of my dress. I didn't care how ridiculous I looked waddling through the sand with fabric gathered up in my arms; I wasn't about to dirty this dress after all the work Mary had put into it. She would've killed me, no doubt.

It was getting darker along the beach, and I found myself hoping that we'd reach our intended destination soon. In a horror film, this was exactly the point in which the man would turn around and kill me, tossing my body into the approaching waves.

Eventually we made our way inside a narrow cave hiding along the rocky coast at the back of the beach. It was filled with candles, which illuminated the circular haven. And with an assortment of cushions and blankets lying on a rock ledge near the back, most of my fears subsided. It was a romantic setting, not the kind of place you would take someone before sending them away, and not the kind of place you would take someone before chunking their lifeless body into the ocean.

Inside the cave the ground was rocky, and without the fear of sand getting caught in the dress, I relaxed my arms and let it fall down to my feet once more. Eoin smiled and took my hand as he led me to the blankets at the back of the cave. Once I'd comfortably crawled on top and situated myself next to him, he turned to me to speak.

"Lass, I need to confess something to ye, but I'm not so sure I can bring myself to tell ye."

Maybe I was wrong about this being romantic. Maybe he was about to tell me he loved someone else, and he was ready for me to go home so that he could get on with his life. A million thoughts ran through my mind as all the fear from earlier came rushing back, and I suddenly felt foolish for thinking I would be brave enough to tell him I loved him.

Instead, I squeezed his hand, encouraging him to just get whatever he wanted to say over with. "All right. You have to tell me now. Just get on with it."

He could see that I was shivering, from nerves more than cold, but he couldn't tell the difference. He politely wrapped one of the blankets around my shoulder.

"Lass, I know that ye have been searching for the ring so that ye can go home. While, we were away, Arran found it."

"He did?" Shocked, I tried to normalize my expression as he continued.

"Aye," he paused to retrieve it and held it out to me, eventually setting it in between us when I didn't reach out for it. "I almost threw it in the ocean."

"You what?" The pitch of my voice was oddly high and screechy, making me sound angry rather than shocked.

"Aye, lass. I'm verra sorry, but I dinna want to give ye the ring. I know that I canna keep it from ye, but I'd like to ask ye something before I let ye have it."

"Of course." My heart restarted as hope began to crawl through the fear rooted in my stomach.

"Doona go, lass." He squeezed my hands tightly in between his own, and I was sure my heart was going to burst with happiness. "I've fallen in love with ye, Bri, and I doona wish to be parted from ye. If ye doona love me, I shall give ye the ring, but I could not let ye leave without telling ye."

My voice cracked as I spoke to him, and a tear broke free from my left eye. "No."

He didn't give me a chance to finish. "I'm so verra sorry for keeping the ring from ye, lass. I just wasna ready to let ye go."

I pried my hands loose and reached up to grab hold of his face. "No, listen. Let me finish."

He stopped talking, pursing his lips awkwardly like a fish, and I couldn't help but laugh.

"It's not so funny, lass. Ye're breaking my heart. I only ask that ye do it swiftly."

"Hush. It is funny. Your face looks ridiculous. I meant, 'no,' I'm not mad at you. I had something to tell you tonight as well."

"Aye?"

"I was going to tell you that I wanted to stop looking for the ring. I can't leave here. This is my home now and I've fallen in love with everyone. Mary, Kip, Arran, Griffin, even you." I winked at him before continuing, "Before, I only thought I had to go back because of my mother and Blaire. She deserved the chance to return to her home, but she doesn't want it.

"How do ye know, lass?"

"It's the spell book. We can write messages to one another that cross over through time. My mother knows I'm safe here, and as long as she knows that, she'll be okay with my decision. And Blaire, she said she wants to stay. That means I'm free, Eoin. I'm free to stay with you. If you'll have me?"

"Have ye, lass? Did ye not just hear what I said to ye? I'll have ye and ye alone."

We fell into each other then, our lips meeting with a sort of elation that comes with knowing your feelings are matched with the one you love.

He undressed me slowly, marveling at my bra as he took in the lacy, blue material.

"Ach, lass! I dinna think it possible for a lass's breast to look so wonderful, while covered. Is it expected that ye wear such material in yer time?"

"Yes, but for goodness sakes, just get it off of me now."

"As ye wish, love."

And as he took me in his arms, we rocked our bodies together against the stones in a motion that mimicked the crashing of the water against the sand, expressing our love for one another through the night.

CHAPTER 34

*A*rran squatted behind the first building on the edge of the village, peering around the corner as he watched the runaway wait for someone to join him outside the ale house. The lad reached into a small bag he carried around his shoulder and removed an item which he'd wrapped in a cloth.

Arran knew he'd been right to follow him. The lad had been given no chance to acquire anything for trade, unless he'd stolen it from Kip or some other area of the castle.

Only a few moments passed before a man Arran had never seen before walked out of the ale house and extended a hand in the runaway's direction. He watched as they spoke quietly for a few moments, ending their conversation when the runaway patted the stranger and handed the unknown item over to him.

Arran couldn't make sense of the strange transaction, but he knew he'd just witnessed the runaway betray them.

As he watched the runaway turn to head back toward the castle, Arran pulled his head back around the corner, out of sight from anyone walking by. He waited until the lad moved past him, then quickly ran up behind him, ramming his fist over the back of the runaway's head. Arran caught the man around the middle, shrugging his unconscious body over his shoulder.

He'd take the betrayer to the dungeon, and he'd get the truth out of the lying bastard by whatever means necessary.

I moved about the spell room, putting away books and materials for what I hoped would be the last time. With my mind made up that I would be staying, and now knowing the location of the ring, I saw no reason to leave the room in such a state of dishevelment.

With each lift of a book, I was reminded of my activities the night before. I knew my back was covered in bruises from being pounded against the rocky surface of the cave, and every muscle in my body was sore from our nightly acrobatics. I'd never been so happy to be so uncomfortable.

As I continued to shuffle books around the room, I realized that the real reason I seemed so preoccupied with re-organizing the space is that I was doing my very best to put off the inevitable. I had to write to Mom and let her know I wasn't coming home.

I was completely confident in my decision. Regardless of the unusual circumstances that had brought me into this time, it had landed me exactly where I was supposed to be. That being said, it didn't make it any easier for me to go about saying goodbye to my mother for what was most assuredly forever.

The thought brought forth a familiar lump inside my throat. The same lump that had lodged itself into place when I'd attended my father's funeral, the same lump that I'd been forced to choke down after laying eyes on Donal MacChristy.

I knew my mother wasn't dying. She would undoubtedly go on to live a happy life, endlessly dating men either too young or too old for her, and traveling the world on whatever dig caught her fancy. But she'd not only been my mother but my very best friend for my entire life. And while I knew she would understand, I also knew it would hurt her to know that I'd chosen not to return to be her partner in crime.

Once I'd rearranged every book in the room at least twice, I knew it was time to sit down and just get it over with.

I tore a blank piece of parchment from one of Morna's old journals and practiced what I would say to her.

Twenty-five drafts later, I knew that the truth was that it didn't matter what I wrote. It was going to hurt her regardless. It was best that I keep it simple and only touch on the most important things: that I was safe, that I was happy, and that I hoped she would understand.

In the end, I wrote only four sentences, ensuring that I left room in case she wanted to write a reply.

"I don't want you ever to doubt how much I love you, Mom, but I found it. That love you talked to me about at the inn? He's here, and I have to stay with him. I'm safe and happy, and I know that's all you've ever wanted for me."

It was done. And while I knew I'd made the right decision, it had cost me the best mom in the world.

I was unsure of how long I sat there, staring blankly at the wall, feeling oddly cold and hollow. I'd been shattered when my father had been killed in a boating accident. Losing someone so suddenly wraps you in a sort of black shock that takes years to shake off.

Somehow, this seemed harder. It was just as sudden a break, and the knowledge that she was alive and well and would go on living and sharing her fun, witty, and wild self for the world to see, but not for me to get to witness, left me feeling utterly lost.

The hand that touched my shoulder was my anchor, and I gladly turned into his embrace. He too understood the grief of loss, with his father's death occurring shortly before my arrival. He didn't ask what I'd been doing. He looked around at the tidy room and at the words on the page and silently sat down beside me, wrapping me in his arms.

He held me without saying a word, silently stroking my back, bending occasionally to plant a gentle kiss on the top of my head, letting me know that he was there for as long as I needed him.

Eventually I pulled away and managed a smile to reassure him that I wasn't re-thinking my decision. He smiled back and reached for my hand.

"I know it may not be customary. My parents kept separate bedchambers throughout their marriage, but how would ye feel about moving into my bedchamber? I doona like the thought of ye being so far away. I want to fall asleep each night with ye next to me, wrapped in my arms."

I stood and pulled him toward the doorway. "I would love to. I'd already asked Mary this morning if she would have someone move my belongings across the hall. In my time, it would be uncustomary for us not to share a room. Besides, I don't want to be alone tonight."

CHAPTER 35

*K*innaird Castle

"*W*hat does the lad want with me?" Ramsay marched from his bedchamber, furious that someone would dare have the nerve to arrive unannounced.

"I doona know, sir. All he said was that he must see ye straight away. He had an item to give ye."

"The damned fool had better be bringing me Eoin Conall's head on a spike if he's to wake me at this hour." Ramsay burst through the doors of the study where the father of his two stable lads stood uncomfortably at the end of the room. "Well, what do ye possibly have that ye think is warranted to disturb me?"

"I . . . I met with the man ye sent to Conall Castle. He gave me this ring to give to ye. Said it's the signet of the late Alasdair Conall, and he believed it could be of some use to ye since Eoin has asked that the MacChristy clan gather at the castle as well."

"Give it to me." Ramsay thrust his hand eagerly in the man's direction. He knew he'd done right by sending the man. The lad was a quick thinker, and he'd just proven that he was worth more than

Ramsay had previously expected. He studied the ring, recognizing Alasdair's signet immediately. "Thank ye, lad. Now, get out."

The man's face dropped, obviously disappointed at a lack of reward, but he retreated quickly, leaving Ramsay alone with one of his messengers in the study.

"Dress in the colors of the Conalls and take this ring to MacChristy Castle at once. Doona give this ring to anyone but Donal, do ye understand? Ye will have no trouble gaining an audience. Donal will welcome any Conall. Once ye have given him the ring, tell him that Eoin no longer requires his men or his presence for the battle. The situation has been taken care of, and there is not going to be an attack."

"Aye. O' course, sir."

With one less clan to worry about, Ramsay was certain his plan to annihilate the Conalls would succeed. In three days' time, he would gather his men and everyone at the castle. Together they would march to the aide of the Conalls, gladly assisting them in their bloody deaths.

onall Castle

"*I* assure ye, lad, I'm in no hurry. I'll gladly spend as many nights down here with ye as ye wish. But we willna be leaving until ye tell me what it was that ye gave to the stranger in town and where ye got it from." Arran threw a fist into the stomach of the man who was now strung up by both wrists in the center of the dungeon.

The runaway groaned painfully as one of his ribs snapped at the impact of Arran's fist. "I already told ye. The man was my uncle, and I was only returning an item I borrowed from him."

"Ye lie. The man was not old enough to be yer uncle, and ye had no such item when ye arrived here."

"I did so. I keep it in my bag. Ye dinna search me when I arrived. I've had it with me all along."

Arran thrust another fist forward, this time hitting the man's other side. "What was the item ye borrowed from him?"

"Only . . ." the man paused as a cough racked his chest, sending blood spewing out onto the dungeon floor. "It was only a coin."

Arran shook his head at the runaway's pathetic attempt to lie, this time sending his fist for the man's jaw. He wrung out his hand as the runaway spit up a few of his teeth. "Like I said. Doona expect to see daylight until ye tell me the truth."

CHAPTER 36

The days following my decision to remain here passed by in a blur of hurried activity, with everyone in the castle and village rushing to make preparations for the arrival of the MacChristys and Kinnairds as well as preparing for the upcoming battle.

It was the night before the expected attack, and while both Eoin and Arran seemed confident all would be well, I found my anxiety building. They'd not seen the devastating ruins of our home, as I had. And while I knew that having two clans join us for the fight increased our chances, knowing what happened before made me uneasy and it made me wonder why there were still ruins on Mom's side of time, if we were going to succeed in battle.

Mom had responded to my message the following morning, playing it upbeat as always, but I could see the tear stains on the parchment where she'd cried. She was happy that I was happy, but she was as heartbroken as I was at our separation from one another. We'd written back and forth over the days leading up to the battle as I did my best to assure her that the fate of the Conalls would no longer stay the same now that we had reinforcements headed our way.

I wondered how it would affect everything on the other side of history if we succeeded. I hoped that I would still be able to use the book to communicate with my mother if the castle never ended up being destroyed. If we were defeated, it didn't really matter.

Dusk had long since crept over the castle, and with each passing hour the tension throughout the castle heightened. Both the MacChristys and the Kinnairds should have arrived at the castle by now, and, although Eoin was trying his hardest to remain calm, I could tell that my hovering, nervous energy was doing nothing to help the situation.

I walked over to him and placed a hand on his shoulder as he sat in one of the studies on the main floor staring out the window for any sign of the clans' arrival. "Would you like me to leave you alone for a while?"

He reached up, latched onto my hand, and pulled me down onto his lap. "Aye, lass. It's not that I doona want ye here. But there's no need for ye to stay up so late worrying with me. I'm sure they were only delayed and will arrive sometime during the night. Go on up to bed, lass, and I'll join ye once both clans have been settled around the castle. It will calm me to know that ye are soundly asleep."

I knew I wouldn't sleep until he came up to the bedchamber, but he was doing his best to politely tell me to beat it, and I didn't blame him. Leaning in to give him a quick kiss, I turned and made my way upstairs.

It was well into the deepest part of the night when Arran alerted him that Ramsay's men were almost to the castle. Eoin stood from the seat in his study and went to the castle's entrance to greet them.

He'd expected Ramsay to burst through the doors with some elaborate tale which would explain their late arrival and have them all laughing and breaking into the ale within minutes. Instead, as Ramsay Kinnaird pushed his way into the castle's main foyer, Eoin knew instantly something had gone terribly wrong.

Ramsay and his men, their clothes wet from the rain and splashed with mud, looked as if they'd been riding hard through the night. Their faces were panicked and frightened.

Eoin didn't bother with greetings as he rushed to grab Laird Kinnaird, who appeared as if he was about to fall over from exhaustion.

"What is it, man? What's happened?"

"Ach, Eoin! I'm afraid we've all underestimated Laird MacLyrron's forces. We only just escaped in time. And I was forced to bring not only my men, but my daughter and all the women and children."

Eoin blanched and suddenly felt unsteady on his feet as he took in the news. "So they doona only plan to attack us. They tried to attack yer territory as well?"

Ramsay spoke in between over-exaggerated gasping breaths. "Aye. I believe he split up his men and sent half to my keep and half to the MacChristy's. For when we passed through Donal's territory . . ." Ramsay paused as if unable to finish.

A terrifying sense of dread crept over Eoin's heart.

"What is it, man? What did ye find at Donal's?" Eoin ushered Ramsay over to the staircase in the center of the room, and they both collapsed onto the stone steps next to one another.

"The MacChristys will not be coming to our aide. They're all gone, Eoin. The clan MacChristy has been completely wiped out. Women, children, livestock, all. Laird MacLyrron left nothing alive. And now he's headed in our direction."

Bile rose in Eoin's throat. If what Ramsay said was true, their hopes of surviving the attack were greatly diminished. "Do ye think with our combined men we can stand against them?"

Eoin took in Ramsay's pained expression and knew his response before he spoke.

"Nay. I doona believe we can. He has three times the number of men we do. The best we can hope for is to hide our women and children as long as we can, and not let them take us without a fight."

"How far away are they? Do we have time to prepare at all?"

"Aye. A group of my men were scouting their location. Tis how we were warned they were headed our way. They are reconvening to gather after splitting directions. They've camped for the night in between my castle and what was the MacChristy's keep. They canna make it here before tomorrow night."

"A small mercy, but at least yer men shall be able to get a short time of rest before we prepare for battle and hide the women tomorrow. We shall all need our strength. While I know sleep is likely to escape us all tonight, I think we should all try. Tell yer men they are welcome to set camp anywhere on castle grounds. I will show ye to yer chamber. Yer daughter may stay in my mother's old room. Blaire resides with me."

"Thank ye, Eoin. It calms an old man's heart to know he will die beside such a fine laird and ally. Let us reconvene in the morning."

*oin opened the door to his bedchamber as quietly as he could, although he knew Bri would still be awake waiting for him. He kept his back to her as he blew out the candles next to the bed. Then he undressed and crawled in beside her.

If he let her see his face, she would know something was wrong, and he couldn't bear for her to know just yet. He wanted one last night, as sleepless as it would be for him, to hold her in his arms and thank the heavens for sending the lass throughout time to find him.

He finally knew the love that his own father had shared with his mother. When his mother had died, it had taken every fiber of strength his father possessed to keep on living. His love for her never ceased, and Eoin had known it had been her name on his father's mind and heart as he'd watched his father take his last breath.

He'd never understood how a lass could have such a hold on someone's heart. Eoin grew up wondering why his father never remarried; he would've if it had been he who'd lost his wife. It was unnatural for a man to live alone so long, and how many years did it take for a heart to heal anyways? Surely not a lifetime.

But all of that was before Bri. And now, as he held her in his arms, feeling the warmth of her skin so vibrant and alive against him, he knew exactly the power a woman could wield over a man's soul.

He loved her beyond reason, beyond hope, beyond time.

Her voice in the darkness, rattled him from his thoughts and he pulled her in closely against him, kissing her hair.

"Did they finally arrive? What kept them so long?"

"Aye, lass. Only some bad weather slowed them. All is well."

It was the only lie he would tell her, but he would allow himself to be selfish, just this night. For Eoin loved the lass too much to watch her die. And after sunrise, although it pained him more than the thought of his own death, he would take the lass down into the spell room one last time. And whether she wanted to or not, she would do the spell and return home.

CHAPTER 37

*M*acChristy Castle

*D*onal MacChristy found himself unable to sit still. He felt an unexplainable sense of unease as he paced back and forth down the halls of his castle. He suspected this was what life felt like for the many ghosts that roamed the halls of the ancient castle, and when he unexpectedly collided with a figure around the corner he thought momentarily that perhaps he'd run into a real one.

He started at the sight of his most trusted housekeeper, Blaire's old maid and tutor, reeling back from the impact. "What are ye doing awake at this time o' night, lass? Ye should have been away long before now."

The elderly woman nodded and extended a plaid cloth in his direction, nearly screaming to accommodate the laird's bad ear. "Aye, perhaps. I've not been sure whether I should show ye something, but I've decided tis best that I do."

Donal took the strip torn from the bottom of a kilt into his hands and turned it over as the sense of unease crept back into his mind. "Where did ye find this?"

"It was in the bedchamber of the lad that came from Conall Castle."

"Aye?" The colors on the tartan were not the same as the Conall colors.

"Aye, sir. And there is something else as well, sir."

"Get on with it then. Tell me please."

"When the lad set out this afternoon, he didn't ride in the direction of Conall Castle. He rode in the opposite direction. I thought it odd at the time, but when I found this in the room, my suspicions grew. Are these not the colors of Ramsay Kinnaird?"

Donal instantly understood, and his heart nearly stopped for fear of his daughter and allies. "Christ, the bastard's fooled us! Sound the alarm and gather all the men at once. We must ride for Conall Castle immediately and hope they are not all dead already!"

onall Castle

*O*nce Arran was certain Eoin was retired for the evening and Ramsay and his men had set up camp, he quietly snuck away to the dungeon to continue his interrogation of the runaway.

Arran had stood quietly in the castle's main entrance, listening to Ramsay's story, and while it was worrisome, there was an untruth laced in Ramsay's sad words and somber face that Arran could see—even if Eoin was too besotted with his wife to see anything else clearly.

His brother was a good man, better than himself, but at least Arran knew that sometimes a person's eyes told more truth than their mouth. Eoin was too trusting of the man their father had called friend, but Arran could see the almost pleased expression in Ramsay's eyes as he told Eoin his tale of woe.

And he was now more certain than ever that the lad he kept in the dungeon knew something about what was going on.

"It seems that yer master has already attacked one of our allies. Why did ye not tell us that he would attack other territories as well?" Arran twisted the leather and wood contraption he'd laced around the runaway's arm, popping the lad's shoulder out of socket.

The runaway screamed in agony before choking out a response. "He's not my master."

Arran smiled at the small progress. "Nay? Well, that's a start at the truth. Let me leave ye with something to encourage ye to tell me the rest." Arran wrapped the leather around the man's other arm and quickly twisted the wooden handle until a snapping sound caused the man to nearly pass out from pain.

"I'll visit ye in the morning, and if ye are not ready to tell the truth, expect to lose some of yer less necessary bits, piece by piece."

Even if he had to kill the bastard, the truth of what the lad knew would come out tomorrow.

CHAPTER 38

J did my best to feign sleep, and while I did drift occasionally, Eoin's tense arms wrapped around me told me everything his reassuring words hadn't. Something was definitely wrong, and I suspected he was just waiting until daylight to tell me.

Anxious to hear whatever it was he didn't want to confide in me, I stirred in his arms at first light, trying to make it seem as if I was just waking up.

"Did ye sleep well, lass?" He didn't release me from his hold, and I was forced to look up at him awkwardly with my head pressed against his chest to respond.

"Better than you, I think. Something's wrong. Just tell me."

He stood then, and I was able to see just how dark the circles under his eyes were. Not only had he not gotten any sleep, something was bothering him terribly.

"Aye, lass. I need to take ye somewhere. Put on yer clothes and join me. I'll wait for ye out in the hall."

Once he'd gone I leapt out of the bed, throwing clothes on as quickly as I could manage, desperate to put an end to my wondering. I knew men had arrived late into the night; I'd listened to the commotion from the windowsill and watched as they'd set up camp.

With reinforcements here, I couldn't imagine what had Eoin so upset.

He pulled me down the hall quickly as he yanked me into the stairwell leading to the spell room, an imaginary knife slipped into my side. No way was he about to do what I thought. No way was he about to send me home after everything. He was a damned fool if he thought I was going anywhere.

I jerked free from his grasp as he reached to light the candles around the dark room. "What the hell do you think you are doing, Eoin? There's nothing for us to do down here. We should be upstairs, preparing for the battle."

I watched as he pulled out Morna's ring and set it on top of the open spell book. "There's not going to be a battle, lass. All that's left is a slaughter, and I'll not let ye stay here to die."

Shock coursed through my system, making it hard for me to understand his words. "What are you talking about? Everyone's arrived. Odds are they'll show up here, see your numbers, and there won't be a fight anyway. I know you're worried, but don't be so dramatic."

He shook his head somberly. "Nay, love. Not everyone did arrive. The MacChristys were slaughtered, lass. All. The Kinnairds barely escaped before their own castle was taken. Even with Ramsay's men, we will be outnumbered. All within the walls of this castle will greet death today, and I canna let ye join us as well. Ye had a life in yer own time. Return to it. Leave, so that I can die knowing that I at least saved ye from my own fate."

I ran to him them, shock and desperation making me cold as I threw my arms around him, seeking his warmth. "No. I won't go, Eoin."

"Ye must, lass. I'm not a controlling man, but I canna give ye a choice. Ye will do the spell."

Tears broke loose, and I sobbed uncontrollably against him, my fear of losing him pushing away any embarrassment over my behavior. "I can't . . . I can't go back to my life before." Sobs racked through my chest, and my head throbbed as if it might explode. "Not after you! I didn't know before. I didn't understand how little I had. I'd never be able to survive there now."

He pried my arms loose from around his waist so that he could look down at me. He shook me roughly. "Now, listen to me. Doona ye tell me that ye won't survive. Ye must. Knowing that I've kept ye safe is the only thing that will allow me to fight and die with my men and not flee from here like a coward. If ye love me, Bri, ye will go. And ye will live a long and happy life in yer own time."

I shook my head as I sobbed, wailing uncontrollably, all rationale gone. "This is my time now. Don't make me do it, Eoin. Please. Don't send me away. If you loved me, you wouldn't ask it."

He slapped me, stunning me enough that my sobs subsided briefly.

"Doona ever say that I doona love ye. Do ye not understand what it takes of me to send ye back?"

"No! Because I would never ask it of you." He'd released his grip on my arms, and I crushed myself against him once more, holding on less tightly, slowly surrendering. I knew his mind was made up.

"Aye, I expect ye would, love, but I know tis hard for ye to see now."

"I'm scared, Eoin. I can't stand the thought of leaving you. I'd rather die here."

"Nay, lass. I'd be no help to my men if I had to worry about ye. Ye must go now so that we can prepare the best we can. If by some miracle we are spared, I swear to ye, I shall find a way back to ye. Even if I must don awful shreds of clothing like the ones ye love so much and travel into that strange place to get ye."

I laughed against his chest. "I would love to see that, Eoin."

"Aye, lass?"

"I need you once more. To feel you in me so that I can hold onto that memory and always know that you were real." Despite my tears, I could hear how corny I sounded. I didn't care.

He responded only by lifting my dress and picking me up off the ground so that he could plunge inside of me. We fell to the ground with a desperate passion that had us moving against one another so we both reached release almost instantly. It was over too quickly, but instead of standing he removed my dress so that I lay before him naked. Silently he scattered a trail of warm kisses down my body.

"I am glad I shall die tonight, lass. For I doona think I could live a day without ye by my side. With each kiss I take a piece of ye to keep with me, and when I take my last breath, however it may find me, it shall be yer face that I see when my eyes close the last time."

"Eoin," I reached down to place my hand in his hair, coaxing him back up to me so that I could kiss him once more.

"It's time, love. I canna stay to watch ye do the spell. I'm afraid I would stop ye from doing it. But ye must, just as I must now go to prepare the men. When I leave, change into yer strange clothes and do the spell as quickly as ye can."

We stood, and he wrapped his arms around me one last time. "I shall always love ye beyond time itself. Even after I'm dead and buried, ye shall feel my love for ye wherever ye may go."

He released his hold, and by the time I looked up he was gone. Dutifully, I set about to follow his last instructions.

CHAPTER 39

J should've been gone by now. Hours had passed since he'd left me standing naked in the spell room. And while I did break down and cry for the better part of an hour after he'd left, I was now strangely calm and collected.

I'd really had every intention of doing what he asked. I'd changed into my jeans, bra, t-shirt, and tennis shoes. I'd gathered all the materials for the spell and even started burning the herbs. But when I sat down to read the spell out loud, I realized the words just weren't going to come out of my mouth.

There was no way in hell I was going through with the spell. I didn't care that Eoin wanted to die knowing I was safe. That would be no comfort to me as I moved miserably through life without him, scrubbing snot off the backs of school chairs. I'd said vows, albeit while I thought I was in a coma. But I meant them now, and I was not going to oblige him. Screw the sense of duty he felt over keeping me safe. Deep down he didn't really want me gone, even if he was too noble to let himself admit it.

Blowing out the burning herbs, I quickly changed out of my modern clothes and back into the dress I'd put on this morning. I didn't know what time the battle would begin, but I wanted to be certain I saw Eoin before the men took their positions. If he wanted me to hide with the other women during the fight, fine, but he needed to know I hadn't completed the spell.

I was running up the stairs in my rush to get out of the basement and find Eoin when voices from around the corner caused me to slow my pace. Stopping only a few steps away from the noise, I listened to try and make out what they were saying.

After a moment I recognized the first as the always-slurred voice of Ramsay Kinnaird. The second, I could only assume, was the daughter whom had oddly been absent from our sight, during our stay at Kinnaird Castle.

"Unless, ye want me to beat ye half to death, doona ye dare let me find ye talking to someone from Conall Castle again. Do ye understand?"

"I wasna going to tell them anything, father. I was only visiting."

The mousy voice sounded quiet, frightened, and I immediately felt uncomfortable with the situation. I heard his hand as it made hard contact with the girl's face, undoubtedly bruising her, and I stepped out from around the corner so that they both could see me.

Ramsay instantly stepped away from the young girl, and I was shocked at how quickly he was able to change his face from one of malice to one of pure sugar. "Ah, Lady Blaire, my daughter only stepped away from the crowd for a moment to have a private conversation. If I'd known ye were down here, we would not have disturbed ye."

"Yes, I can see that." I turned to the girl whose face was already red and inflamed, not attempting any semblance of a Scottish accent. "What's your name? We haven't met before."

The girl hesitated, her gaze darting between mine and her father's. When Ramsay stayed silent, she spoke. "Edana. Pleasure to meet ye."

I smiled at her. "The pleasure's mine. Are you all right? Would you like to accompany me on a walk?"

Ramsay reached out and grabbed Edana by the arm. "Aye, she's fine o' course. Just worried about the battle is all. And I'm afraid she's been a bit ill. Best if she does not leave the castle."

"Thank you, Ramsay, but I didn't ask you if you'd like to walk. Edana looks old enough to answer for herself."

Ramsay turned his cold eyes on me, all semblance of kindness gone. "Ye overstep, Lady Blaire. Tis not yer place to tell me when my daughter may speak for herself. And if I may say so, I believe ye are overtired yerself. Ye are speaking quite strangely, lass."

Ramsay was accustomed to obedience from women, and he expected me to apologize at once. He didn't know me very well at all. "No, Laird Kinnaird. You overstep by laying foul hands on your daughter. If I see another bruise or red mark on her while you are staying here, I can assure you Eoin will no longer be requiring your assistance, battle or not. It would suit you to remember whose home you are in. Do I make myself clear?"

Ramsay's face flushed red, but he managed to keep his anger under control as he replied curtly, "Aye. Now, if ye will excuse me." He released Edana's arm, and after flashing her a look of undisputable warning, turned and stormed from the stairwell.

I reached forward to touch Edana's shoulder. "Are you really okay? He shouldn't have touched you so."

"Aye, miss. Ye should not have spoken to him as ye did. It will not mean good things for ye."

Her fear for me was evident in her eyes, and I was certain that what I'd witnessed was little to what often occurred between them. "I'm not afraid of your father. He seems a right bastard, though. Listen, if you need anything while you're here, just come and find me. You don't have to go back with him after the battle if you don't want to."

"Thank ye, miss. It's best that I go now."

With her head down, she followed in the direction of her father, and I wondered briefly if perhaps I'd made things worse for her.

I hoped not, but I couldn't allow myself to think much on it right now.

I had to find Eoin.

CHAPTER 40

*a*rran left his brother's bedchamber with a heavy heart. He'd never seen Eoin so devastated, and it made him realize how wrong he'd been about Bri. Eoin loved her just as much as he loved Blaire, and seeing that made him feel guilty for how ardently he'd tried to send her away.

It was selfish behavior, and now that Bri was gone, he found himself wishing that he could do something to get her back. Even if Eoin was right and they'd all be dead come evening, Arran knew Eoin was weaker without Bri by his side.

He nearly jumped out of his skin, then, when he passed Bri on his way down to the dungeon. She said nothing to him; she only smiled briefly in his direction before hurrying on her way. It was such a normal interaction that it took Arran a moment before he realized that she shouldn't have been there. He whirled around to catch her attention before she got too far away. "Bri! Come here, lass."

He moved in her direction, meeting her halfway in the middle of the room.

"I'm sorry, Arran. I don't have time. I've got to find Eoin."

Arran reached to grab her arm. "What the hell are ye still doing here? Ye should be gone by now."

"I'm not going, Arran. I know he wants to keep me safe. But I can't do it."

Arran smiled and waved her away, dismissing her. "Get on with ye, lass. Ye will find him in his chambers. I'm glad ye dinna listen to him. He needs ye here."

With Bri remaining here during the battle, it was even more important that he get the truth out of the runaway.

The lad was close to breaking, and as he entered the dungeon and laid eyes on the man hanging unconscious from his wrists, he grabbed the pail of the man's urine and threw it in the runaway's face.

"Time to wake up. I've no more patience for ye, lad. It's time for ye to make a choice. Ye can either tell me who yer real master is and the real reason that ye're here, or I'm slowly going to slice each one of yer wee toes off, and ye'll find them served to ye this evening."

The runaway groaned, unable to raise his head to look Arran in the eyes. "I doona believe ye will do it."

Arran grabbed the knife he'd left lying near the entrance to the dungeon. Moving quickly, before he could talk himself out of it, he grabbed the runaway's big right toe, swiftly sliced it off, and tossed it to the ground.

The man's screams bounced off the dungeon walls. "No one will hear ye, lad. It's just ye and me. Now, do ye want to lose the others or are ye willing to talk?"

"Aye. Aye. Doona cut another. I work for Laird Kinnaird. He's the one that plans to attack ye, not Laird MacLyrron." The runaway puked out onto the floor; the pain radiating from his foot made him ill.

"Is what ye say true, lad?"

"Aye, I swear it on my father's grave."

"Aye? Well, ye shall meet him there now." Arran drew his blade quickly across the runaway's neck, jumping back to avoid the spray of blood as the man took in his last breath.

Bri wasn't the only one who needed to find Eoin. Perhaps now that Arran knew the truth, they would have time to stop Ramsay's treacherous plan.

CHAPTER 41

*P*resent Day

"*W*hat did you say, Blaire? I can't hear you up here!" Adelle continued to dig into the soft moist earth, intent on digging up Alasdair Conall so that she could get the ring. It was the last day the spell would work, and daylight was fading fast. She'd resigned herself to the fact that Bri was going to stay, but she would be damned if she allowed Blaire to stay separated from her home forever as well.

Blaire's voice was suddenly clearer, and Adelle poked her head out of the hole she was digging to see Blaire standing at the top of the entrance to the basement.

"I said, stop digging. I doona know how, but the ring is here. Right on the spell book. Come and see."

It was impossible. She must've set her own ring down in the room, but no, she glanced down at her own hand to see all of her rings securely in place.

"Are you sure, Blaire?" Adelle followed Blaire down into the spell

229

room, nearly swallowing her own tongue when she saw the ring sitting right on top of the switching spell.

"I told ye. Perhaps, it works the same way as the writing. I doona know what made me come down here, but I saw it right away." Blaire smiled at her, and Adelle rushed to swallow her in a large embrace.

"I'm so happy for you, Blaire! This means you can go home. We should start the spell right away." She pulled back when she felt Blaire stiffen in her arms. "What is it, Blaire?"

"Aye, we should start the spell, but I'm not going back."

Adelle's voice came out even higher than usual. "What? Blaire, if you don't go now, you'll be trapped here; the spell won't work after tonight."

"Aye. I know. I canna go back, but ye can. We are gonna do the spell for ye. I doona know if it will work, but we must try."

"Me? It never crossed my mind. The portrait is of you and Bri. It won't work, I'm sure."

"Perhaps if ye hold a piece of me. Here." Adelle watched as Blaire reached for a small knife, quickly cutting a lock of her hair and extending it in her direction.

Adelle took it, cradling the gift as she allowed herself to consider the possibility that she might be reunited with her daughter. Not only that, she would be able to live in the very time and with the very people she'd dedicated her life to studying. It was an archaeologist's dream come true.

"Adelle, if ye want to try, we must try it now. Daylight is almost gone."

"Are you sure you won't go back, Blaire?"

"Aye. There's nothing left for me there. I shall start anew here."

Adelle smiled, hope and fear of disappointment building as they quickly gathered the materials for the spell. When all was in place, Blaire turned to leave.

"I think it best I leave. I doona want to risk the spell taking me back. I shall wait in the car. If it doesna work, join me there. Thank ye for yer kindness. I shall never forget ye."

They hugged briefly, and once Blaire had gone and she heard the car door slam in the distance, Adelle placed the ring on her finger and slowly sounded out each word in the book.

———

1 645

*M*ary ran through the castle as fast as her short legs would carry her. The moment Kip had informed her of Eoin's decision to send Bri back, she'd fled from her own chambers at the edge of the castle grounds and raced to stop the lass.

How Eoin could be so foolish, she couldn't begin to understand. Did the lad not understand that their love made them both stronger? Passion was wasted on the youth, she was certain.

She nearly slid down the stairwell in her hurry to get there before the lass started the spell, and as she rushed through the spell room door, she was afraid she arrived only moments too late. The room was humming with an unseen energy, just as it had done the day she'd watched Bri arrive.

Suddenly the room trembled, and Mary found herself staring at the second-oddest looking lass she'd ever seen, next to Bri. The woman looked about with an expression of awe, scaring Mary nearly to death as she cackled gleefully and jumped around the room.

Taking in the lass' strange clothing, Mary could only draw one conclusion.

"Ye must be her mother, aye?"

CHAPTER 42

*E*oin took his time dressing for battle in the solitude of his bedchamber. All his men were as prepared for battle as they could be. It mattered not anyway; his men would fight valiantly by his side. He had failed them all, and he knew the ground would run red with the blood of all his clansmen in a few short hours.

He was no longer afraid to die. He'd sent his heart to live hundreds of years away from him. Eoin would gladly meet his death on the battlefield. He glanced out the window, watching his men prepare for the eminent battle. A reflection in the glass caught his attention, but he quickly closed his eyes against the vision. It was good he was not long for this world; he'd lost his mind, and was seeing his strange, lovely lass in places where she was not.

A hand on the middle of his back caused his eyes to spring open as he spun to see the realest vision he had ever seen standing before him. His feet grew suddenly unsteady and his throat was dry as he worked to choke back tears. "Lass, if ye are not real, leave me be and doona torture me so. My heart canna bear it."

Her slender arms wrapped around him, and his tears ran freely as he scooped her up tight.

"I couldn't do it, Eoin. I know you told me to, and you're going to be angry. But I just don't care. My place is here."

"Nay, love. I'm not angry with ye. Why, I doona believe I've ever been so pleased in all my life." He pressed his lips against hers, seeking entry with his tongue, desperate to lay claim to as much of her body as possible.

A squeaky noise at the doorway caused him to break his kiss as they both turned to see Ramsay Kinnaird's daughter standing uncomfortably in the doorway.

*T*hank God he wasn't angry. I knew eventually he would be glad I'd decided to stay, but I was worried that his fear for my safety would be enough to make him react negatively to my unexpected reappearance.

When we broke our kiss, I started at the site of Edana Kinnaird watching us from the doorway. I pulled away from Eoin and went to greet her.

"What's the matter, Edana? Is everything all right? Did your father hurt you?"

Eoin interrupted and walked over to join us. "Hurt her? Why would he do such a thing?"

"I accidently walked up on them in the stairwell. He hit her hard across the face, Eoin. Look at the mark."

Edana obligingly turned her head to the side to show Eoin, and the angry grumble from Eoin's throat was a sure sign he was angry. "Do ye have something to tell us, lass? I willna stand for it if yer father is hurting ye."

Edana looked down at her hands, fidgeting nervously. "Aye. I know he will kill me if he learns, but I could not live with myself if I let him do what he plans."

"What is it lass?"

"There's no . . ."

She was interrupted by Arran's presence in the doorway, who was hollering for Eoin even before he entered the room. "Eoin! I must speak with ye!" He stopped when he caught sight of Edana and me standing together with Eoin.

Eoin held his palm up in Arran's direction as if to stop him. "Wait just a moment, Arran. The lass has something to tell us."

Arran shook his head, making his way to stand among us in the circle. "It canna wait, Eoin. Laird MacLyrron is not the one attacking us. It's Ramsay."

I immediately looked in Edana's direction seeking either a confirmation or denial of Arran's words.

Hesitantly, she spoke up. "Aye, he tells the truth. That's what I came to tell ye. Laird MacLyrron sits comfortably at his home, and the MacChristys are not dead. My father plans to attack ye this evening."

I reached out to gather Edana in my arms, who now cried freely, terrified of her father's wrath.

Eoin touched Edana briefly on the shoulder. "Doona worry, lass. We willna let him hurt ye again. I'll not say I'm not relieved, despite the betrayal. Now that we know he's planning to turn on us, we should have a much better chance in battle."

Arran nodded. "Aye. Would ye like me to go and kill the bastard now? I doona think his men will fight us, unless under his command. They all know the wretched arse he really is."

Eoin shot Arran a look of disapproval before glancing in Edana's direction. "Nay, we need to discuss a plan of attack first."

Before anyone else could respond, yet another visitor entered the room hurriedly, and I was nearly knocked to the ground as Mary threw her arms around me.

"Oh my God, lass. I thought for certain I'd missed ye. I'm so pleased ye were smart enough not to listen to the foolish lad." She reached out from my side and wacked Eoin in the side of his arm. "What is the matter with ye? Ye are a foolish boy!" She returned her attention back to me. "I went down to the spell room to stop ye from doing the spell, but ye were gone. I found someone else in yer place."

It was only then that yet another figure in the doorway caught my focus.

"Mom?" I broke free from Mary's grasp as I charged in her direction. I could feel everyone's eyes on us as we clung to each other tightly, both of us weeping into the other's hair.

After what seemed like ages, she pushed me away and smiled. "If you weren't going to come back to me, I decided I was just going to have to come to you."

"Oh, I'm so glad. Is Blaire with you, too?" I didn't miss Arran, as his eyes grew wide at the mention of my look-alike. "I placed the ring on the spell book, hoping it would possibly transfer to her."

Mom shook her head, and Arran quickly masked his expression, doing his best to hide the pain that only I could see. "She didn't want to come. She allowed me to go in her place."

"Oh." I was unsure of what to say and was glad when my mother interrupted, easing the tension in the room.

"Bri, honey. I can certainly see what made you decide to stay. Which one's yours, and is it okay if I touch them both?"

CHAPTER 43

*A*fter taking a few brief moments to introduce my mother to everyone in the room, Eoin hushed us all, taking his place as leader among us so that we could make a plan of attack.

"It's nearly dark, and we must decide how to act quickly."

Arran gave him little chance to continue before interrupting. "I doona see why we need to decide anything. The best thing to do would be to cut the bastard down, at once."

"Nay. I want to allow him the opportunity to change his mind. Perhaps, he will take it, and no blood will be shed."

It was Edana's turn to speak up, albeit nervously. "He willna do it. Once he's set his mind to a task, doona expect him to back down only because he's been found out."

"Ye may be right, lass, but I will not kill a man for something he's yet to do. Mary, do ye think tis too late to prepare a meal?" Eoin looked in Mary's direction, smiling at the irritated expression on her face.

"Do ye really think that's what we should be speaking of now, lad? I know I'm no warrior, but that seems a shoddy battle plan."

"Aye, Mary. Ye are quite right about that. But if Ramsay willna change his mind, he will call his men to battle when I confront him. If we are sitting down for a meal, at least it will take them a moment

237

to gather for a fight. It will give us an advantage. Ramsay will wonder why I would have us sit to eat when we should be preparing for battle. It will make him nervous, and I'd like him to be so."

Mary crossed her arms and looked exasperatingly in his direction. "Aye. I expect he shall think ye've gone and misplaced yer brain, and I'm not likely to disagree with him. But if ye want food, ye shall have it. I know better than to try and change yer mind, ye stubborn fool."

Eoin smiled. "I'd ask something else of ye, Mary, as well. We canna let Ramsay see Edana again. Give yer kitchen maid instructions as to the meal, and then make yer way up to the top tower to hide with Adelle and Edana."

"Aye, o' course. Where do ye expect Bri to be?" Mary glanced in my direction as if she thought he'd forgotten me.

"Ramsay will expect to see Bri at the table. He knows that at Conall Castle, the laird dines with his wife. He thinks it mad, but he knows tis our custom. 'Twill arouse suspicion if she is not there." Eoin paused and turned his gaze to Arran. "If fighting begins, ye are to take Bri away at once. Doona let anyone harm her. I must handle Ramsay, myself."

Arran nodded. "Aye, she will not be harmed, Eoin."

Once everyone knew our plan of action, we all dispersed into our positions. Mary quickly attended to dinner and then escorted my mother and Edana up to the castle's top tower. It was difficult to get to and was certainly the safest place for them to stay.

Arran left to ensure that men would be waiting outside every door of the dining hall, ready for entry into battle if it came to that.

I sat nervously in our bedchamber, waiting for Eoin to come back from his talk with Ramsay. He'd left shortly after making plans to invite Ramsay to dinner. I glanced up as Eoin made his way into the room.

"What did he say?"

"Well, I doona think he believes I suspect him. He only said I was a fool to worry over my stomach at a time such as this, but if I wanted to spend the last moments eating before Laird MacLyrron's men arrived, then he'd not stop me."

"So he's coming?"

"Aye. It's of no concern to him when Laird MacLyrron's men should be arriving, since it is he who shall start the bloodshed."

I walked over and leaned gently into his side. "When is it starting?"

He took my hand and made for door. "Now, lass. I'm eager to end this; I doona like waiting for the unknown. And the sooner ye are truly safe, the better."

CHAPTER 44

ension laced every inch of the dining hall as Ramsay made his way to seat himself on Eoin's right hand side. I sat on his left, and as we positioned ourselves at the table, I could see in Ramsay's eyes that perhaps he was more suspicious of this impromptu and poorly timed meal than Eoin had thought.

Ramsay's dark, blood-shot eyes, consistently glazed from too much drink, made my skin crawl as he glared at me across the table. I'd angered him earlier, and he was not one to forget someone crossing him.

I met his gaze head on, determined not to flinch from his sight. Finally, he tore his eyes away from my own and turned to speak to Eoin.

"I see not much has changed under Conall Castle's new laird. Ye have yet to learn that meals should be shared in the company of men."

Eoin's face was hard, no longer concerned with placating him for the sake of maintaining him as an ally. "It is ye, Ramsay, that have yet to learn that the company of women makes everything more pleasant."

He reached over to squeeze my hand, and it immediately released some of my tension, if only momentarily.

"Aye? If that be the case, why doona ye have my daughter join us as well?" Ramsay gestured with his hand at the other empty chairs at the table.

I could see by the way he glanced around the room that Ramsay knew something was off. His hand rested uneasily to his side, giving himself quick access to some sort of weapon concealed from my sight.

"She wasn't feeling well. I had Mary take food to her bedchamber."

Ramsay ignored me, offended that a woman dare speak in his presence. "Yer wife speaks verra strange, Eoin. I dinna notice it before when ye came to visit me."

Eoin was finished putting off the confrontation; I could tell by the way he shifted in his seat, leaning forward so that he could leap into action at a moment's notice. "Ramsay, before I tell ye what I have to say, I'd like to remind ye that our two clans have been allies for generations long before us. We have both come to the other's aide, and I know my father considered ye a friend. It would be a shame for that alliance to come to an end, aye?"

Ramsay had an unsettling ability that made the words coming out of his mouth drip with sincerity while his eyes oozed poison. "Aye, lad, that it would. Good thing we have come together to fight our shared enemy."

"I doona know if that is so, Ramsay. I have reason to believe that it is ye who plan to attack us—that perhaps Laird MacLyrron is not on his way here at all."

Ramsay stood quite suddenly, throwing his fist violently down on the table. I could hear shuffling outside the dining hall doors, and I knew the action had been his signal to his men. Outside these doors, the sound of battle was already ensuing.

"Do ye now? And why would I do that?"

Each door to the dining hall swung open as both our own men collided with Ramsay's in a horrific dance of death. Metal clashed around us as I stood watching the interaction between Ramsay and Eoin, neither of whom had yet to draw a sword.

"I doona know, Ramsay. Perhaps, ye could explain it to me. Surely there's no reason for bloodshed."

"Ye are wrong, Eoin. There is a need for bloodshed, and there will be plenty of it this night. Ye are a damned fool, just like yer father. He knew that it was expected that ye wed Edana. Instead, he married ye to this ignorant whore! Our clans would have been made stronger by such an arrangement. Without it, I've no desire to stay allies. Instead, I shall claim the Conall clan and castle as my own."

Eoin didn't have a chance to respond as I screamed at the sight of a sword swinging in his direction. Eoin unsheathed his own just in time and, as he sliced the man across the middle, there was no doubt that battle had begun.

I knew my life was in danger, but every swing of a sword and every horrifying sound of a man groaning as he met his death seemed to slow down in my mind as I kept careful watch on Ramsay.

I could see Arran making his way toward me out of the corner of my eye, but he was delayed as he worked to cut down two of Ramsay's men. I'd expected Laird Kinnaird to head straight in Eoin's direction, but instead I watched as he snuck away from the crowd.

I knew he could be headed in only one direction.

CHAPTER 45

I ran as quickly as I could, damning floor-length dresses with every step. I was unsure if he knew that they would be in the tower, but I knew from Eoin that Ramsay was familiar enough with the castle for it not to take him very long to figure it out.

I was worried for Eoin, but at least he had the means and skills to defend himself. Edana, Mary, and mother were defenseless, and I was not going to allow him to hurt any of them. With each step I feared I was going to be too late. I was still a good distance from the tower, but when I passed the small hidden door at the end of the corridor, I knew I could take the shortcut Eoin had shown me on that one stormy night.

I stumbled up the stairs in the darkness, ripping off the wooden door that concealed the window entrance, slicing open my fingers as I threw it aside. Though it was dark, I could still make out the castle wall, and it was thick enough that I knew it left me plenty of space to walk along it.

As I scooted along the outside perimeter of the castle, I counted windows until I was almost sure I stood in front of the window that would place me in the tower staircase. I didn't have time to second guess myself. Unable to pry the window open, I reared back and shattered the glass with my heel, cutting wide gashes down my leg as the blood spread over the end of my dress.

It was the right window, and as I made my way up the spiral staircase I could hear Ramsay fumbling with the lock.

"Edana, it will be far worse for ye if ye doona let me in. Now open this door, ye wee bitch!"

I could hear all three women screaming on the other side of the door as Ramsay budged it open a half an inch with the impact of his shoulder. I screamed at him as loudly as I could to draw his attention away from the doorway.

"Stop! Leave her alone!"

He spun toward me, sticking a finger in my direction. "Doona ye tell me what to do with my daughter. I shall slit yer throat after I'm through with hers!"

I ran, throwing myself in between his oncoming shoulder and the door.

His shoulder hit me square in between the breasts. I cried out as all the air in my lungs rushed out of my body. Gasping for air, I struggled to speak. "No . . . take me! Eoin will surrender, if you have me! You've won the battle if you take me captive." I hoped to God I was wrong, but I could think of nothing else that might tempt him to leave Edana, Mary, and my mother in peace.

"Aye, lass. Ye are right."

I didn't struggle against his arms as he pulled me against him. Holding the edge of a dagger across my neck so tightly that it broke the surface of the skin, he dragged me back down the stairs and into the ongoing battle.

***

*A*rran scanned the room in between swings of his sword. He'd lost Bri in the crowd, and he was certain his brother would never forgive him. Not that it would matter. He couldn't find his brother or Ramsay in the crowd of fighting men.

They were losing too many. He glanced around to see men he'd known his entire life open and bleeding onto the stone floor as their lifeless eyes gazed upward. With each lad he watched fall, his hope of their success waned.

Just as one of Ramsay's men narrowly missed sending a sword straight through his stomach, a surge of men from all surrounding doors shocked Arran into dropping his own sword.

The room suddenly filled with men he knew not to be Ramsay's or their own, and he smiled as he watched Donal MacChristy walk into the center of the room, his booming voice successfully slowing the pace of men clashing their swords against one another.

"Clan Kinnaird, if ye doona wish to die, ye should lay down yer swords at once. For we fight for the Conalls, and ye are far outnumbered now." Donal paused to scan the room, and Arran knew he was looking for Ramsay. "Look around, yer laird is not even fighting with ye. Doona lose yer life for such a cowardly leader."

It only took moments for Ramsay's men to see the wisdom in Donal MacChristy's words. They'd lived under fear of Ramsay for far too long, and there were not many willing to give up their life for his.

Arran smiled as he allowed it to sink in that the battle was over. Laird Kinnaird must have fled in an act of cowardice, but that mattered not. He was no threat without an army of men at his side.

Arran's relief at their survival was short-lived as he scanned the room twice more, still unable to locate his brother or Bri.

A strange hush settled over the room as men who'd only just been engaged in battle stood unsure of how to now act.

Just as Arran was about to leave the dining hall to go in search of Bri and Eoin, a figure shouted from a shadowy corner of the hall. Ramsay stepped into the light of the room, his arms wrapped around Bri, his knife ready to slice her throat.

*I*t had only taken Eoin a few short moments after the battle had broken out to register Ramsay's and Bri's absence. He'd not hesitated to set out in search of them. Arran could lead the men. He would not lose her again.

He'd just made it to the bottom of the stairwell leading to the back tower when he heard someone moving down the stairs. He silently slipped around a corner, unseen, as he watched Ramsay drag his beautiful wife out of the stairwell with a knife at her neck.

It had been all he could do to keep from launching himself at Ramsay that instant, but he knew that once the devil entered the dining hall, Ramsay would expect to see him fighting the battle. When Ramsay realized Eoin was not in the room, that was when he would be at his weakest.

Eoin stayed covered in the darkness as Ramsay stepped into the light in front of the silent crowd. He was only a few short steps from Bri, and his hand twitched on the handle of his sword, desperate to run it through Ramsay's heart.

Ramsay screamed for him as he revealed himself to the onlookers, but Eoin didn't move from his location behind Ramsay.

"Eoin! Surrender yer castle and yer men, or watch yer wife bleed to death in my arms."

Eoin watched as Arran cautiously took a step in Ramsay's direction. "He's not here, Ramsay. And surely ye see that ye are outnumbered. This is finished. Doona shed blood when ye have already lost."

Eoin could tell Ramsay was on the brink of panic. He worried that Ramsay would slide the knife across Bri's throat in a fit of madness. Slowly he crept up so that he stood directly behind Ramsay. Eoin locked eyes with Arran, quickly shaking his head so that he wouldn't alert their foe to his position.

"Where is he? Someone find him at once," Ramsay shouted at the top of his lungs.

Eoin could see the man's hands shaking on the handle of his blade. The time for him to act was now. He nodded at Arran, who quickly rushed to grab Bri from Ramsay's grasp.

Eoin ran his sword through Ramsay's back and into his heart. "There's no need to look for me, Ramsay. I'm already here."

EPILOGUE

February

I scooted myself out from under Eoin's heavy arm as gracefully as I could. He grumbled as the bed shifted, and he reached to grab me toward him. I crawled out of the bed but leaned forward to kiss him gently on the forehead.

"I'll be back in a while. There's something I need to work on."

Taking one of the candles from my side of the bed, I slipped on a thin gown and wrapped a blanket around me as I slipped into the night-filled corridors of the castle. I was slightly surprised to see the castle so quiet and lifeless, I was sure we'd woken everyone with the sound of our lovemaking.

It had been several months since the defeat of Ramsay, and while peaceful relations ruled the clans once more, Ramsay's men still remained camped on our castle grounds as they tried to find a solution to whom would now be their new laird.

Despite the flurry of people in and out of the castle each day, things were back to normal, and everyone was safe and happy once more; everyone except Arran. I'd watched him as he dutifully put on a brave face in front of his brother but silently fell apart in private.

Each day he found his way to the bottom of more goblets of ale than he had the day before. I couldn't stand to see him so unhappy a moment more.

It was for this reason that I snuck my way into the spell room in the wee hours of the morning once again.

I'd stumbled across a promising spell book this afternoon but had fled the room after I heard a noise at the top of the stairs. I didn't want to tell anyone what I'd found until I was certain.

Situating myself on the bench, I held my candle carefully over the yellowed page, reading the words as I smiled wide.

There were other spells that could reopen the portal. Perhaps Arran could find his way to Blaire after all.

*T*urn the page for a Sneak Peek of *Love Beyond Reason*, Book 2 of Morna's Legacy Series.

SNEAK PEEK OF LOVE BEYOND REASON (BOOK 2)

CHAPTER 1

Just Outside the Ruins of Conall Castle—Scotland—Present Day

Three days I'd sat in the small room at the inn, only a short distance from the castle ruins. Surrounded by what were now considered artifacts of the castle, I took my time, spending days feigning illness so I could decide what I should do next.

Gwendolyn, the kind innkeeper, and her husband, Jerry, were growing impatient. I knew they wouldn't allow me to stay in the room much longer without explanation, but what was I to tell them? I could hardly believe the truth myself.

With Adelle's help, I'd been able to fool the innkeepers into believing I was Adelle's daughter Bri, by remaining for the most part silent when interacting with them. With Adelle no longer here to speak for me, I knew they would notice my lack of an American accent.

A knock at the door meant it was evening, and Gwendolyn was

bringing my supper. She'd graciously and unquestioningly brought each meal and left it outside the door since I'd arrived back at the inn claiming to be quite ill. She'd given me the privacy I'd so clearly desired, and so it surprised me to hear her speak from the other side of the door.

"I'm sorry to disturb your rest, but Jerry and I are both worried about you, dear. You've spent far too much time inside the room, so you've left me no choice I'm afraid. You can either clean yourself up and join us for dinner downstairs, or I shall be calling a doctor to come see to you at once."

Gwendolyn paused, waiting for my response. I wasn't ill, only worried, and I wouldn't have them send for a doctor for a non-existent sickness.

"'Twill be...I'll be down shortly." A short response was best. Perhaps, my accent wouldn't be as noticeable with only a few short words. Not that it mattered. I was going to have to tell them all I knew, not that they would believe me.

At this point, I had nothing left to lose.

I walked down the stairs and into the small kitchen to be met by kind smiles from both Gwendolyn and Jerry. The old man gave me a thorough look over before speaking bluntly, true to form.

"Ye must be feeling much better, lass. Ye doona look sick at all. Now sit down here and tell us where yer mother is. We know something has happened, and it is time that ye tell us what that is. Gwendolyn is too polite to ask ye, but I've no problem with tellin ye that yer behavior has been quite strange."

The old man stood to usher me to a chair across from both of them. Once I was seated, he resumed his place next to his wife. I sat silently for a moment, quite unsure of where to begin. I knew my accent would garner questions from them right away. "Aye, I'm no longer feeling ill, but I do need to tell ye both something."

Gwendolyn pinched her eyebrows together oddly in my

direction. "Well, my goodness, Bri. I know it's tempting once you've been here awhile to try and speak like everyone around you, but I've never been very successful at it myself. You sound as if you've lived here forever."

Jerry laughed in response as he patted Gwendolyn on the shoulder. "Aye, my lassie's voice holds nothing of Scotland, although she's lived here for forty years now. She still speaks as if she arrived in the country only yesterday."

Gwendolyn leaned sweetly into Jerry before glancing back in my direction and continuing, "The accent really is great, but why are you doing it?"

I glanced down at my plate of untouched food, not quite ready for either of them to think I'd lost my mind.

Jerry reached across the table to gently squeeze my hand and, as I looked up at him, I could see the concern in his face. "Where's yer mother, lass?"

"She's not my mother. And I'm not Bri. I doona think ye will believe what I must tell ye, but will ye listen to all of it before ye decide that I'm mad?" I lifted my head to look them in the eyes as I waited for their answer.

Jerry and Gwendolyn exchanged an unreadable sideways glance before Jerry spoke first. "Aye, lass. O'course we shall listen to ye. Let us move next to the fire though. The chairs in there are much more comfortable."

Gwendolyn simply nodded before they both stood and left me to follow them into the next room.

Once seated, I fumbled uneasily with my words, unsure of how to begin. One question had sat at the forefront of my mind since the first night I'd left Adelle at the castle ruins. I'd been too afraid to ask, for if the answer was not what I hoped, it meant everyone I'd known and loved had died only days ago, unable to change history. I knew that I must learn the truth before I explained anything further to Jerry and Gwendolyn.

"Might I ask ye a question first?" I dinna wait for their response. "The castle ruins, I suppose they're still ruins, aye?"

Hope fluttered in my chest at the quizzical looks by both Jerry and Gwendolyn.

Jerry pointed in the direction of the castle. "Do ye mean Conall Castle, lass? If so, I wouldna go calling the place a ruin. It's still beautifully intact—a fine structure and a popular visit for tourists."

I was unsure of what a "tourist" was, but if what he said was true, it meant that they'd been successful at stopping the attack. Adelle, Bri, Eoin, Mary, Arran, had most likely all gone on to live for many more years. That knowledge was enough to rid myself of any other fears I had about moving on in this time alone.

"Do ye really mean it? The castle is not just a pile of rocks? It wasna destroyed long ago?" I needed just one more reassurance in order to let myself fully believe him.

Gwendolyn nodded and spoke this time. "Yes, dear. The Conalls have been one of the most powerful and beloved clans in Scotland for centuries. Descendants still own the castle, but they've partnered with the historical society to open it up for visitors. Are you sure you're not ill?"

I nodded, relieved beyond explanation. It was time to explain to them what had happened. Then regardless of their reaction, it was time for me to move on from this place and start a new life here on my own.

"Aye, I feel fine. But I need to tell ye what's happened, and 'tis a long story. I doubt that ye will believe me."

Jerry smiled and sat back in his chair, settling in. "Why doona ye just get on with it, lass? Then we will decide what we believe."

"Aye. I'm not sure of where to begin. The first thing I should tell ye is that I'm not Bri. My name is Blaire MacChristy. My father was laird of MacChristy Castle during the seventeenth century. I was betrothed to Alasdair Conall's eldest son, Eoin, but on the day of our wedding in the year sixteen hundred and forty-five, I found myself swept up by a spell cast by Alasdair's late sister, Morna Conall, a witch who died when I was very young. As you can see, Bri and I look verra much the same with our hair dark and our eyes blue, and Morna knew that we would. She cast the spell so that if Bri and I ever laid eyes on the same spelled plaque in a spell room beneath the castle, we would switch places in time. Nearly two months ago, her spell worked. Bri was sent back, and I was brought forward." I paused to look up at them and was surprised to see that they both seemed rather unsurprised by my words.

Instead, Jerry asked a question as if we were having the most normal of conversations. "Lass, why did Morna want ye to switch places? And where is Adelle?"

It took me a moment to speak. Was it possible that he believed what I was saying? "Ye see, that's why I asked ye if the castle was ruins. When I arrived here, it was. When Adelle and Bri came here, it was in ruins. Only a few short months after my wedding, the Conalls were murdered and the castle destroyed. No one ever found out who murdered them and that was why Bri and Adelle came to Scotland, to search for something that might reveal who had murdered the Conalls. Tis for the same reason that Morna cast the spell. She hoped that if Bri and I switched places, Bri's knowledge of what was to come would enable her to stop it. And she did. If not, then the castle would still be in ruins now."

"And Adelle?" Jerry continued to stare at me as if he wasn't shocked by my story.

"Once Adelle realized that we'd been switched, we spent weeks searching for a spell that could switch us back. We found one, but Bri dinna want to return. She married Eoin, and they fell in love. I dinna want to go back either, there's not much left for me there." I paused as an uncomfortable knot lodged itself in my chest. I swallowed hard, pushing it down, and continued. "Adelle wanted to be with Bri. So she did the spell instead, and it worked. She's with Bri now. 'Twas three days ago when I arrived here alone telling ye I was sick. I dinna know what to do." I leaned back in my own chair and crossed my hands in my lap.

Gwendolyn had remained silent when Jerry had spoken up, and I could tell nothing by her face.

The three of us sat in silence for what seemed like much longer than I'm sure it was. Eventually, Gwendolyn stood and walked to the other side of the room behind me and reached up to the top of the bookshelf lining the wall and pulled a small box from the shelf.

She returned to her seat next to Jerry and smiled at him quickly before extending the box in my direction. "I'd like to tell you a story myself if you don't mind, dear."

Confused, I only nodded and took the box to sit it in my own lap.

Gwendolyn pointed at the box. "Open it, and pull out the photographs."

I obeyed, lifting the small metal latch that kept the lid closed and looked down inside the box. I remembered the first time I'd seen a photograph, the first day I'd arrived in this time. Adelle had shown me one of Bri to emphasize just how much we resembled one another. Despite all the strange and wonderful things I'd seen, it was still miraculous to me that moments could be captured forever on a small piece of parchment.

Only three photographs lay inside, all facing down, and I lifted them out and closed the lid before turning them over. As I did, the air around me chilled suddenly as I gazed at the images.

The first was of Conall Castle, but not as I remembered it. It was the castle in ruins as it had been when I arrived in this time.

The second was of the spelled plaque, still painted with my portrait staring back at me. A reminder of the day my life had changed forever.

The first two images were shocking, but it was the third that caused my hands to shake and my breath to come out unsteadily as I glanced up at Gwendolyn. She only smiled softly, waiting for me to speak.

The third photograph was less a picture and more of a painted portrait, depicting people I'd known in my old life. Alasdair, young and vibrant, holding a baby Arran in his arms, while Eoin, no more than five, stood next to his father, only knee high. Alasdair's other arm was draped around a woman's shoulder, squeezing her tightly with affection. The woman was not Alasdair's late wife. She'd died giving birth to Arran, and I knew there was only one other person the woman could be. The witch, Morna.

While her face in the portrait was younger, it matched Gwendolyn's exactly.

Gwendolyn eventually gave up on waiting for me to respond. Laughing heartily, she reached out and squeezed my hand. "Come, dear. Surely after all you've been through, nothing can be too much of a surprise to you."

I looked over at Jerry who only nodded in confirmation. "Do ye mean? How could ye be her? She died when I was a verra small child."

"There are a far manner of things, dear, that seem impossible. Surely this is no more impossible than you sitting here in this century when you were born in another, aye?"

Gwendolyn slowly lost the American accent she'd been using the entire time I'd known her. She was right. After all I'd been through, I had no trouble believing her, but I didn't understand why.

"If ye could end up here after yer own death, then why would ye bother with the spell for me and Bri? Could ye not have stopped the massacre yerself?"

Gwendolyn, or Morna, I wasn't sure which name was now appropriate, smiled as if expecting my question.

"Because, lass, there are more important things than life and death. My spell put into motion other things just as important as saving the lives of my family members. Souls needed to meet. Souls that belonged together, despite being born centuries apart. Without my spell, that could never have been."

"Do ye mean Eoin and Bri?" Looking at her more closely, I noticed a resemblance to Alasdair, Eoin, and Arran that I'd never seen before. The shape of their eyes, the slant of their smiles, all strong Conall traits that made me trust her story even more.

"Aye. Eoin and Bri. Not to mention, there was my own lad, who dinna exist in my own time. Instead of saving my family myself, I chose to sit back and watch over those who would save them, while at the same time finding the man I was meant to love."

"Ye mean, Jerry isna like ye?"

Jerry cackled and coughed before he spoke. "Oh no, lassie! I was born right here, in this time and if I had the gift of magic like her, I'd have stopped my knees from cracking long ago."

Morna frowned in Jerry's direction. "I've told ye before, I could stop it for ye myself, but ye willna let me." She turned toward me once more. "He accepts the truth, but it all still makes him a wee bit uncomfortable. He willna let me use magic on him."

"So ye mean ye knew I wasna Bri?"

"Aye, lass. But I'll tell ye, I dinna expect ye to stay here and Adelle to go back. My visions dinna show me that. Perhaps they dinna want me to try and stop it from happening. Are ye certain that ye wish to stay here?"

Panic shot through me at the thought of going back. I answered too quickly, startling both Morna and Jerry. "Aye! I canna go back."

Morna's face softened, her eyes showing that she understood. "All right, lass. Well, what is it that ye want to do now? We shall help ye get settled wherever ye'd like to go. Do ye wish to stay in Scotland?"

I'd given it no thought. I'd been too concerned with what I was going to tell them and whether or not Adelle and Bri had been able to stop the massacre to think much further into my future than a few moments. "I'm not sure. I doona know what to do."

Jerry leaned over and squeezed my hand, and there was no doubt in my mind that Morna had chosen well. Her husband was the best of men, kind to his core.

Morna waved a hand in the air as if dismissing my concern. "Doona worry. Why doona we help ye get settled in Edinburgh? We could get ye a job and a place to stay, and ye can see how ye like it for a while. If ye decide later that ye'd like to go elsewhere, then we'll be more than happy to help ye."

"Aye, that will be fine. Thank ye. I suppose ye shall be glad to have another empty room for guests, aye?"

Morna stood and motioned for me to do the same as we made

our way to the stairs. Clearly, we were all about to retire for the evening.

"Lass, we doona allow other guests. Ye are the only one who knows this house is here. Only yerself and those I wish to see it can see this house along the side of the road. We'd be overrun with tourists, otherwise."

Get *Love Beyond Reason to* read the rest of the story.

Love Beyond Reason
(Book 2 of Morna's Legacy Series)

READ THE WHOLE SERIES

And More To Follow...

SWEET/CLEAN VERSIONS OF MORNA'S LEGACY SERIES

If you enjoy sweet/clean romances where the love scenes are left behind closed doors or if you know someone else who does, check out the new sweet/clean versions of Morna's Legacy books in the Magical Matchmaker's Legacy.

Morna's Spell

Sweet/Clean Version of *Love Beyond Time*

Morna's Secret

Sweet/Clean Version of *Love Beyond Reason*

The Conall's Magical Yuletide

Sweet/Clean Version of *A Conall Christmas*

Morna's Magic
Sweet/Clean Version of *Love Beyond Hope*

Morna's Accomplice
Sweet/Clean Version of *Love Beyond Measure*

Jeffrey's Only Wish
Sweet/Clean Version of *In Due Time*

Morna's Rogue
Sweet/Clean Version of *Love Beyond Compare*

Morna's Ghost
Sweet/Clean Version of *Love Beyond Dreams*

LETTER TO READERS

Dear Reader,

I hope you enjoyed *Love Beyond Time (Book 1 of Morna's Legacy Series)*. Eoin and Bri became a real part of my life during the writing of this book. I was so immersed in their world, it was hard to pull out of it at times. I found myself saying things like, "I doona think so" even when talking to my family.

You are probably wanting to know what happens between Arran and Blaire, at least I hope you are. Their story continues in *Love Beyond Reason (Book 2 of Morna's Legacy Series)*. Will they find a way to be together, or are the obstacles just too hard to overcome? I hope you choose to continue the journey and find out.

As an author, I love feedback from readers. You are the reason that I write, and I love hearing from you. If you would like to connect, there are several ways you can do so. You can reach out to me on Facebook or on Twitter or visit my Pinterest boards. If you want to read excerpts from my books, listen to audiobook samples, learn more about me, and find some cool downloadable files related to the books, visit my website.

The best way to stay in touch is to subscribe to my newsletter. Go to my website and click the Mailing List link in the header. If you don't hear from me regularly, please check your spam folder or junk mail to make sure my messages aren't ending up there. Please set up your email to allow my messages through to you so you never miss a new book, a chance to win great prizes or a possible appearance in your area.

Finally, if you enjoyed this book, I would appreciate it so much if you would recommend it to your friends and family. And if you would please take time to review it on Goodreads and/or your favorite retailer site, it would be a great help. Reviews can be tough to come by these days, and you, the reader, have the power to make or break a book.

Thank you so much for reading *Love Beyond Time*. I hope you choose to journey with me through the other books in the series.

All my best,

Bethany Claire

ABOUT THE AUTHOR

BETHANY CLAIRE is a USA Today bestselling author of swoon-worthy, Scottish romance and time travel novels. Bethany loves to immerse her readers in worlds filled with lush landscapes, hunky Scots, lots of magic, and happy endings.

She has two ornery fur-babies, plays the piano every day, and loves Disney and yoga pants more than any twenty-something really should. She is most creative after a good night's sleep and the perfect cup of tea. When not writing, Bethany travels as much as she possibly can, and she never leaves home without a good book to keep her company.

If you want to read more about Bethany or if you're curious about when her next book will come out, please visit her website at: www.bethanyclaire.com, where you can sign up to receive email notifications about new releases.

ACKNOWLEDGMENTS

Many thanks to my family. Without your love and support, I would have been unable to pursue my dream of writing. You have given me the gift of pursuing my passion by trusting my, albeit sometimes shaky, judgment. Few people could be so lucky.

A special mention certainly belongs to my Mom and sister, Maegan. Thank you for reading, and re-reading, and re-reading yet again until I know you weren't actually reading, but you still graciously accepted the task of allowing your eyes to roam over text you'd seen a hundred times, all while still managing to look excited to be doing it. I hope one day I can repay the favor.

Thank you to Charlie and Flag, the two sweetest, most handsome dogs anywhere. Their ability to lie patiently at my feet while wondering why on earth it's taking me so long to get up out of my chair and go play frisbee is the very definition of love.

To DeWanna Pace, thank you for the suggestions.

Jodi Thomas, Tim Lewis, and all the others who help run the WT Writer's Academy each year, I hope each of you know the impact that week has had on me. It helped spark the fire in me that started my journey as a writer. For that I will always be grateful.

Alexandra Sokoloff, your screenwriting techniques for authors helped get me un-stuck when it came to my writing and allowed me to tackle the stories trapped in my head in an approachable way. My oversized storyboard now hangs proudly on my wall as the centerpiece of my office, and I implore its use every time I sit down to write.

To Nona, Deann, Jolene, Storm, Matt, Linda, Marilyn, Sheri, and Sherill. I'm so glad that I had the privilege of spending a week with all of you creative people. Thanks for helping with the brainstorming process and helping with some of the hang-ups in the story.

Jonathan Baker, for your professionalism, kind words, and advice. Your work has certainly helped improve the quality of this novel.

Janet Collins, thank you for your encouragement at the first Writer's Academy we attended together and for your emails of encouragement ever since.

Niki and Abbie, simply because how could I not? Our girls' nights are amazing, and I am definitely in need of one soon.

Thanks to my other team members, Madee at xuni.com for building an awesome website, Damonza.com for creating a cover that I just can't stop staring at, and Rik Hall for the great formatting.

Lastly, to my grandmother, Mims. I've heard you whispering words of encouragement for years. I got my love of writing from you, and I know you would be so proud. I miss you daily. I sure hope there are eReaders in heaven.

10884044R00164

Made in the USA
Lexington, KY
02 October 2018